Praise for Camille Bordas

'So smart. Writing comedy is difficult enough, but writing comedy bits that fail and comedy bits that succeed requires some brilliance. That brilliance is on display here' Percival Everett

'Utterly charming … moving, witty, funny and especially wonderful for the mature kind-heartedness of its view of humanity' George Saunders

'Profound, deeply engrossing, dark and generous, a great novel about humans making art right now' Sam Lipsyte

'Wryly funny and painfully awkward, populated by an irresistible cast of overthinkers and second guessers. It's a deep and illuminating pleasure' Tom Perrotta

'Not only very funny, but also incisive and insightful. Come for the laughs, stay for the observations so deadpan and accurate that you may be blinded by your own reflection' Ling Ma

'There's definitely a ⸱　　　　　　　　　　　　't explain why somethi⸱　　　　　　　　　　　　here. This is the fictional e⸱　　　　　　　　　　　　 *Spectator*

'Thoughtful … Borda　　　　　　　　　　　　 about the narcissism and insularity of creative types are very good and her deadpan delivery means they tend to land. She proceeds with a spry, associative logic' *London Review of Books*

'A disquisition into the nature of comedy and creativity. Like the best comedians … Bordas is alert to the deeper joke' *Sunday Times*

Also by Camille Bordas

The Material

How to Behave in a Crowd

ONE
SUN
ONLY

Camille Bordas

First published in Great Britain in 2026 by
Serpent's Tail,
an imprint of Profile Books Ltd
29 Cloth Fair
London
EC1A 7JQ

www.serpentstail.com

Copyright © Camille Bordas, 2026

1 3 5 7 9 10 8 6 4 2

First published in USA in 2026 by Random House, an imprint
and division of Penguin Random House LLC

Printed and bound in Great Britain by
CPI Group (UK) Ltd, Croydon CR0 4YY

Some of the stories in this collection were originally published in the
following publications: *The New Yorker* ("Most Die Young," "The
State of Nature," "The Presentation on Egypt," "Only Orange,"
"Offside Constantly," "One Sun Only," "Colorín Colorado," and
"Chicago on the Seine") and *The Paris Review* ("The Lottery in Almería").

A CIP catalogue record for this book is available from the British Library.

Our product safety representative in the EU is BGC Sustainability
& Compliance, 7 avenue du Général Leclerc, Paris, 75014,
France https://baldwinglobalconsulting.com

ISBN 978 1 80522 014 5
eISBN 978 1 80522 016 9

For Adam Levin

Contents

ONE
SUN
ONLY

One Sun Only

THIS IS NOT A REWRITE OF THAT STORY IN WHICH PLANTS AND animals and people keep winding up dead over the course of a school year, but it starts the same, and it feels odd not to acknowledge, so I will. I just did. Things kept dying. My father first, in June, then the puppy my ex-wife had adopted to help the children get over their grandpa, and then the school janitor, Lane. Right after Halloween, Lane had died during lunchtime in the cafeteria, in front of the kids. Heart attack. A few weeks later, my son, Ernest, came home from school and told me that he hoped there was no afterlife.

"I hope there's no afterlife," he said. We were in the living room, looking through the window, waiting to see if the rain would turn to snow. "I hope he's not watching over me."

I asked who he meant. I thought maybe he was talking about my father, but perhaps it was Lane on his mind. I didn't think it could be the dog.

"I just don't want there to be an afterlife, is all," Ernest said, after thinking about it for a few seconds. "For anybody. I think when you're dead you should stay dead."

I had him and his sister for the weekend. Sally, who was now eleven and exploring Catholicism (to her mother's alarm), kept talking about her hope that my father was watching over us. My father had been very fond of her. He'd taken her to the Art Institute every Wednesday, taught her painting techniques and a lot about art history. They'd been obnoxious together, playing games like who could most quickly recite the titles of all the artworks in Gallery 397 (Sally's favorite), or all of Pablo Picasso's middle names in order. (The full name was Pablo Diego José Francisco de Paula Juan Nepomuceno María de los Remedios Cipriano de la Santísima Trinidad Ruiz y Picasso, a succession of sounds I came to know as well as the alphabet.) A few weeks before my father died, he had asked me if he could take Sally to the Venice Biennale, where one of his paintings was being shown. We both knew that this would likely be his last trip abroad. I'd told him he could take Sally to Venice if he took Ernest, too. "Ernest doesn't care about art," my father had said. "He's eight years old," I'd said. "He cares about his grandpa." They'd all spent two weeks touring Italy—Venice, Florence, and Rome—a trip Sally still mentioned at least once a day. A trip that I, alone with my father as a child, had also taken a version of.

"Can you look up Bill Murray's net worth?" Ernest asked me, turning away from the window.

He'd watched *Groundhog Day* again at his mother's the day before. He could've asked her to search for Bill Murray's financial situation, but for some reason he kept these kinds of requests for me. I looked up Bill Murray's fortune online.

"And how rich are we?" Ernest asked.

"A lot less than that," I said.

I don't know why I wasn't ready to tell him the actual number, why it felt wrong. My father had left behind a significant amount of money, and I was still getting used to it. I hadn't known him to have so much.

My phone rang. Nikki couldn't help checking on the kids whenever they were with me for the weekend.

"I got a call from Ernest's teacher," she said.

"How are you doing?"

"Sorry. Yes. How are you doing? She says Ernie's drawings worry her. She says he keeps drawing dead people."

I left the living room.

"We know this already," I said, once I reached my office. "It's just a phase. Little boys are drawn to violent scenes."

Nikki asked me to look through our son's backpack for what he'd drawn at school that day.

"Describe what you see," she said, once the drawing was in my hand.

What I saw was a single page with the instruction "Draw yourself many years in the future!" and my son's response: a drawing of his own gravestone, with mine, his mother's, and Sally's surrounding it.

"Are there dates on the gravestones?" Nikki asked.

"Only on mine," I said. "According to our son, I'll die in . . . almost exactly two years."

My ex-wife audibly shivered at the other end of the line.

"It's just a drawing, Nik."

I was pissed that Ernest's teacher had called her instead of me.

"He shouldn't be thinking about death so much," Nikki said. "I think he might be traumatized."

"Let's not bring trauma into this. He's had a rough year."

"I'm surprised he didn't draw your father's grave," Nikki said. "He misses him."

"Does he?"

"We all do."

I heard some glasses clink in the background.

"Do you have company?"

"Just Franny," she said. "Just having drinks with Franny."

"Hi, Franny," I said.

Nikki echoed my hello, and I heard Franny say, "Is he offering you more money again?" (I kept suggesting that I increase Nikki's alimony, but she kept refusing, on the grounds that she'd married—and divorced—a struggling novelist, not an art-world heir.) "Take the fucking money," I heard Franny say.

"I've been using this wine-delivery service," Nikki said, at random, hoping, I could tell, that I hadn't heard Franny. "They're so responsive. Every time I have the smallest question, the slightest issue, they answer right away. I wonder if I'm their only customer."

Sally came into my office then.

"Is that Mom on the phone?" she asked.

"Yes, honey. Do you want to talk to her?"

"I just saw her this morning," my daughter said, and left the room.

"They really make you feel special," Nikki said.

"At least *she* didn't draw me dead in two years," I said.

Sally wanted to hang some art. She thought that my new apartment lacked life, and since I'd inherited (on top of all his money and books) my father's last series of paintings, a series Sally had seen take shape in the old man's studio for months, she thought that what we should hang was a no-brainer.

"There's no room for all four," I told her. "You'll have to pick one."

"I like the walls white like that," Ernest said.

"It's depressing," Sally said. "It feels like a hospital in here."

"You've never been in a hospital," I said, deciding, apparently, to side with my son.

"There's stuff everywhere at Mom's," Ernest went on. "It's suffocating."

" 'Suffocating'?" Sally said. "That's a big word for you."

"Shut the fuck up," Ernest said.

I should have said something, and maybe I would have, had I been given more time, but Sally lost a tooth then, her last cuspid, on the breadstick she'd been snacking on. She spit the tooth onto the coffee table, and the sound it made hitting the glass was the last thing Ernest and I heard for a while, as Sally quickly left the room, leaving us to stare at the piece of bone she'd just expelled, sitting amid a little blood and half-chewed dough. *Was* it a piece of bone, by the way? You always hear that your smile is the visible part of your skeleton, but are teeth made of actual bone? Ernest started blinking rapidly, every blink drawing the left corner of his mouth up with it.

"Are you okay?" I asked.

He dipped a finger in the blood next to Sally's tooth. This seemed to calm him down, so I let him do it. He drew a red circle on the glass.

The reason my father had liked Sally more than Ernest was that Ernest wasn't very good at drawing. Or, rather, he wasn't curious about how to get better at drawing. He'd gone with his grandfather to the Art Institute once a week, too, for a time, but soon he asked to be excused, and my father never forgave him. One thing he'd recognized in Ernest, however, was a talent for drawing near-perfect circles freehand. I think that's why he was so pissed at him, in the end. An assured freehand circle was a sign that you could be great at drawing, according to my father, if only you put your mind to it.

"It's a nice circle," I said to my son.

He clenched his fist and, with the meaty side, erased what he'd drawn.

The rain had now acquired the consistency of mucus, each drop sticking to and sliding down the window.

How could it only be six P.M.? Time moved so slowly when the kids were around. I couldn't wait to experience what everyone said: *They grow up so fast.* Even seeing them every other weekend, I noticed no changes.

I guess Ernest had changed somewhat, though. One time, when he was in kindergarten, I picked him up and the teacher's summary of his behavior read, "Cried often but participated!" I'd shown it to Nikki (we were still married then), and we'd both laughed at it for minutes, commenting on how wonderful an epitaph it would be, before pretending that we hadn't just joked about a day when our son would be dead. We hadn't, really. We'd joked about a hypothetical epitaph, for a hypothetical person, way in the future. And now the real Ernest was drawing all of us dead, and I couldn't remember when I'd last seen him cry. Not at his grandfather's funeral, not for the dog, and not for Lane.

Sally came back into the room with a toothbrush to polish her tooth and a little cup to place it in. She informed me that she would leave the tooth right outside her bedroom door tonight, as opposed to under her pillow, because she didn't want to be woken up by the tooth fairy (whom we all knew she knew was me).

She didn't say anything about Ernest messing with her blood.

Instead, she jumped back into the conversation we'd been having before the tooth, preparing to offer a compromise.

"I can tell you're not ready to hang Grandpa's paintings," she told Ernest. "Maybe it's too soon."

Ernest didn't seem to understand what Sally meant by "too soon."

"Grandpa hated me," he said.

"No, he didn't," Sally said.

It would have been better if I'd said it myself, or immediately backed up Sally, but looking at Ernest I had the most vivid memory of being his age, of having to go to my father's studio to show him the drawings I'd made that week, something that I'd had to do every Sunday night. I remembered him discarding drawing after drawing, and how convinced I'd been that he hated my guts.

"He thought I was stupid because my favorite part of the Italy trip was the Trevi Fountain," Ernest said.

"He didn't think you were stupid. He just wanted you to like the museums and the churches more."

Sally again. I still hadn't spoken to reassure my son that his grandfather had loved him. I thought it was pretty weird of Ernest, too, after seeing the Bargello, or the Bridge of Sighs, for that matter, to have liked the Trevi Fountain so much. My own favorite part of the Italy tour, as a child, had been the San Marco convent in Florence—a good choice, according to my father, though he'd seemed surprised by it. Perhaps he'd been more surprised by my capacity to make good choices than by the choice itself.

"I was going to say let's not hang Grandpa's paintings anyway," Sally went on, "but maybe we could hang some of our stuff, you know? Just so it's less sad in here."

"That's a great idea," I said.

Even Ernest thought so.

While I made dinner, I let them pick their best work to Scotch-tape on the walls. After dinner, there would be bedtime, I determined. After bedtime, I could try to work, maybe finish that chapter I had been writing for weeks. The nights I had the kids were usually more productive. Since I'd bought myself a new apartment, a new desk, the right ergonomic chair, and a year off from my job, I'd discovered that I was the kind of writer who worked better when he was stealing time from other obligations. An hour here, two hours there, in between meetings, on my lunch break. I was better in a rush. Three months now of entire days at my disposal, and I'd written so little. In the mornings, I looked at what I had, despaired, and then read better writers than me for the rest of the day. Lately, I'd been looking at art books, too. My father's collection had made its way to my living room. But tonight I would work well, I told myself, breading the cutlets. Because I'd been deprived of the possibility for a few hours, I would work well. Dinner, put the kids to bed, then work. I'd told Nikki I would talk to Ernest about his drawing of our family graves, but I knew I wouldn't. How did one start a conversation like that? How did one keep it on track? It always looked easy in the movies. Mothers telling daughters how hard it was being a woman, fathers explaining death to sons in less than a minute, and, in both cases, explanations making sense, big warm hug, conversation over. I couldn't do it. And what was wrong with drawing your own grave anyway? There was something therapeutic about it, wasn't there? We'd done it since Ernest was old enough to draw stick figures—drawn the things he was afraid of.

. . .

This reminded me of a book I'd read as a college student, one weekend when I was visiting my father. I'd taken it from his shelf, a slim volume about the drawings made by children in war zones, what could be learned from them. I don't know why it had appealed to me. I guess I'd always been attracted to technically poor drawings—lines for limbs, squares for buildings, things that looked like I could've drawn them myself. My father had tried to make my interest sound fancy, said I liked "art brut," but I don't know if I *liked* it, exactly, or if I simply found comfort in it, its naïveté. If I could reproduce a drawing easily, then it meant that I could've been its creator in the first place, right? At least that's what I thought as a child, when I copied Bill Traylor's crooked houses and Henry Darger's little girls with penises. My father had this rule that I had to make at least one sketch a day. I could keep copying, sure, you learned a lot from copying, he said, but it was important to come up with things of your own, too, your own way of rendering the texture of a lemon on a wooden table, for example, your own way of interpreting shadows on a sill. It was a person's way of dealing with the small things that made him unique.

I drowned the cutlets in boiling oil, and realized as I watched them golden that I remembered quite a few things about the book. The book about children in war zones and what they drew. I remembered that roads that suddenly stopped, or mouthless faces, could be interpreted as signs of trauma. I remembered that traumatized children tended never to draw the sun. Ernest didn't draw suns anymore, hadn't drawn a sun in months, but maybe it was all right. Maybe he thought the sun was implied in most drawings, or boring to draw. And no sun in a child's drawing was still better than several suns, according to the book, if memory served. Several suns could indicate developing psycho-sis, or even psychopathic tendencies. What you wanted, really, as a parent, was for your child to draw one sun and one sun only. But where would a sun have fit in Ernest's drawing, anyway? The drawing of our family plot? Wouldn't it have been worse if Ernest had drawn a sun there, over all our gravestones?

We ate dinner. Sally made a big deal out of her missing tooth, but all in all she was happy, a happy girl who kept talking and talking—about the exhibition she'd just prepared in the living room, her day at school, her memories of Florence. It was hard to relate to Sally sometimes. When she was too happy, I could sometimes feel like I was in a commercial. Like I was watching a commercial, rather. For healthy snacks. I'd be happy that she was happy, of course, but I'd also feel like I was losing her, like I couldn't reach her where she was. I'd had this fear, before be-coming a father, that my children would be like me, mostly sad and overanxious, but Nikki had promised me they wouldn't, that we would raise them to be happy and only reasonably wor-ried. I'd told her that the fear, then, became that my children and I would have nothing in common. She'd laughed at that. She'd thought that I was joking.

The exhibition in the living room was mostly of Sally's work. She went everywhere with the leather case her grandfather had given her years ago (her "portfolio"), but most of Ernest's pro-duction was at Nikki's, and so he hadn't had much to pick from. Sally was a big fan of the cross section, always had been. Through the years, she'd drawn countless variations of apartment build-ings whose façades had been cut away to reveal what every family was doing, each in its little square. Tonight, she'd hung cross sections I'd never seen, of our local supermarket and of her pregnant aunt (Nikki's sister), who was expecting twins.

"I don't understand something," Ernest said as we observed the twin fetuses. "Are the babies going to be from two different dads?"

Sally told him he was an idiot, that even though Aunt Sophie had used a sperm donor, it was still only one guy's jizz, that they didn't just mix a bunch of different jizzes in a glass before they gave it to the woman to drink.

Ernest had only three drawings in the exhibit: two he'd made in a rush right before dinner of the Trevi Fountain (piles of shiny coins at the bottom of the fountain in the first drawing, and then, in the second, nothing left after the cleaning crew had come—no sun in either picture), and one he'd made the day before at his mom's, a still from *Groundhog Day*—the scene where Bill Murray orders the whole diner menu for breakfast. He liked drawing food. What he'd done best there was the glisten on the blob of wine-colored jam in the middle of the doughnut, and I congratulated him for it.

"Great job on the jam," I said, and he asked me to look up how much money was at the bottom of the Trevi Fountain.

"It changes all the time," I said. "You know that."

Ernest actually knew a lot more about the Trevi Fountain than I did, fascinated as he'd been after seeing it scraped clean one morning under police surveillance. He'd been the one to tell me that the fountain had to be cleaned once a week, because people threw so much money in it, and that the money went to the homeless of Rome.

"I think there should be a website that tells you how much money they pull out of the fountain every week," Ernest said.

"The Trevi is so boring," Sally said. "At first, I thought you

could wish for anything there, but the wish is actually mandatory. You have to wish to go back to Rome one day."

"I think that's just a guideline," I said. "You're always free to
wish for whatever."

"I wish for Grandpa to be able to see us right now," Sally
said, closing her eyes.

Mine met Ernest's as she said this, and I saw sheer panic
there, and I saw that he saw me see it. He broke eye contact immediately.

I pretended to look at my watch and said that it was time for
bed.

"But I didn't finish my placards!" Sally said. "I haven't named
all my drawings yet!"

I said that she could finish tomorrow.

Sally said, "I can't wait for tomorrow!" and I felt it again, the
distance between us.

While her brother brushed his teeth, Sally told me we could just
hang one of her grandfather's paintings in her bedroom, if Ernest was really dead set against seeing them in the rest of the
apartment.

"It could be just for me," she said. "I could fall asleep looking
at it, like the friars in San Marco fell asleep to their own personal
Fra Angelico every night."

It felt wrong to me, hanging such an expensive work of art
in an eleven-year-old's bedroom. Like jewelry on a newborn.

"I'll think about it," I said.

That was good enough for her.

.   .   .

Ernest, as I tucked him in, asked me if he was going to die during the night, something I knew he asked his mother every night as well. I promised he wouldn't. I'd been afraid of sleep at his age, too, of being unconscious, of what could happen then, that perhaps I would go too far in and unplug my brain forever instead of just turning it off for the night. I remembered asking my father once, "Will I die during the night?" and him saying that he didn't know, that no one could know these things. I never asked again. To Ernest, though, I'd always given the only answer a modern parent could give—"No, honey, of course you won't die during the night"—which reassured him but also made it so that he had to ask again and again every time he went to bed. And made me worry that, on the off chance that he did die in his sleep, the last thing my son would have heard from me was a lie.

I think that's why I'd loved my father, in the end. His honesty. It turned people off—it had turned me off, too, when he started applying it to Ernest—but it was meant to help. It had taught me not to be a wimp. Not that I thought Ernest was a wimp. But he definitely hadn't come out of his visit to the San Marco convent with my father as transformed as I'd been by mine. At San Marco, going into cell after cell with my dad, one friar's bedroom after another, in utter silence, I'd realized that what he wanted me to understand was that one slept alone and didn't complain, that being alone was not only fine but what one had to aspire to. At least I think that's what he'd meant.

I cleaned up the kitchen. I wanted a drink. I never drank when I was alone with the kids, though, not even a glass of wine once they were down. In case something happened and I had to drive them to the hospital. Even when Nikki and I were still married, I waited until she was home at night to have one. She didn't drink when she was alone with them, either, but when we were together, we often had a glass or two, and didn't worry about who would do what in an emergency. We were good drunks together. We would figure it out, was the thought. I wanted to talk to her again. I looked at the weather forecast on my phone instead, even though I knew that the only way Chicago could work, as a city, was if we all agreed to stop doing that. Outside my windows, twentysomethings, but also people my age, were flocking along Damen Avenue to gather at Gold Star, Big Star, Violet Hour, Rainbo, to drink and forget about something, or think about it harder. It was barely nine, the night was only starting for them. I understood that the reason people moved to the suburbs to raise their kids had little to do with the schools— it was because they had to stop seeing how much fun the childless were having.

I sat at my desk and looked at the last few lines I'd written, but I'd forgotten to put my phone on silent and was immediately interrupted by a string of texts from my friend Henry, who was on his way to Paris to promote his sixth novel, which had just been translated into French. He was still at the airport, taking off in an hour, but he'd already met a French fan (he was fairly famous), a cute lawyer who was on the same flight as him. He sent me a selfie of them eating tortas at O'Hare's Frontera, Henry's latest novel on the table between them. "Lucky bastard," I texted back. "All that happened to me tonight was Sally lost a tooth." "That's amazing," Henry responded. "You should write a story about it." I couldn't tell if he was being serious. Henry was constantly telling me that I should write more personal stuff, that the reason my first (and so far only) novel had sold so little was that people didn't want to read about hundred-percent-fictional characters anymore, they wanted real humans, real life, and I'd had such an interesting life, being the son of a big-deal artist, traveling the world with him as a boy, losing my mother so young, meeting Nikki after having been originally set up with her sister (yes, the one expecting twins), and then the divorce. People loved divorce stories, Henry said. The book he was going to Paris to promote had, in large part, been inspired by his own. For a minute, I considered writing about Sally's tooth. I texted Henry, "Are teeth actually bone, or some other material?" and he answered, "Look it up!" which I did. I learned that bones were made of living tissue and could therefore heal, but teeth couldn't. Teeth were deader than bones. My daughter had lost something that had been dead inside her for a long time. I wondered if Nikki still kept the kids' teeth.

I looked at Ernest's drawing again. He'd drawn some flowers on his mother's and his sister's graves, at least. Both of ours were just gray. I wondered for the first time what happened to children of divorce when they died, which parent they got buried next to, if they died before having families of their own. Now that I'd split with Nikki, and planned on never remarrying, I assumed I would be buried with my own parents at Rosehill, and not with her at Hebrew Benevolent. I'd converted to Judaism to put her mind at ease that we would rest together for eternity, but now she'd either forgotten ever wanting this or felt ridiculous for having wanted it, which were two completely different things but still looked exactly the same to whoever wasn't in Nikki's head.

.   .   .

Ernest's drawing wasn't that bad, I thought. Technically speaking. Why had my father insisted that he was weak? He'd never told Ernest this directly ("I know you can't tell children they're weak anymore"), but he'd told me. I hadn't wanted to make too much of his obvious preference for Sally before then. I'd wanted to believe that it was only natural, that the first grandchild always had to hold a special place in an old man's heart, but he'd explained to me one day that it wasn't so: he preferred Sally because she was smarter than Ernest. Ernest was about three at the time. My father couldn't help comparing them, noting what Sally had already achieved by the time she was Ernest's age, how she'd spoken in full sentences and shown curiosity for the written word long before age two, how early she'd asked about God, when her brother seemed concerned only with what was in front of him— if that. I'd told my father that girls and boys developed at a different pace, but he'd countered that even *I* had been smarter than Ernest at his age, and that *I* had been a boy. I'd felt a split second of relief at not being last, at not faring as poorly in my father's estimation as Ernest did. A relief immediately followed by guilt, of course, which had driven me to defend Ernest's honor with even more passion—to no end. "Look at this drawing," my father had concluded, pointing at one of Ernest's maroon crayon storms on our fridge, ruining it for me. "Sally already had the intuition of perspective at his age. What is this shit?" I'd believed before then that all children's drawings held some interest, that they could never be bad. But of course they could.

I went to the living room, Ernest's drawing in hand, to look for the book about children in war zones. I didn't think my son was traumatized by his grandfather's death, or the dog's, or Lane's, but maybe? How could you tell trauma from fear, or from deep sadness? When my mother died, I'd been horribly sad, not traumatized, I don't think. My father had taken me to Italy the following week, to see the San Marco convent and other things that lasted longer than people. It had helped.

I found the book and started reading it, taking occasional breaks to look at the drawings on the wall. I had children who drew supermarkets, I thought. I had children who drew well-lit places, an abundance of fresh produce, an abundance of food, babies about to be born, flowers on some of our graves—not massacres, not enemies, nothing like the drawings I was seeing in the book, which their creators had titled "Nuclear Winter," "Dead Dad on Threshold," "Three Bodies at a Crossroads," "Headless Children in Ditch."

As I checked my kids' drawings for signs of trauma, it occurred to me that my father might have been doing the same for me at the time, on Sundays. Not checking for signs of trauma, exactly—I don't think he much believed in that word applied to upper-class American children—but perhaps the reason he'd asked to see my drawings every week wasn't so much that he'd hoped I would become a great artist (he had to have abandoned that idea quickly) but that he'd wanted to make sure I was all right, that I was developing properly. For the first time since he'd died, I wished I could give him a call.

Around one A.M., Ernest came in. He'd just had a bad dream and wanted cereal. The way I'd always dealt with nightmares was the way my father had taught me to deal with them: you had to draw what had happened in the dream, and burn the result in the sink, to prevent the nightmare from ever coming back. The technique worked exactly a hundred percent of the time, and when Ernest came into the living room, he already had his box of crayons and a piece of paper in hand. I took him to the kitchen, so he could eat his cereal while he drew.

"What did you dream about?" I asked.

"Lane," he said.

He never spoke of Lane. There'd been counseling at school for the kids who'd seen him fall dead in the cafeteria, and the counselor had reassured us that Ernest's mental health was sound, that our son would let us know if and when he needed to talk about Lane.

"What was Lane doing in the dream?"

"He was dead. I'm not sure it was a dream, though. Maybe I was just remembering when he died."

"Okay," I said. "Do you want to . . . draw it?"

Ernest nodded. He'd had what he was sure was a nightmare before dreaming/thinking about Lane, though, and he wanted to draw that first. He drew us all murdered by an octopus-like creature, the whole family torn to pieces. All of us but him—he'd simply witnessed the scene. He knew as he drew it that that monster in particular would never come haunt his dreams again, and so he applied himself: this was goodbye. We burned it.

When the time came for Ernest to start drawing Lane, the scene of his death, I paid attention. I watched my son work. The book I'd just been reading had taught me that the order in which children drew episodes from their lives was significant, that a traumatized child would always start by drawing the most frightening aspect of a scene, and only then move on to décor, tweaking secondary elements and polishing up details at length without ever going back to the first part. Ernest sure drew Lane first, Lane lying on the floor, eyes closed and mouth open, his tongue sticking out, then went on to sketch the tiles he lay on, a group of kids gathered around the body, all connected to arrows that stated their names. Then he filled the background with a food counter, rectangles of mashed potatoes, fish nuggets, and peas—each nugget and pea drawn individually. I'm sure that all of this had been on the menu that day. The day Lane died. When scared, children were able to commit a great amount of detail to memory, the book had said. Even running for their lives, they were able to catch glimpses of military logic, they noticed how many planes were in the sky, in which direction they were flying. They remembered where bombs had fallen and what had been destroyed, who'd jumped in the river. Ernest went to pee, and I assumed he was finished with the drawing.

"Do you want to burn it in the sink?" I asked when he returned.

"I'm not done," he said, and went back to work on Lane's body, to which he hadn't added a detail since he'd first drawn it, to which he hadn't even added any color. He drew Lane's right hand, which had been a strange hand, one with a thumb the size of a slider bun. I knew the thumb had made Lane the object of a lot of jokes. Macrodactyly, his problem was called—Lane himself had told me about it once. Though I knew the kids made fun of him for it, I wasn't sure whether Ernest ever had.

"Did Lane's hand frighten you?" I asked Ernest.

He shrugged.

"I didn't care, really," he said. "Matt made fun of him all the time, but I didn't care."

"Do you wish you'd defended him, though?" I asked. "When Matt made fun of him?"

I thought maybe that was what was haunting my son, his first-ever regret, not having stood up for Lane and his enormous finger, but Ernest shrugged again.

"I guess it was a little weird," he said. "But when you're weird people make fun of you. You have to accept it."

After a while, during which he added and colored more peas, he asked me if there was anything I wanted to draw and burn in the sink myself. I said there wasn't, but he insisted.

"Don't you want to draw Grandpa?" he asked.

I waited too long to say anything.

"It would be nice if we forgot about him," he said. He wasn't looking at me, was still coloring peas.

"Why do you think that?" I said. "Did you not like Grandpa?"

"It makes you sad to think about him. You've been sad since he died. I think we should all forget about him. It was a long time ago."

I told him that it wasn't that easy, that you had to remember the people you loved, but he seemed impervious to the argument.

He'd put a roof on top of the school cafeteria, and was about to get to work on the sky above it.

They said never to act shocked when your child told you what was on his mind, to welcome any thought of his with an open heart, and I guess I'd internalized the advice well enough. I didn't tell Ernest how fucked up it was, suggesting that we all forget about my father, that we treat any memory we had of him the way we treated nightmares. I didn't tell him he worried me.

"Was it sunny that day?" I asked him instead. "The day Lane died?"

I thought of Nikki's sister then, for some reason, the twins in her stomach, the four hands, the twenty fingers growing in there. I thought of my friend Henry, too, who was going so far and at such speed right now, to Paris, another place my father had loved. He had to still be up there in the dark. Henry, I mean.

Ernest said that it had been raining the day Lane died, and grabbed a gray crayon. He handed me a black one, so I could get started on my own drawing. He was staring at me. He wouldn't stop staring at me until I started drawing. Maybe I could draw a part of my father, I thought. One specific memory. Surely there was something about him that I could stand to forget. Ernest smiled when I took the crayon. Then, right when I put it to paper to get to work on my outline, he asked how much I'd left by Sally's door, for the tooth.

Most Die Young

"MOST DIE YOUNG," PROFESSOR CROZE ADMITTED.

"Define 'young,'" I said, not looking up from my notebook. Professor Croze was not a pretty sight. There were white spots on the back and the sides of her tongue, and she seemed unaware of them, or unconcerned, at least—she opened her mouth wide to say even the smallest things.

"Under the age of thirty-eight," she said.

I wrote, "Young < 38," and underlined it twice. It didn't matter that I'd just turned thirty-eight. I never took anything personally.

Professor Croze went on to list the main causes of death among the Pawong, a Malaysian tribe that she'd studied as a young anthropologist.

"They get murdered, of course—they're such easy targets— or they go hang themselves in the forest when they've had enough. Sometimes they convince themselves they've been cursed, and they fade out and die within a few weeks, without any evidence of infection or disease."

I was writing a story on the Pawong for *Wide,* a cultural magazine with interests so broad that no one knew quite how to think about it. From one month to the next, I'd seen it shuffled around among the entertainment, politics, and women's-interest sections of the newsstand.

The Pawong were a small tribal society that my boyfriend, Glauber, had told me about a couple of months earlier. Glauber is a name, in case you're wondering, and it was Glauber's name. I'm not just making it up for the sake of the story. Glauber had been an anthropology minor in college, and random facts about faraway cultures would pop into his head on occasion, usually over dinner, when there was a lull in our conversation. "The Mehinaku are so strict about female and male task attribution that a bachelor would rather starve than cook for himself," he would say, or "The Aztecs believed that the goal of war was to take prisoners, not kill the enemy, and that's why they lost to the Spanish so quickly."

What he'd told me about the Pawong, though, on the night we broke up, had been meant not as edifying trivia but as an insult, I think, even though I hadn't taken it that way—as I said, I take nothing personally. We'd just had an argument about a four-day weekend: Glauber wanted to go visit his parents in Burgundy, I wanted to stay in Paris. "How surprising," Glauber had said. "What is it now? Is it the thought of getting on a train full of strangers that frightens you? Or is it seeing an old man on the verge of death?" (Glauber's father had cancer.)

"You know what it is," I'd said. "I can't sleep in the country."

"You hate it."

"I don't hate the country," I'd said. "It's just I get bored there during the day. And then at night I get scared."

"So it *is* fear," Glauber had said. Such triumph on the "is." "It's always fear with you." He'd closed his eyes at this point, which was something he did whenever he planned a sentence more than four words long. "There's this tribe somewhere in South Asia, the Pawong, if I remember it right, and they don't understand war or even conflict at all. Neighboring tribes come and slaughter them and rape their women, and the Pawong don't know to defend themselves or retaliate. It doesn't even occur to them that they could respond."

"I can't see how this relates to Burgundy," I'd said.

"The Pawong," Glauber had resumed, eyes still closed, "live in fear that their enemies will come back, but they don't prepare for it. They just dread it and dread it, and teach their children to dread it, and then, when their children are properly scared, it makes them incredibly proud. 'My son is so much more afraid than your son,' they boast to their friends and neighbors. They value fear more than we do courage, or anything else, really. You would be right at home with the Pawong."

"You want me to go there and get raped and slaughtered?" I'd said.

"No," he'd said. "I think you should go live with the Pawong and be their god."

Within the hour, he'd packed and left, and although it's true that things hadn't been great between us for a while—we'd run out of things to say to each other, and our silences were, frankly, boring—I would have appreciated a little notice, a little time to get used to the idea of breaking up before the breakup's implementation.

A few days after he left, I started researching the Pawong and stumbled on an article about warless societies by Professor Croze. She had only a few lines about the Pawong, but they confirmed what Glauber had said:

Shyness, fear, and timidity are highly valued among the Pawong. "To be angry is not to be human," goes one of their sayings, "but to be fearful is." Pawong children are taught to express and show their fear to their peers, as well as to avoid conflict at all costs. The Pawong flee at the first sign of danger, and don't see a need to make excuses. "We are frightened," they say, and that is explanation enough.

Two months after reading these lines, I was in Professor Croze's office asking the obvious questions.

"How did the Pawong accept your presence among them if they're so fearful? Aren't they afraid of strangers?"

"Well, I guess I wasn't that scary!" Professor Croze answered with a burst of laughter. "I mean, look at me!"

Because she asked directly, I had no choice but to look up from my notebook. I wondered if whatever was on her tongue was contagious and if she was going to die.

"In fact, they were way more concerned about my own lack of fear in coming to them than anything else," she went on. "They said, 'But what if we had been bad people? Did you think about that?' They couldn't understand why I would leave my home and take chances staying with them. They thought I was brave, which made me weirdly proud—except they see no value in bravery. They think bravery is a form of stupidity, actually." I held my breath every time Professor Croze spoke, in case her tongue infection could be airborne, and then for five seconds after she was done, to be sure.

Leaving her office, I got lost in the same maze of university hallways that I'd always had trouble navigating as a student. I'd noticed, back then, that the more prestigious the professors, the more carefully hidden their offices were. I assumed that the Sorbonne ranked Professor Croze fairly highly, because her office had been particularly hard to find. In my time, there had been a legendary office, Professor Sarrazin's, and every year I would hear of a student having a meltdown in some hallway during registration week, trying to find it. The "Sarrazin Triangle" had direct consequences on Professor Allan's class enrollment—that's how I knew about it. I'd taken Allan's class my first semester. His office was the one you stumbled upon when, after looking in vain for Sarrazin's, you were ready to give up on Venice in the Middle Ages to take a shot at Advanced Latin. Allan's class was always full.

At the restaurant, waiting for my sister, I refrained from googling "white spots tongue." My sister wasn't late, by the way. I'm always early. This used to drive Glauber crazy. "Nothing horrible will happen if you're a little late," he'd say. I don't understand why people say things like that. I mean, I know the chances that my being late would lead to any catastrophic consequences are low, maybe exactly as low as my being early would, actually—I don't know, I'm not a math person—but I'm sure they're not zero, they're not "nothing," so why say anything at all?

"Sorry I'm late," Delphine said. "My last dog took forever to die."

"You're not late," I said.

"I know. It was just a way to introduce the fact that my last dog took forever to die and maybe fish for a little sympathy."

Delphine is a veterinarian, which is not something that she's dreamed of doing since she was a little girl, contrary to what people assume when she informs them of her profession. As a little girl, Delphine wanted to be a secretary at a travel agency. We both did.

"I'm sorry about your dog," I said.

"Well, it wasn't *mine*," Delphine said. "But, yeah, thanks. I treated that guy his whole life. It's never easy, I guess."

Delphine is married with two kids, so we never talk about her life over lunch. She's the first to admit that it's a boring topic.

"You need to get back on the horse," she told me, after asking about my sex life since Glauber. She sat up straighter, scanned the room for a horse.

"I liked Glauber," I said. "I think it's healthy to mourn for a little while."

"You didn't like Glauber," Delphine said. "No one likes Glauber. Please don't get back together with Glauber."

I'd had an erotic dream about Glauber a few nights before (telescopic hard-on, lavender fields) and had made the mistake of telling Delphine about it. She'd invested it with meaning. Drawn conclusions.

I guess it wasn't really a *mistake*. I tell Delphine everything.

"Glauber wasn't all bad," I said.

"He wore oxfords sockless."

"He was rich, though."

"He wasn't *that* rich," Delphine said. "And you don't care about money as much as you think you do. I mean, you don't travel, you don't smoke, you don't eat meat . . . you're literally allergic to most jewelry." She paused, knowing she was forgetting a major money pit that didn't concern me. "You don't have dreams of any kind," she added, not at all definitively, going high-pitched on the word "kind" and leaving her sentence suspended there, in the hope that I would contradict it.

I had nothing. Rather, my dreams were so humble that normal people would have considered them laughable. My dreams were to not get murdered, to not suffer a ludicrous death, to not think about death all the time, to live in an apartment small enough that I could see all of it from anywhere I stood. (I had already fulfilled that last dream.) I was about to capitulate when I saw Professor Allan, twenty years older than when I'd last seen him but still unmistakably Professor Allan, walk into the restaurant. Since we were close to the university, this wasn't hard to believe, but because I'd just thought about him after so many years spent not thinking about him, the surprise made me yell his name across the room. Allan turned in our direction. He looked at my face, and then right past it, to see if there was someone else behind our table. There was nothing behind our table but a chalkboard listing the daily specials. Allan walked over to us, squinting the whole way, as if he could crush my features into recognition.

"You probably don't remember me," I said when he was close enough to hear. "I took your class about twenty years ago."

"Oh. Yes. You've been long forgotten then." Allan relaxed his eyes.

"I wasn't a very noticeable student to begin with," I said. "Although, once, I made you and the whole classroom laugh by mistranslating *clavicula Salomonis* as 'Solomon's clavicle.'"

"Oh . . . of course I remember you." His voice softened. "Of course, of course . . . Julie, right?"

"I'm just the sister," Delphine said, although no one had asked her anything.

The translation fiasco appeared to have placed me in Allan's memory, but his change of tone seemed to indicate that he also remembered me as the poor Julie whose parents had died during her freshman year. My parents had been poisoned by their water heater—carbon monoxide—and people tended to remember that because it had happened on the same day that terrorists had bombed the Saint-Michel Métro station, right next to the Sorbonne. I'd been in Allan's class when the bombs had gone off.

"I'm guessing you didn't pursue a career in ancient languages," Allan said. "What are you doing these days?"

He put his hand on my shoulder. Poor little Julie.

"I'm a journalist," I said, a little embarrassed.

"An essayist," Delphine corrected, encouragingly. I realized that she thought I was interested in Allan on a sexual level. I guess I'd yelled his name pretty loud.

"She's actually writing an essay in defense of ancient languages right now," Delphine went on. "With the new education reform and all."

"Oh, are you really?" Allan asked. It was unclear whether he'd picked up on Delphine's matchmaking signals or was just feigning interest in my career because he thought my life had been ruined forever during one of his classes. "Maybe you should interview me."

"That's a great idea," Delphine said.

"Over lunch, perhaps?" Allan suggested. His hand was still on my shoulder.

"Why not?" I said, only to please Delphine.

"She might never have been good at actual Latin," Delphine said, "but she was always so fascinated by the ancient Roman lifestyle, you know? When we were kids, she read all the *Astérix* comics and actually cheered for the Romans. I always thought that was the weirdest thing. Same thing happened later, when she read the Bible."

"Is that so?" Allan said.

It wasn't so, of course. Delphine had just invented a family memory right there on the spot so that I would have a better chance of sleeping with the guy. I'd never read the Bible, or *Astérix,* though I knew that the Romans weren't supposed to be the good guys in either. As a child, I'd mostly just played travel agent with Delphine; we'd take turns picking up a disconnected phone and setting up imaginary people with imaginary trips. Some of our clients went to Rome, sure, but my recommendations to them were only ever make-believe pizza places.

Allan gave me his cell number, I gave him my work number, and he went to have a quick coffee at the counter. I felt nauseous.

"Is there something on my tongue?" I said, and stuck it out.

"Dude, put that back in," Delphine said. "We're in public."

"Is there?"

"Why would there be?"

I told her about Professor Croze's tongue and requested her medical opinion.

"Could be papillomavirus," Delphine said. "Or just a fungus. Were the spots cauliflower-like in shape?"

"Are funguses airborne?"

"Come on. Eat your vegetables. You're fine. Plural of fungus is fungi, and you don't have tongue fungus, just like you didn't have Parkinson's last week or psoriasis last summer."

I wasn't fully convinced that I didn't have Parkinson's. Sometimes I held both my arms straight in front of me and the right one shook a little. Glauber thought I worried too much. "It's useless," he'd say. "I can assure you that no human beings ever wished, on their deathbed, that they'd spent more time worrying." "Except what if they died crushed by their own house?" I would say. "Don't you think their last thought would be something along the lines of Gee! I should've worried about that sag in the ceiling more actively!" Glauber would dismiss this kind of response on the grounds that, sure, there were always exceptions, but that we should be led by the rule and not be ruled by the exception. I hated when he said that, because he made it sound as if the reason I kept looking for exceptions was that I thought of myself as exceptional, whereas I believed, on the contrary, that it was my ordinariness itself that made me a better candidate for exceptional scenarios. Exceptional people died of cancer and heart attacks; it was the nobodies who suffered stupid and puzzling demises, to make up for the lack of surprises in their lives. At least, that had been my parents' experience. I suppose they'd even been given a double dose of last-minute reparations, having died an uncommon death on an exceptional day.

Delphine called me a "good girl" after I finished my vegetables. She used the same tone that she used on her dogs sometimes, but that was all right. She loved her dogs.

Back at the office, I had a voicemail from Allan—I'd given him only my work number, in an attempt to keep things professional—informing me of his lunchtime availability for the following week. He didn't sound very busy, which made things difficult. Coming up with an excuse or two is always doable, but no one believes you when you line up four in a row. Perhaps I could agree on the latest possible date he'd offered and then follow it with a last-minute "Something came up." Just as I was deciding to do so, I realized that I'd forgotten to ask Professor Croze to confirm my suspicion that the Pawong people, owing to the disdain they felt toward bravery, didn't have a word for cowardice. I'd noticed that, for readers eager to learn something about a different culture, the lack, in said culture, of a concept that they were familiar with was more likely to pique their interest than any other factoid. A foreign language having a single word to define something that they would need a whole sentence to express in their mother tongue would also be, conversely, a pleasure-giving piece of information. Highly quotable. That's why everyone knows about *Schadenfreude* and how the Inuit have forty-something words for snow. That's why, even though I don't know much about Japan, I do know that the Japanese have a word for one of my habits, which is to buy books, pile them up, and never read them (*tsundoku*). No word for cowardice in the Pawong language would mean that I had found my lede. I wondered what Glauber would think of my article. He'd probably think that I was a coward for going to an old—maybe even dying—professor to investigate, and not straight to the Pawong themselves.

"What's up?" I heard Delphine say on the other end of the line.

Sometimes my sister answered the phone before I even realized that I was calling her.

"Do you think I should go to Malaysia?" I asked. "For my article?"

"Absolutely not."

"I was thinking maybe it would make for a better story."

I heard Delphine take a deep breath. "I have trouble believing you would consider leaving a city you haven't gotten two miles away from in more than a decade for the sake of an article. You don't even like your job. Is someone threatening you? Does your boss want you to go?"

"No. It was just a thought."

"Did that thought pop into your head at a moment when, I don't know, you were mulling over grand gestures to win Glauber back?"

"I *like* my job. I just feel it's one that people tend to think very little of."

"Fucking Glauber," Delphine said.

"Everybody thinks they could be cultural journalists, because they, too, can write sentences and have opinions. Investigative journalism, on the other hand . . . I don't know. I was just thinking maybe it's time to take my career to another level. Nothing to do with Glauber. Glauber wanted me to go to the Pawong and be their god, for fuck's sake."

I was almost starting to convince myself that the idea of going to Malaysia had sprouted from my professional drive.

"You'd make such a terrible god," Delphine said. "You'd never know what to command. You'd beg for everyone's input all the time."

"Gods don't command," I said. "They just sit there and get adored."

"You wouldn't be too comfortable with adoration, either," she said.

I tried to picture a life among the Pawong. I knew that they lived deep in the forest, so I sat my imagined self on an ancient tree, whose dark trunk had been carved out as a throne for me. I don't know many kinds of trees, so I pictured a cedar, even though I'm pretty sure cedars aren't indigenous to Malaysia. Its massive roots popped out of the ground here and there to make sporadic benches on which the Pawong sat facing me. They looked frightened and wore only headbands and penile sheaths. I didn't picture any women. It would probably smell divine inside a cedar tree, I thought, but I realized I couldn't imagine scents.

"Maybe I could get used to adoration," I said to Delphine. "It's not like the total lack of it has made my life too terribly exciting so far."

"Life's not supposed to be exciting," Delphine said. "Only certain things are, like a good soccer game, or when you fall in love and stuff. Other than that, the way life works is, it gets you used to absolutely everything too fast, so that it becomes harder and harder to really enjoy anything other than maybe the repetitiveness itself, if you're one of those people, and that's that."

"But life *contains* those exciting things you list. It contains the soccer matches and the men worth loving, so why should we not expect the whole thing to be exciting?"

"That's very poor logic," Delphine said. "A bottle contains wine, yet the bottle itself is not exciting. Sometimes you'll get a nice view from a train window, but then the same train goes through miles and miles of shit. The train is not—"

"I get your point," I said. "There's never a need for more than one metaphor."

"I wasn't sure where that last one was going anyway."

I was still partly in my cedar-throne fantasy. I wrote a brief email to Professor Croze, asking for pictures, and Delphine must have read part of my mind, because she asked me what the Pawong looked like. "Maybe fear makes them incredible lovers," she said.

I'd been told I was a fantastic lay over the years, and after a while I'd decided to believe it. Maybe I had my pathological fear of everything to thank for it.

"I have to go now," I told Delphine. "To Group."

"No one has to go to Group," she said. We hung up.

Group. I found it unfair of Glauber to have left me on the grounds that I was afraid of everything, since we'd met at Group: a group for people suffering from generalized anxiety disorder, which I'd joined after dropping out of the group for hypochondriacs, because it didn't encompass all of my worries. Glauber's anxieties had been only a temporary affliction—they plagued him after he found out about his father's illness—and he soon got over them, but still. Where had his empathy gone? He'd behaved like one of these poor people who become rich and start looking down on the poor with more contempt than even the born rich do, because they're convinced that anyone can decide to stop being poor (they did it!), that it's all hard work and willpower and nothing to do with luck, and that, therefore, poor people are just lazy and weak minded.

I usually didn't share much at Group. I mostly went to take

comfort in the knowledge that I wasn't the only person who couldn't help thinking, whenever she bought a sweater, that she might be found dead in it. Group allowed me to really know where I stood on the scale of worried people, whereas a shrink never told you anything about other patients.

"I'm really worried that I might go blind," Ilse said at Group that evening. "I can't think of a worse fate. I know certain blind people are very happy and all, but I don't think I would have the inner resources to be one of them. And, if I have to be completely honest, which I guess is the purpose here, I think I'd rather be able to see what's in front of me than be happy."

Patrick nodded once and deeply at this confession.

"I never believed my thoughts originated in my brain, the way everyone else does," Ilse went on. "Or that my emotions came from my stomach. I feel like all of it comes from my eyes, you know? If I close my eyes longer than a blink"—she closed her eyes here to illustrate—"nothing happens. I don't feel anything. I can't think. So how would I manage without eyesight? And how would I watch my shows?"

That second question, which I believe was asked in jest, caused Helena to talk about her inability to commit to a TV show, out of fear that she would die before every plotline was resolved, even though she was in perfect health. Patrick told her about a website that streamed short films for free. "World-class directors," he said. "Foreign. Never more than thirty minutes long." As he was offering to give Helena the name of the website, his phone started ringing and he apologized profusely for forgetting to turn the sound off. He couldn't find the phone, though. Manically rummaging through the mess of his briefcase, he kept saying "Shush" in its general direction.

"Maybe you need to take that?" Colette offered, in her signature nice but firm tone. Colette was the moderator.

"I'm so very sorry," Patrick said, and at that point I felt my own phone vibrate in my pocket. I wouldn't have looked at it if my neighbor Yann hadn't looked at his. It was a text message from Delphine: "are you ok?"

"There's been a bombing at the Sorbonne," Yann informed us all, in an admittedly shaky voice—but no more shaky than the one he'd used, week after week, to talk about his fear of bay windows and open water.

"What do you mean, there's been a bombing at the Sorbonne?" Ilse asked, as if the sentence could have meant anything other than the sum of its components.

"everything ok," I texted Delphine. "i'm at group"

"stay where you are"

"you?"

"still at work. kids at the nanny's, seb at office"

This quick exchange reassured me of the safety of pretty much everyone I cared about. I'd changed phone numbers after publishing a damaging profile of a National Front official (not that he'd threatened or harassed me, but I was concerned that he might) and gotten rid of Glauber's number in the process (it had felt like the mature thing to do), so I couldn't check on him. I wasn't even sure that I would have. Everyone in Group was riveted to their screen, though; they had longer lists of loved ones to get through. I broke our circle to go stand by the window. The little square park, three stories below, was empty. Night was falling, and in the building across the street a TV was lit behind every other window.

"It was a long time coming," Ilse said.

"What?"

"The attack. They've been threatening to hurt us for a while."

I wouldn't have bet on Ilse being second to run out of people to check on, but there she was, looking through the same window as I was.

"I guess you're right," I said.

My phone started showing concern for my survival. It blinked with government-issued injunctions to take shelter immediately and await further instructions. Notifications from news agencies gorged the home screen with partial and temporary information. Twenty-nine confirmed deaths. Mostly students. Bomb had gone off in the library, open 24/7 and, during winter finals, packed at all hours. A suspect wearing black gloves seen fleeing the scene. Two explosions, actually. A possible second suspect on the run. List of subway stations closed to the public.

"You're a journalist, right?" Ilse said. "Shouldn't you have more information than us about what's going on?"

"I'm not that kind of journalist," I said.

"What kind are you?"

"How do you know I'm a journalist?" I asked. I couldn't remember ever having disclosed my profession at Group.

"Oh, Glauber told me. You know, after you guys got together, he started coming to Group on Mondays, so that you wouldn't be in the same circle of sharing."

"I know he did," I said.

"It's not advisable for couples or friends to participate in the same circle of sharing," Ilse recited.

"I didn't know he'd shared about me."

"Well, he didn't exactly *share* about you. We just got to talking after Group now and then, you know, over cookies and tea. It was more like private conversations."

Glauber had never told me about lingering after Group.

Behind us, Helena burst into tears. I checked my phone. Another bomb had gone off, this time in the lobby of a hotel near the American embassy. Possible hostage situation. Patrick retrieved a crumpled paper bag from his briefcase and started breathing into it.

"He seemed to be quite taken with you," Ilse resumed. "Glauber. I was surprised to learn you'd broken up."

"And how did you learn that?" I said.

"He came here last week. We hadn't seen him in *months*."

"Did his anxiety come back?"

"It's unclear," Ilse said. "His father just died. He said he was coming for closure, because we'd helped him a lot, you know, dealing with the whole thing, but I think he'll be back."

"You seem pretty happy about it," I said.

"Always nice to see familiar faces."

I received a text from an unknown number. "Are you all right?" it said. The signature followed immediately: "This is Bernard Allan, by the way." I don't think I'd ever known his first name. Only a few seconds had elapsed between getting the mysterious text and the revelation of its author's identity, but I'd somehow managed to convince myself that it was from Glauber, that he'd tracked down my new number. The disappointment made me actively hate poor Allan. Why was he writing to me? Didn't he have actual friends? How had he found my number? Why hadn't Glauber been able to?

"Everything all right?" Ilse asked. "Did you hear from everyone you might be worried about?"

"And others," I said.

"Do you think this is the end of the world?" Ilse said, and she wasn't looking out the window or vaguely at the horizon, in the way I assumed people did when they asked questions like that, but straight at me.

"Glauber told me you had an arrangement," she went on. "He told me that when you started dating you agreed on a place

to meet if the end of the world was coming and you weren't
already together."

Glauber hadn't lied. We'd once had a conversation about a
meeting place for the Apocalypse. We wanted to be out in the
world when it collapsed. I can't remember why.

"We actually had two," I told Ilse. "Two places. In case the
Apocalypse struck exactly our first meeting point."

"Clever!"

"I thought so, too, at the time. It was Glauber's suggestion.
Very foresighted. But then it made it complicated to decide
which of the two places to go to in the event—more than
likely—of the Apocalypse not striking one of the agreed-upon
meeting points. We thought we would have to go to the one
that was farthest from ground zero, but I'm not always good at
evaluating distances. Or what if the end of the world started at
different places simultaneously?"

"Yeah, like today, right? What would ground zero be? The
university? Or that hotel?"

"Exactly."

"I see," Ilse said, and she broke eye contact. Our fellow wor-
riers were mumbling stories that, judging by their grave faces,
involved us all dying in a very near future.

"Do you think he's waiting for you?" Ilse asked. "At one of
the two meeting points?"

"I sincerely doubt it," I said. "I'm not so sure what's happening right now qualifies as the Apocalypse. Also: we broke up."

"Well, as of last week, he didn't have a new girlfriend or
anything. And he did ask about you."

"What did you tell him?"

"There wasn't much to say," she said. "You never share."

"I guess I don't," I said. "I come here to listen. Just listening
helps."

Ilse nodded and squinted all at once. She didn't know what I meant.

"Do you mind telling me what they were?" she said. "The rendezvous points?"

"Why? Do you want to go?"

I'd meant it as a joke, but Ilse was dead serious.

"If that's okay with you, of course. I mean, it would have to be. Otherwise, I'd never know where to meet Glauber anyway!"

I told her what the two meeting places were—the Nespresso boutique by my office and the nicer Nespresso boutique by the Luxembourg Gardens—and she just left. No one tried to stop her.

The Pawong wouldn't have let me or Ilse leave without trying to stop us. They would have reminded us that the subways were closed, that subways were dangerous places anyway, with all the germs, or that it was a long walk, that walking contained its own threats, like low-flying birds, or things falling from buildings (flowerpots, bodies), that we would expose ourselves to potential chemical fallout (none of the authorities seemed to be considering the possibility that the bombings were a chemical strike; I was), that Glauber wasn't worth the trouble. And he wasn't. Delphine, on the other hand, was alone at her practice, worrying about her children, her husband, me. Delphine wasn't used to worrying the way I was.

As I walked, I forced myself to be amazed by the efficiency of those government warnings I kept receiving, forced myself to have grown-up, level-one social thoughts about how our government, so divided, so pathetic, so disrespected, still had the power to send a message to us all, to have everyone, for a brief moment at least, be on the same page. Well, everyone but the terrorists, of course. And me. Although the terrorists were probably following instructions and hiding out, too. Chances of running into them were low.

My phone vibrated in my hand. It wasn't Glauber.

"You didn't respond to my text," Allan said. "I'm worried."

I answered something along the lines of "I'm fine," but in a far more convoluted way. I'd answered Allan's call only because it meant that I would have to talk, and hearing my voice shaping correct sentences dictated by my brain reassured me whenever I felt panicky. It meant that I was still there. An ambulance passed.

"What are you—walking around town?" Allan said. "Don't you know what's going on?"

"May I ask how you got my personal number?"

"I called your office."

"And they just gave it to you?"

"I was *worried,*" he said.

"Eight hours ago, you didn't even remember who I was."

"Well, you've changed. Last time I saw you, you were a teenager. But of course I remember you."

"Only from a couple of faculty meetings they made you go to back in the day. How to deal with a bereaved student. Look, I'm not even writing an article on the second death of dead languages. I'm writing an article about the Pawong tribe. Unless you know anything about them, I don't see a reason for us to have lunch."

"I read Croze's books," Allan said. "I'm worried about her, too, actually. She stays late at work sometimes. She's not picking up her phone."

It surprised me that Allan and Croze were friends. He didn't seem the type to have older women friends.

"Her office is nowhere near the library," I said, trying to reassure him. "Plus, this morning, her tongue was covered in white spots. Maybe she's at home, nursing some kind of virus. Maybe she doesn't even know what's happened."

"That's just how her tongue is," Allan said.

"Is it a fungus?"

"I don't know. I think it's just discolored."

I was silent.

"I'll ask her about it, if you want. If she ever picks up the phone. Would that leave you more inclined to have dinner with me?"

I don't know which part of our conversation had gotten him thinking he could upgrade to dinner, but I appreciated his boldness.

"Only if whatever it is she has isn't contagious," I said.

I managed to have the phone call last exactly until I reached Delphine's practice.

"i'm here, about to knock," I texted Delphine. "don't be afraid. it's just me."

She came to the door immediately.

"Do you still keep beers in your vaccine fridge?" I asked.

Delphine opened the black drawer at the bottom of a small refrigerator full of vials.

"Help yourself," she said.

There was a dog on her consult table, a big freckled thing with front paws the size of smaller dogs, on which its head rested. The other two were missing. The other two paws.

"Her owner left when we heard about the first bomb," Delphine explained. "She wanted to get home to her kids. I was about to put her dog down, and she just left."

"Are you supposed to wait until she comes back to do the injection?"

"She said I should just go ahead and take care of it. She wrote me a check and everything."

The dog shivered when I touched her head. "You're going to die," I told the dog, but I said it nicely. "It's okay to be afraid."

"That's just mean," Delphine said. "Give her a break."

"She's standing up for you," I told the dog. "You're in good hands."

Delphine had been watching the news on her desktop computer. She'd muted it when we came in, but her eyes were still drawn to images I couldn't see from where I stood. She'd had three beers already.

"How long does she have?" I said. "If you don't put her down?"

"One, maybe two months of increasingly horrible pain."

The dog started licking my forearm. Her tongue was freckled like her body.

"Can you turn the screen around?" I asked my sister. I wanted to watch the news, too.

"The wires are too tight, actually. Come sit by me."

Delphine turned the sound on and dragged another chair over. I didn't want to leave the dog alone, so I carried her to the chair and nestled her hind-leg stumps into my lap.

The news showed people who had gathered on the security perimeter of the university. Some held flowers, as was customary, I guess, since I'd seen on TV other groups of people bring flowers where catastrophe had struck. I'd never questioned the practice before, but, having just walked through empty streets for more than forty minutes, I wondered where they'd found their bouquets. As far as I could tell, all the shops were closed. Delphine and I had had a real hard time finding flowers for our parents' funeral, because so few florists had been able to meet the demands that the attack on the Saint-Michel station had engendered.

There was a picture of them, our parents, on Delphine's desk. The dog yawned.

"Is she in pain right now?" I asked Delphine.

"She doesn't seem to be."

The dog had no idea what was going on. TV had bought her two more hours of life.

"Maybe we can wait a little to put her down then, no?"

"You mean until the next time she has a seizure? Like, in two days?" Delphine looked at the dog, then at the news, then at me. "Sure," she said. "If you take her home until then."

My phone chimed. An email from Professor Croze. "Here you go!" it read. She'd attached four black-and-white pictures. A Pawong house, a Pawong dinner, two Pawong men fishing, a Pawong family. They didn't look afraid. Or cowed. Or meek. Or, for that matter, friendly. They actually looked kind of scary.

I texted Allan to let him know that Professor Croze was safe, and that he should email her. The news now showed images of windowsills all over town on which people had lit candles. I had candles at home, I thought. There's a certain type of man who believes that scented candles are a romantic gift. Glauber was one of them.

Around six A.M., after a tired news anchor announced that two suspects had been arrested, I walked Delphine to her nanny's, then home. Her husband and kids asked me to stay for breakfast, and they wanted to know everything about the dog I was dragging in a dog wheelchair, but I told them that I needed some sleep, that I would come over for dinner instead.

Glauber was waiting for me in the hallway of my building, by the mailboxes. He apologized for showing up unannounced, but he'd had no other way to make sure that I was all right. "You changed your number," he said, and then sneezed. He was allergic to dogs, but it seemed a bit fast acting.

"I'm still at the same email address," I said.

"Who checks their *email* during a terrorist attack?"

"Did you see Ilse last night?" I asked. "She told me about your father. I'm really sorry."

"Why would I have seen Ilse?"

"She was looking for you."

I invited him upstairs. We fucked, but it was meaningless. I didn't even tell Delphine about it. After he left, I fed the dog leftover mashed potatoes and lit some candles.

Four days later, the dog had a seizure. Delphine came over to give her the injection. I held her while she died. I felt her getting heavier almost instantly, and her body seemed to shrink in my arms, compacting the way that my winter clothes did when I vacuum-sealed them for storage each spring. She would only take up less and less room from now on. I held her until I was completely sure that she wouldn't wake in a panic, and then for a few more seconds after that.

We buried her in Delphine's yard that night, and Delphine kept the wheelchair at her office, to give to the next dog who needed it.

The Lottery in Almería

ELENA, HIS SISTER, WAS GOING TO STAY WITH HIM ALL AUGUST. Maybe it would bleed into September a little, she warned, and Andrés said that was fine. What else could he say? The house in Almería was as much hers as it was his, on paper—they'd inherited it from their father twenty years earlier. Andrés and Elena were French (they grew up in Paris), but their parents had been Spanish, Spanish exiles. When it had become possible for their father to go back to Spain, he'd bought a house in his hometown, a few blocks from the sea, and Elena had taken up the habit of visiting for a week every summer, with her husband and her daughter. Andrés would come as well, stay longer. After their father's death, Elena had kept treating the house as a vacation home, but then she divorced, and her daughter grew up, and what the daughter, Sofía, didn't tell Elena was that she found it sad now, coming to Almería to "explore her Spanish roots" without her grandfather around. After she graduated from high school, no one went to Almería for a while. Andrés often daydreamed about retiring there, but one evening, after a tedious

parent-teacher conference (he taught high school Spanish), he
had an epiphany, as he called it (Elena, when Andrés wasn't
around, called it a breakdown), and decided not to wait, to quit
his job right there and then and move to this sunny place where
a house was paid for, where he could live on his savings for a
while.

Moving from Paris to the south of Spain in the middle of the
school year, he felt like he'd won the lottery. Off-season was for
the rich, wasn't it? Except he hadn't won the lottery. His savings
ran out after two years and he now worked remotely for a French
publisher, cranking out schoolbooks and conversation manuals
for French people traveling the Spanish-speaking world. Every
two years, he had to update his manuals, come up with new
dialogues, keep them fresh. This was more work than people
imagined, and more creative, too: he had to come up with situations, with characters. Well, he didn't have to come up with
characters exactly, but he wanted to, and so he did. People, even
his editor, didn't notice their existence, they weren't named, but
Andrés knew who they were: the horny exchange student, the
overachieving dad who wanted to make the most of his only
week off and ruined the vacation for the whole family, the gre-
garious pilgrim on his way to Santiago. There were specifics,
and an order to respect—you couldn't get around the "Where
Are You From?" section, for instance, the "Book a Hotel Room"
or the "Car Accident" bits (even though he couldn't imagine
anyone taking out their conversational Spanish book after a car
crash), the essential "At the Bar" (a dialogue in which the horny
student shone bright)—but within these compulsory sections,
provided he included a few mandatory vocabulary words, Andrés had some freedom. He could give his characters a voice.
That's what he told himself.

He had to complete his least favorite section that week,

"Flirting." You had to have a "Flirting" section in conversation guides. To fuck abroad was one of the main reasons people traveled. Andrés always felt a little uneasy when he reached that point in the process, he, the overeducated Baltasar Gracián scholar, putting himself in the shoes of a twentysomething French idiot trying to get laid in San Sebastián. He'd tried to turn it around every possible way, to have a woman character initiate the flirtation, to have it happen in a museum. He'd tried to make it a lesbian thing, tried to make it an encounter between older intellectuals, but that was even worse. And his editor had said no. He wanted a douchebag and a pretty girl to resist that douchebag. "But if she resists the douchebag," Andrés had said, "we're admitting that our vocabulary and compliment suggestions are insufficient." "Well, of course they are," his editor had said. "You're not rewriting *The Game* here. Just a pedagogical tool to learn a little Spanish." Andrés hadn't gotten the reference. He'd last read a book written after 1985 in 1989 (Deleuze's *Le Pli*). Hadn't flirted in years. Last dated in the eighties. Would've taken holy orders if he'd believed in the thing. The monastic lifestyle had always appealed to him, was indeed very close to his own—small meals, a lot of contemplating, a lot of silence. Andrés did like women, but he'd decided it was easier to do without them. One had broken his heart long ago, and hadn't even noticed, didn't know it to this day (she was still Elena's best friend). The way Andrés saw it was, he'd tried love and it hadn't worked out. He'd tried sex without love, too: not for him. So he just lived his life without either. Writing from the contemporary French douchebag perspective was a personal challenge.

Some mandatory words or concepts for the flirting section were "flirt," "love at first sight," "clingy," "hot," "condom."

. . .

Elena knocked as Andrés was considering deleting the sentence "How are you doing?" He deleted it.

"Still haven't fixed the doorbell," Elena said.

Elena and Andrés never said hello or exchanged pleasantries. They hadn't seen each other in months, but they emailed often.

"When I win the lottery, I'll fix the whole house," Andrés said.

Elena left her suitcase near the door and helped herself to a beer.

"Speaking of which," Andrés said, "I should go get my Euro-Millions ticket before Rafa closes. Should I get you one? The jackpot's at eighty-seven million euros."

"I'm good," Elena said.

"You don't want eighty-seven million euros."

"I can't play that stuff," Elena said. "The chances of me winning are about the same as my plane had of crashing today, and I prayed it wouldn't. Seems a bit hypocritical to ask for the same numbers to rearrange themselves and act in my favor now."

"You *prayed*?"

"You know what I mean."

Andrés wanted her to try the lottery, up their chances of becoming rich. He believed in beginner's luck, that Elena had a better chance of winning than he did. She would share the money with him if she won. He knew that. She might even give him most of it.

"Maybe you should buy a hundred tickets, then," he told her. "You'll never be on a hundred planes at once, so that wouldn't be tempting fate."

Elena didn't say anything, and Andrés took it to mean that she was considering the idea, but she was just exhausted from the plane and the Xanax. Half her beer was gone already. She was half gone herself.

"Well, I'm going," Andrés said. "Only ten minutes before they draw. Sure you don't want me to buy you a ticket? Turn that two-euro coin into eighty-seven million?"

The two-euro coin in question was the Greek one, Europa abducted by Zeus.

"Think of your offspring," he insisted. "Think of Sofi."

"She's doing just fine without me," Elena said.

Andrés played the European lottery every Tuesday and Friday, and the charity lottery to benefit the visually impaired on Mondays and Wednesdays. He played the national Christmas lottery every Christmas, too, but that didn't mean much: everyone in Spain, even the king, played the Christmas lottery. Most every Spaniard, too, could be guilted into buying a ticket from a tired blind man once in a while—they were all around, these blind men, hamming it up by wearing socks that didn't match, bumping into your café table while they tried to sell you your lucky number, or stationary behind their street kiosks, their long faces not easy to ignore when you were having a good day. But the European lottery, that was Andrés's little guilty pleasure. The Spanish were a bit dubious about it, because the lottery, in their country, was supposed to be a communal thing—you played as a group, you won as a group. That was what made the Christmas lottery so popular. If you won, it meant your friends won as well. Andrés, however Spanish, had been raised in France. Was closer to the northern European every-man-for-himself sensibility. A sensibility that had, apparently, begun to spread: every week, more and more Spanish people played the EuroMillions.

He wasn't the only player around with a last-minute fetish, either. Six men stood in line before him, two-euro coins in hand, glancing at the clock above Rafa's register. Four minutes to nine. At nine, they drew. If you managed to convince yourself and people around you that playing had been an afterthought, something you almost forgot to do, then you upped your chances of winning, these men felt. Because it made for a better story. And luck seemed to have a thing for good stories, to leave alone the guy who'd played the same numbers for the past thirty years. Real players let the machine pick their numbers. They didn't waste any time, and the line to Rafa moved like an escalator, quick and steady.

Andrés didn't like Rafa much. Rafa always made fun of him for not giving up—Andrés had absolutely never won anything, not even the two euros that chance routinely threw back your way after a certain number of losses, to keep the hope alive and fund your next ticket. Also, Rafa was an Argentine, and Argentines always thought they were better than you. Rafa didn't play and didn't smoke, just sold lottery tickets, scratch-off games, and cigarettes to addicts for whom he had contempt. Really, he was an artist, he'd tell you. At night, he wrote songs. Andrés had tried to show interest in the songs, to befriend Rafa, but Rafa had told him that at this stage, he only wished to share his work with professionals. He was concerned people might steal his melodies. He said it had happened before, someone stealing a song of his, making millions off of it. He wouldn't say who, or what song. He was wary of professionals, too, but if he didn't show his work to them, then he would never get the fame he deserved, so he had to take a chance there. One had to take risks. Andrés thought about that joke whenever Rafa talked about himself, the one where the kid asks, "Daddy, Daddy, what is the ego?" and the father answers, "The ego is the little Argentine we all have inside our hearts." He'd tried to sell his editor on the idea of inserting a note, in the cultural pages of their conversation guides, on the complex web of hatreds within the Spanish-speaking world (Uruguayans hated everyone, everyone hated the Argentines, Argentines hated Peruvians, Mexicans hated the Spanish, the Spanish hated the Portuguese—and yes, sure, the Portuguese didn't speak Spanish, but the animosity was still worth mentioning to travelers of the Iberian Peninsula), but his editor had said no, to stick to soccer and flamenco and Javier Bardem. He'd okayed a sidebar on the Spanish Christmas lottery, though, because the Spanish Christmas lottery was such a beautiful idea.

Andrés was the last to buy a ticket that night (making his chances to win even greater, he thought). Rafa took his two euros and made a comment on how they would go straight to thickening the next jackpot.

What will I do with €87 million? Andrés asked himself on his way home. The question was philosophical. He wasn't interested in drawing up a list of products and experiences (and perhaps emotions) that money could buy. He wondered what actions and obligations this kind of cash could buy him out of. *The real question is, What will I be able to not do with €87 million?* he thought. He would still be required to shower and eat, no way around that. He wouldn't hire a cook, no. He liked cooking, just not eating. You couldn't hire someone to eat for you. Would he hire a cleaning lady? He doubted it. He cherished his solitude, didn't like having people around. People came with their little habits and their ways of doing things. Elena was going to do the dishes a certain way, for instance, he knew this already, he knew it would bother him. Letting the glasses dry next to the sink, open mouths up . . . who did that? He wouldn't hire anyone to do anything.

He waved at different neighbors on his way back, people

he didn't really know but heard all about from the baker. Mauricio, Teresa, Antonio . . . he knew who was having money trouble, whose children hit whose at school, whose wife had left him, and for whom. It was all a bit boring, but he kept track. Those were the people he played the Christmas lottery with, his neighbors. Would he still write conversation manuals? With all that money? Probably not. But then who would he talk to? Other than his sister and his editor, he didn't really talk to anybody. He wrote emails to his niece once in a while, but she rarely wrote back whole sentences. Would he travel the world? He didn't think so. He realized people would wonder what was wrong with him, if he suddenly had all this money and his life didn't change. Maybe he would just not tell. Not telling anyone was the key. All he really needed to do was hire a team to rehab the house, and that would be what, €50K, tops? People could believe he paid for it with his earnings from conversation manuals. No one knew how much authors made. Elena knew, because she'd lent him money the past few years, but if he won the lottery, he would tell *her*.

The house was getting old. New cracks had appeared in the walls since Elena's last visit. Andrés expected to find her staring at them in silence, and the chipped paint, the swollen wood floor from Easter's water leak, the broken tiles. She never said a word about the collapse, only commented on the doorbell. The broken doorbell was code for everything else that had fallen apart.

When he came home, he found she'd retired upstairs, to the less decrepit of the two guest rooms. Andrés went to check on her, see if she wanted some dinner, but the door was shut; no light filtered out from under it. He could hear the fan: a sucking more than a blowing sound. She was out for the night.

He worked on the "Flirting" section some more. If he could write the whole dialogue without thinking about the lottery results, if he could come up with all the lines without checking the EuroMillions website, he would increase his chances of winning, he thought. "Is your father an astronaut?"

Did that pickup line even still exist?

The internet confirmed that it did. It also offered a link to 120 other "funny" pickup lines. Nothing wrong with clicking, Andrés thought, nothing wrong with looking for inspiration there.

None of the lines were funny, of course. They couldn't be. *Maybe* if we knew more about the speaker, the context, *maybe* if we were given a scene in which a geeky youth goes out for the very first time in his life, and he happens to have an obsession with magnetic fields and iron alloys, then perhaps the lines "Did you swallow magnets? Because you're very attractive!" wouldn't be so terrible. Perhaps there was a way not to cringe at "If beauty were time, you'd be eternity." Perhaps. But a blunt list of such lines didn't amount to comedy. Andrés imagined a lonely man looking at those lines in earnest, memorizing his favorites, trying to learn something about women. How far removed from reality some people could be, he thought, going down the list. Seeing the bad lines accumulate, Andrés started worrying for the women receiving them.

"My parents always told me to follow my dreams. Can I follow you home?"

Who wanted to hear that?

He emailed his niece. Had she ever heard a decent pickup line in her life? he asked. He also wanted to ask if she'd gotten more creepy lines than corny ones, on average, over the years, but then he would have had to think about that, so he didn't. Certain things he didn't need to know. Sofi answered immediately. She was in a bar right now, in fact, not having a great time. But it so happened that someone had just walked over to tell her that she looked like Lionel Messi, and it wasn't exactly a great line, she said, but at least it was one that she'd never heard before. Andrés tried to work with the Messi line, but he realized, as his niece had a few minutes earlier, that there was nothing to do with it, nothing a woman could say in response, and no good follow-up for the guy, either. That pickup line had been dead on arrival. He checked the EuroMillions website. He hadn't won.

He went downstairs and cooked some rice. He was careful not to make too much noise. The house was full of echoes, any of which could wake up Elena. After dinner, while he did the dishes, he reminded himself not to sing. He wasn't really in the mood to anyway. By the time he finished cleaning up, he was sweating heavily. Under normal circumstances, he would've done the dishes shirtless, but with a visitor in the house, he favored modesty over comfort. Also, Elena'd seen him shirtless many years before and told him to take care of a mole on his back that he had yet to attend to. It had grown bigger. Another one had sprouted next to it. He stepped outside, onto the sidewalk, to see if the air was any lighter. Purita spotted him from across the square. Purita waitressed at Casa Juan and always waved at neighbors from over her trayful of drinks. That evening, however, she brought the drinks to those who'd ordered them and walked all the way to Andrés, ran to him, almost, her empty tray dangling at her side like a hoop.

"Did you win?" she asked Andrés before she even reached him. "Is it you?"

"EuroMillions?"

"Shit, it wasn't you? The TV says the winning ticket was printed at Rafa's!"

"The whole eighty-seven million?"

Purita tucked her tray in her armpit to light a cigarette. An-drés understood she didn't believe he wasn't the winner, which made the situation even worse. He wouldn't have told her if he'd won, but still.

He had the losing ticket in his shirt pocket and showed it to her. Purita, who'd committed the winning numbers to memory, sighed enough smoke to hide the entirety of her face.

"We all hoped it was you," she said, her nose reappearing first through the cloud. "You play so much. God, I hope it's not one of those Erasmus assholes."

Every waiter and bartender in Almería despised the Erasmus students. It wasn't clear to Andrés what their crime was, other than having a good time studying abroad and drinking too much. They couldn't possibly be louder than the local youth, nor worse tippers.

"That would be terrible," he said.

"If an Erasmus guy won, I'll kill myself," Purita said, exhaling more smoke.

She glanced at the bar. Rafa was entertaining a table of regu-lars, making big hand gestures, miming, it seemed, strong waves followed by giant explosions.

"Doesn't Rafa know who won?" Andrés said.

"He says if he knew what time the ticket was printed, he could tell us, but the TV didn't say. We're taking bets over there, if you want to join."

"You're betting money on who won money?"

Purita nodded. Andrés followed her back to the bar.

"Wasn't him," Purita told the group.

"Of course it wasn't," Rafa said.

Andrés asked Purita for a beer and sat at Rafa's table.

"They're going to come film my shop tomorrow," Rafa said. "For the news."

"I heard it's the first time a Spaniard wins so much money," Jaime, the baker, said.

"Even if it wasn't," his wife said, "they would still come and film Rafa's shop. They always film the shop. And the winner. There's a guy whose job is to go all around the country and film lottery winners."

"Must be one bitter man."

Andrés regretted saying this. His beer came.

"Your sister is visiting?" Jaime asked him. He was pointing his chin at Andrés's house, where a light had gone on.

"She arrived today, yes. Staying all August."

"Good for her." Jaime was a bit drunk already. "Everyone should come to Almería. All the worries: gone."

"*Everyone?*" his wife said.

"You're welcome to host her if you want"—another thing Andrés said and regretted saying.

"Don't start speaking ill of your sister," Jaime said. "Maybe *she* won the lottery."

"She doesn't play games of chance."

"She played a scratch game last year," Rafa said. "I remember, she won six euros. I told her she was lucky, not like her brother."

Purita came with little plates of octopus and Russian salad. Rafa stared at her cleavage as she bent down to place them in front of Jaime.

"Something you want to say to me, Rafa?"

"No, no, I was just thinking," he lied, "whoever the winner is, he should share with me. Not fifty-fifty, but give me some, maybe a million or two. I'm the one who prints the tickets, after all, I'm the one who presses the buttons. If I wait one more second, another random set of numbers comes out."

"Is that so?" Purita asked.

The lights had gone off again in Elena's room.

"Whoever it is, he should give you a million because his winning probably sank your business," Jaime said. "Who's going to buy tickets from you now? The jackpot won't strike your store twice."

"People are dumber than you think. The win will only bring in more customers. I'm ready to bet on it."

"Whoever it is," Purita said, "I probably had to call his sorry ass a taxi at some point, or cover for him one way or another, with his wife or mistress or whatever, so he owes me."

"And he owes every loser who played at Rafa's, for playing a bad combination of numbers when they did and getting the machine to line up the winning numbers when it did."

"Yeah, right, he owes us all . . . You guys are reinventing the Christmas lottery here," Jaime's wife said. "This one is for selfish assholes—no offense, Andrés. He won't share his millions with the neighborhood."

Andrés hadn't said anything since his jab at Elena. He'd been observing Rafa observing Purita, waiting for him to say something inappropriate to her, or corny, or creepy, or—who knows—beautiful. But Rafa never built up the nerve. Just glanced at Purita's ass and tits whenever he believed she wouldn't notice. Andrés thought about his niece now, in some hipster bar in Paris, being told she looked like Lionel Messi. That was not what he'd hoped for her. He remembered the day she was born, thirty-five years earlier. A wonderful day. Everyone still alive then, his mother, his father, and then this new person coming along, yes, a person already—he hadn't expected to feel that way about an eight-hour-old baby. It wasn't so much that she'd had toes, a little hat, fingers that clasped around his, it was how she'd winced at a light being turned on next to her face, how offended she'd looked—*This is unacceptable*—how quickly she'd turned against her surroundings. He'd laughed about it with Elena's husband,

and his father, while his mother and Elena—still in her hospital
bed—whispered things to each other a few feet away. Serious
things, Andrés assumed. The women always talking about important matters in low voices at one end of the room, the men at
the other, giggling, protected. It was too much, of course. You
couldn't just add new people and expect the old ones to stick
around. Andrés and Elena's mother had died six weeks later.

When Andrés woke up the next day, Elena was gone. Downtown to buy rosquillas, he thought. Andrés wanted to pretend
she was disturbing his solitude, but really, Elena was a trained
loner herself, and her routine didn't impinge on his much. She'd
even left her coffee cup and spoon in the sink, for him to clean
the way he wanted.

Andrés had dreamed of strangers that night, of people he'd
never met. Not neighbors, not movie stars: random, unfamiliar
faces. This was happening more and more. He'd been amused by
it at first, taken it to be a symptom of his unleashed creativity,
but it worried him now. What did it mean when you didn't
know the people in your dreams? Were they men and women
he'd seen on the street without having noticed but whose lives
his brain, in its dark little shed, had drawn hypotheses about?
Was it a brain tumor? Was he having someone else's dreams?
Had the wires gotten crossed? Was he just too lonely?

He took his coffee upstairs. An email from Sofi was waiting
for him.

She'd actually sent it minutes after the one about the Messi
pickup line.

> i realize mom is staying with you these days & that's prob
> why you're askin about me. if she's trying to spy on me thru

you, please don't play ibto her game. she needs to learn boundaries.

Andrés didn't make much of the message. He was aware of constant storms brewing around him—that's what family was—but he usually managed to stand clear of these, to not ask for, or encourage, the sharing of details. To not take sides, if it came to that. Most of the time, the storms would pass in the distance, and Andrés would only realize they'd dissipated after not hearing the rumble for a while. He was still occasionally curious to know how certain issues had resolved, but the downside of not participating in a crisis was that you didn't get to ask questions about the outcome. He'd spent a year, years ago, answering Elena's complaints about her then-husband with old proverbs and Gracián quotes concerning lying and dissimulation. Not a word against the husband, not directly. Once the divorce had been pronounced, he couldn't reasonably have started asking about the petty things, like who'd kept the painting he loved so much, the small one they'd had in the hallway, with the dwarf and the elephant. He still wondered about it, though. He hadn't seen it in Elena's new apartment, the few times he'd visited.

He'd heard about his niece's affair with a married man, but never followed along on Elena's dives into the psychology, the drama of it all. When she'd told him about Sofi's trip to Madrid to freeze her eggs, all he'd said was "Science fiction."

He wrote a few bad lines about dreams, some idiot in a bar telling a girl he'd never met before that he'd dreamed about her last night. The Spanish didn't say "I dreamed about you," though. It was "I dreamed *with* you," which Andrés suddenly found a little menacing. The "with" seeming to imply that the woman being dreamed of had willingly participated in the fantasy.

He heard the scrape of the front door against the tile then,

Elena coming home. He typed more, and more furiously, when Elena was around, to give the impression that he was working hard, in case she walked into his office. He had no idea what to type, however, so he imagined a conversation between two boring people about the lottery. Faced with the dullness of the resulting dialogue, Andrés typed, "I can't believe I'm writing such shit. I can't believe what happened to me," then jumped to third person, to escape the house of mirrors of the first, the jump happening without him thinking about it, in an instant—he was still giving the impression, if anyone had been watching, that he was writing in great inspiration. He typed the first few lines of this story.

> Elena, his sister, was going to stay with him all August. Maybe it would bleed into September a little, she warned, and Andrés said that was fine. What else could he say?

But then quickly, what he wrote started diverging from what we've seen, and Andrés went into a different story, exactly as true as this one, but from longer ago.

> Why did he resent her presence so much? His sister had always been on his side.
>   Their parents had told them not to speak Spanish at school, that their last name, with all its o's and a's, was already enough to get them bullied by all these French kids with the silent letters in theirs, the little Henriot, the asshole Durand, and Chaussoix, and Pineault ($e + a + u + l + t$ equating here, as far as he could tell, to the final, single, vulgar o in their own name). Andrés had had to become André for school, drop a letter, while Elena had moved up

the ladder and gained two silent ones, a coveted *h* and a distinguished *e* in replacement of her name's final *a,* plus accents, to become Hélène. In the sixties, they left your last names alone but still Frenchified your first. *Hélène et André.* They were two different people out there, at school, and young Andrés had blamed the silent *h* for the rift in his and his sister's relationship, though the truth was, they hadn't been close before the *h,* either. Elena, four years older, was already used to her *h* by the time Andrés started school. She had no problem sliding into Hélène in the mornings, whereas Andrés/André played marbles alone at recess, far away from the others. When they came for his bag of marbles one day, the French boys, he was going to let them have it, but Elena, who from a distance always kept an eye on her brother during recess, came over and started talking to him in Spanish.

"Hit one," she said, pointing at the group of French boys who'd come for the marbles.

Andrés reminded Elena that they weren't allowed to speak Spanish at school. He did so in Spanish, of course (he wasn't stupid enough to publicly undermine the only person to ever be on his side), but he whispered it.

"Hit one," Elena repeated.

"Which one?"

"The one with the ears."

"He's too big."

"They're all too big for you, it doesn't matter."

He hadn't hit anyone, but the boys with the silent letters in their names hadn't hit him either, had gone quiet, fascinated by the sounds of Spanish. Later, they'd asked him to teach them some words, thinking it could become a secret code between them. Andrés had refused. He'd said it was a secret code between him and his sister, but the truth was, he'd never said anything secret to her.

He kept writing and writing, disjointed episodes from his childhood, quotes he remembered from Gracián, but mostly, he wrote about Elena, because that's who he was performing inspiration for. He wrote things like:

She traveled with a small suitcase, at least. He appreciated that. You always thought maybe she wouldn't stay as long as she'd said.

and:

Even his sister, more laborious, not as good in school as he'd been, had achieved more than him, had had a better life.

Occasionally, he got carried away and used the first person again, but mostly, he stuck to the third. He described a few of the objects lying around, a ceramic pencil holder from Níjar, his father's ashtray, in which no one had ashed since he'd died, but was still there, still waiting. That got him sentimental, the ashtray. He could picture his father carrying it to the garbage can when it was overflowing. The truth of it was that sometimes, at fifty-nine years old, Andrés still missed his mommy and daddy, gone thirty-five and twenty years ago, and he was both grateful for it, for not having gotten over their deaths, and a bit ashamed. He believed that maybe, if he'd had children, this wouldn't have happened, and he thought that the reason Elena didn't miss them, their parents, or didn't seem to, was that she'd prepared for their death by having a child of her own. Could he be holding it against her? Andrés wondered, and wrote. That she'd moved on? Or could he be holding it against himself, that he hadn't? What did "moving on" mean now anyway, at fifty-nine? At this stage in his life, he was only interested in moving back, to when he was eight years old, perhaps. That had been a good time. He hadn't been eight years old for fifty-one years, he wrote, and then because that was too depressing to think about, he wrote more about his sister, whom he called Hélène now (he always thought of her as Hélène when she annoyed him), he wrote everything that annoyed him about her, he wrote mean things until he couldn't help but find nice things to say.

Elena never came into his office, and after about an hour of fake working, Andrés joined her in the living room. She was reading *La Voz,* the local newspaper.

"In case you're wondering," Andrés said, "it wasn't me. I didn't win."

"I know," Elena said. "That's the one thing the whole neighborhood seems to agree on."

"They still don't know who it was?"

"No, but Lucille texted this morning, to ask if it was you."

Lucille was the woman who'd broken Andrés's heart.

"How does she know someone won in Almería?"

"She plays EuroMillions, too, when the jackpots grow that big. She always knows where they end up getting hit."

She was silent for a few seconds, and Andrés thought she was debating whether or not to say more about Lucille (Elena knew it to be a sensitive topic, and Andrés knew that she knew, even though they'd never actually talked about it), but she was, rather, gathering strength to ask about something that mattered to her.

"Have you heard from Sofi lately?" she said.

Andrés never engaged in drama, but he never lied, either.

"She emailed," he said.

"What did she have to say?"

"Nothing much . . . Is everything all right between you two?"

Elena looked over her paper and up at Andrés, trying to figure out what Sofi might have told him about their rift. The mystery of the lottery winner had made the front page, of course, but there was also a narrow rectangle, above the numbers that had made someone rich, news of a dolphin washed up dead on the beach. Andrés wondered if the dolphin would've taken the whole front page, had a local not won €87 million.

"We had a fight," Elena said. "We're not talking these days."

"A fight over what?"

"I had this surgery," Elena said. "Sofi found out, and she got upset. She thinks I should tell her everything."

Elena gestured toward her lower body when she said the word "surgery," and Andrés assumed she'd had surgery on her feet.

"But you're all right now?" he asked.

"Yes."

Andrés could've left it at that, let her say that Sofi had overreacted, let Sofi say the opposite, or whatever it was that Sofi had said in her email, that Elena *spied* on her, and perhaps on another day he would have, left it at that, but there was something about not having won €87 million, about having *nearly* won €87 million (which is how he would think of the event for the rest of his life, that night he *nearly* won €87 million), that pushed Andrés to inquisition. Maybe he wanted to hurt Elena a little bit, also. Or maybe he wanted to understand what it was like to have children, the lies you had to tell yourself to make it bearable.

"Sofi didn't say anything about that," he said. "About you hiding things from her. She seemed to be mad . . . to suggest that you were intruding on *her* life. Or something."

"Well, I think it's all one and the same," Elena said. "Two faces of the same coin. She got upset at the imbalance. Not so much at me intruding on her life as at me closing full access to mine. She got upset because I always ask her about her, and give her advice that she sometimes hates hearing, and meanwhile, I didn't tell her important things about me, and she felt betrayed or something. *Played,* I think she said. Which of course—I'm her mother. Children like to think they play their mothers all the time, with the weed and the cutting school, but really, it's our purview. We're the players. We decide what they can and cannot know."

"What did you say that she hated hearing so much?"

"That she should leave that asshole she's with."

"The married guy? She's still seeing him?"

"She froze her eggs for him. For when he's ready."

"Did he ask her to?"

"No. She says she's thinking ahead. She doesn't want to try for a baby while he's still married. She's giving him time."

The newspaper was closed now, Andrés thinking of frozen babies, and Elena on a roll. She'd needed to talk to someone about this.

"She pretends everything is about her," she went on. "Because she wants a baby now, or soon, she thinks I should tell her everything about my health, about problems I might have down there"—she gestured again to her lower body, and Andrés realized that she hadn't been talking about her feet—"but it's my business, it's private. You don't talk about that with your children. Our mother never told us anything."

"Different times," Andrés said, not sure why. Not sure either which was better in this case, the older times or the newer ones. "But you're all right now?" he asked again.

"I think so," Elena said.

The living room window was open to the sidewalk, Elena had even drawn the thin, dirty curtains to the side, and when Jaime walked by and peeked inside (something that, in Almería, any passerby would've done), it was almost as if he were in the house with them. He let them know he was on his way to see the dead dolphin on Zapillo Beach.

"They haven't taken it away yet?" Andrés asked.

"It's the weekend."

Andrés didn't want to see, but Elena told Jaime she'd join him, so he tagged along. He didn't want to be the guy who didn't have the guts.

Jaime asked Andrés the question he'd probably asked all his customers that morning at the bakery, what he would do if he ever won the lottery. Andrés didn't even have time to make something up.

"He wouldn't know what to do with that much money," Elena said. "He'd just establish a new lottery, on his lottery earnings."

"That would be smart, actually," Jaime said. Then he asked if Andrés was working on a new Spanish manual, and Andrés said he always was, that when one was finished, it was time for another to be updated.

"What lesson are you on?"

"Flirting," Andrés said.

"Ah! The best one! If there's one thing we know how to do here in Spain, it's flirting!"

Elena said the best opener was still "Can I buy you a drink?"

"I mean, I guess in this day and age, a woman might take it badly," she added. "Like it's assuming she cannot buy her own drink."

"Right."

A few minutes later, they were on the beach. Fifty yards

ahead of them, a clustering of people indicated the dead dolphin's location. Jaime said that maybe, nowadays, what a man in a bar ought to do was ask, "Can *you* buy me a drink?" to put the woman in the position of power.

The dolphin had not only been hurt by a shark, or some other predator, but someone had carved out letters in its flesh, forming the word *zorra,* which meant "fox," but also "slut," "bitch," "whore." Elena brought a hand to her mouth when she saw this.

"You didn't read the article in *La Voz*?" Jaime asked. "They talk about this."

"Who would do something like that?" Elena said. "See a dead dolphin and take out a knife to cut it and . . . write that?"

Andrés couldn't tell if she was more shocked by the cutting itself or the word the cutter had chosen. Would it have been different if the criminal had decided to write a nice adjective? A clever maxim?

"Actually," Jaime said, "they think someone did that out at sea, maybe on their boat, and then threw the dead dolphin back into the water."

"How is that better?" Elena asked.

"I didn't say it was better."

"And the shark bite?" Andrés asked.

"They think he got bit *after* he was dead."

That's some streak of bad luck, Andrés thought.

The letters were wide and dug deep into the dolphin's body—you could see the white layer from under the gray skin, then the flesh, not pink or beige exactly, but the color of worms. People were taking pictures.

"Is it a female dolphin?" Andrés heard someone ask.

Elena knelt by the dolphin, motioned to pet its head.

"What are you doing?" Andrés said. "Don't touch it!"

"Why not?"

"I don't know, it might carry diseases."

She moved her hand toward the dolphin again.

"Hélène!" Andrés said, something he couldn't remember doing since childhood, calling her that, but it seemed appropriate—they'd called each other by their French names when they'd wanted to be heard.

Elena wasn't shocked to be called Hélène. That's what most people called her, in fact, back in France. She laid a hand on the dolphin's forehead and left it there a few seconds, before moving down to the nose. A child asked his father if he could touch the dolphin, too, and the father said no, that it was dangerous.

"Why is she doing it, then?" the boy asked, and Andrés thought he recognized them, the boy and his father, from the previous winter, when there'd been that nasty *gota fría* and all these things—chairs, toys, bikes—had washed up on the shore, all coming from a flash-flooded town many towns over. Most of it had been ruined by prolonged contact with water, but a few pieces had still been viable, and the neighborhood had treated the beach as a flea market that morning, gone home with plastic chairs and small objects. Andrés himself had thought of taking home someone's collection of shells, kept in a Tupperware—it had seemed wrong to leave trapped shells so near free shells—but he'd left it there, in the end. The second he'd decided against taking it, a boy had seen the box, begged his father to bring it home. It was the same boy, he realized, the same father.

"Why is she allowed to pet the dolphin?" the boy asked again. "Why?"

"Because the dolphin had a very hard life," the father ended up responding, which answered nothing at all.

Elena wanted to stay until someone came for the dolphin. Andrés insisted she at least wash her hands in the sea, that maybe the salt would kill some of the bacteria the dolphin might have carried. He was ready to wait with her as long as she wanted, but Purita joined their group then. She'd been looking for Jaime.

"We found him!" she said. "We found him!"

No one had *found* the EuroMillions winner, of course: he'd made himself known.

"Who is it?" Jaime asked.

"I don't know, they're going to interview him at Rafa's in a minute, you should come over!"

"Do we know it's a man? Do we know anything?"

Of course it was a man, Andrés thought. Women never won, or they knew not to tell anyone if they did.

"Elena, you coming?" Andrés asked, but the new multimillionaire having been discovered didn't alter her resolve to keep watch over the dolphin. Except for her, all who'd been gathered followed Andrés and Jaime and Purita to Rafa's store, eager for a new adventure. It was not every day that two different things happened in Almería. Purita repeated that she would kill herself if it was an Erasmus student who'd won. "I'll slit my wrists," she specified.

They arrived at the shop as the TV crew was doing their cutaway shots—close-ups of the counter, the scratch-off games trapped under the glass, the wall of cigarettes, the "Tabacos" sign outside. Andrés could already hear the narration they would record over the images: *At first glance, this tobacco shop resembles any other. But today . . .* The winner was in the back of the store, holding his winning ticket, talking to Rafa. Andrés had never seen him before. It was an Erasmus student, of course. A twenty-year-old Frenchman. Thibault Lefèbvre was his name. He had to spell it out for the interviewer. Four silent letters, Andrés counted. A lot of people had crowded in front of the store, but Andrés managed to get closer when they started filming the winner. He'd come with a French-to-Spanish conversation manual for the interview (not one of Andrés's), but he didn't need to look at it. He'd prepared a list of phrases in advance, to describe his level of happiness. He was very precise in his choice of vocabulary. It seemed important to him, to find the right words. He was sweating. It was the first time he'd played, he said. He'd just reread Borges's story "The Lottery in Babylon" for one of his classes, and had bought a ticket just for fun. Andrés assumed he was making this up. Rafa entered the frame there, to say that Borges was an Argentine, and that he was an Argentine, too, so it had all come full circle. The interviewer told Rafa to step away, that he would be interviewed later, one on one.

What was he going to do with the money? the winner was asked. He would have a more beautiful wedding than planned, he said—he'd proposed to his girlfriend the month before. He'd pay for a nice honeymoon. A new house for his parents.

Andrés left before the interview was over. He wasn't even mad that the money had gone to a young guy, a French guy, a guy who'd seemed to have been happy even before winning. He almost felt relieved that it hadn't been him, that he hadn't had to explain to anyone that he had no one to spend the money on, really, that he'd never had a wife, children, that his parents had died before he could buy them anything nice, let alone a house, that he was in fact letting his own father's house crumble over his head.

Back home, he had a new message, from Sofi. She'd remembered a good pickup line, she said. He responded, "You should call your mother, I worry about her," and told her that she'd touched a dead dolphin. He sent another email a few minutes later, to explain about the dolphin, what had happened to it. He felt a bit stupid, telling Sofi to call Elena, when Elena was a ten-minute walk away from him, over there on the beach, alone with the dolphin, and he could go and check on her himself. That would make more sense. But what? What would he say?

Andrés opened a file on his computer, in which he kept all the dialogues he'd ever written, and copied the "Flirting" section from his 2006 manual into the document he'd been working on the past few days, the one he'd send to his editor next week for the 2016 manual. No one would realize it was the same, he thought. Word for word, the same scene.

The State of Nature

I SLEPT THROUGH THE BURGLARY. I CONSIDERED LYING ABOUT this to the cops when I went to report it, but you don't lie to the police. It's like doctors: they can't help you if you lie to them. I mean, I don't always tell my doctor the whole truth, but that's because my doctor happens to be an old friend—some things are just too embarrassing to tell your friends.

One cop asked if I was unemployed, since I had been taking a nap on a Thursday morning.

"I'm an ophthalmologist," I said. "My schedule varies."

She looked at my glasses suspiciously, as if they contradicted what I'd just told her, as if an ophthalmologist were required to have perfect vision in order to practice. I wear contacts when I work, because patients tend to feel the same way.

I told her everything that had been stolen. Most of my living room and a bit of the kitchen were gone: laptop and flat-screen, of course, sound system, but also the Eames chair, the four Hans Wegner Wishbone dining chairs, the two Moroccan rugs I'd brought back from Fez, the two pieces of jewelry I always put on the marble side table (gone as well) when I came home, the china. I didn't care much for the china, and I never used it—it was a gift my parents had received on their wedding day, and the marriage had failed—but I knew it was worth something.

"And an optometrist's case," I said. "An antique from the thirties."

"Does that have any kind of resale value?" the cop asked.

I said that all the trial lenses had been in mint condition, that someone might pay a thousand, twelve hundred, maybe, but that mostly it was of sentimental value, since it had been my grandfather's. I'd never met my grandfather, but I omitted that part.

"That's a widely varied set of items," the cop said, reading over her list. "Either the guy knew exactly what he was going to find or he was pleasantly surprised."

Out of curiosity, I asked if people often slept through burglaries. I hadn't taken a pill, by the way—I'm just a heavy sleeper. People are always amazed at my ability to fall (and stay) asleep at parties, through construction in the building, at condo meetings. I'm convinced that this corresponds to some ancient tribal trait, some remnant of a time when human activity around you meant safety, that it was safe to sleep, that someone was looking out for the group. My mother says that it's a nice thought, but that I shouldn't trust "human activity" to mean "friendly activity," I should be more wary, have less faith in people. I guess the burglary would prove her point—but then what? There aren't any pills against sleeping too well.

"It happens," the cop said. "Not often, but it happens."

I wondered if they had come into the bedroom. How long they'd watched me sleep before deciding it was safe to carry on. The cop had used the singular, but I pictured two burglars, minimum, what with all the heavy lifting. Mostly, it was worse to imagine only one guy.

When I came home, my cat, Catapult, gave me hell and followed me around from room to room to make sure that I wouldn't miss any of her grievances.

"You could've summoned some of that bitchiness earlier, when they came in to steal your bed," I told her. The blue Moroccan rug had been her favorite napping surface. "It's a bit late to make a federal case of it now."

Catapult screamed louder whenever I spoke, so I didn't argue with her any further. Also, yes, I talk to my cat. I think the weird thing is *not* to talk to your pet. Or to expect your pet to answer you. Or to talk to your pet when someone else can hear. I'm not insane. I know the cat matters to me and only to me, so I won't talk about Catapult too much, only when relevant to the story. In fact, maybe I can reveal all of Catapult's arc right now and be done with it: Catapult was not screaming because she missed her fluffy Moroccan rug. (She could sleep on anything, even atop the cast-iron radiator, when it wasn't burning hot, her body sagging into the crenels.) She was pissed because we no longer had a TV. It took me some time to accept it, but that's what it was. Catapult missed Netflix and Larry David, and that was the long and the short of it.

I was late to my three P.M. appointment, because the locksmith thought I was interested in his life story. It was, in fact, somewhat interesting—his father murdered by his mother, lots of traveling—I just didn't need all the details. As I walked the patient into my office, my secretary handed me his file. I'm usually able to read a patient's file and still catch, out of the corner of my eye, what kind of state he's in (nervous, impatient to chat, wishing he were elsewhere), but I got nothing from Mr. Simmons. It was like having a log wearing glasses in my peripheral vision.

I make quick personal notes on patients' files, so I can remember them from visit to visit and be prepared if they're squeamish (certain people will faint when you go near or even just talk about their eyes), or simply have handy a topic of conversation I know they're interested in. For Mr. Simmons, the note I'd made to myself was "State of nature guy." I remembered him.

"Mr. Simmons," I said. "Coming in to see if your eyesight's remained stable enough the past twelve months for you to try LASIK?"

"That is correct," he said.

"Remind me again why you want LASIK so badly?"

I didn't need to be reminded. I just enjoyed hearing it.

"I don't want to depend on glasses anymore," Simmons explained. "They make you look weak, and I don't want to look weak. I want to be ready and have perfect vision when the world collapses—or just the banking system—and we have to go back to the state of nature."

"Right!" I said. "The state of nature."

His eyes shone behind his glasses when I said the words. It had to have been his dream since childhood.

"Also," he said, "I hunt. Glasses get in the way. It would be nice to be able to see my prey better."

I prepared the phoropter with his current prescription.

"Can you read the second-to-last line for me?" I said.

"E-R-Y—"

"Don't squint."

"Okay," he said after a few seconds, and started breathing heavily. "I can't. I can't read it without squinting. Is that bad?"

"Don't worry," I said. "Just relax. Tell me more about returning to the state of nature, how you see it."

I made changes to the lenses while he spoke.

"I think I'd be pretty good at the state of nature," he said. "And it'd be best for everyone, I believe. Fairer grounds on which to judge a person's worth."

"You mean like sheer strength?"

His forearms and shoulders hinted at a steady regimen of lifting, pulling, possibly boxing. The rest of him didn't scream tough guy, though. More like IT guy. But that was probably a balance he cultivated.

"I mean like intelligence, ability to garden," he said. "Good sense of direction will be a plus, too."

I pictured him opening jars for his mom, scaring men away from his sisters by rolling up his sleeves—happy to do it.

"I guess I wouldn't last very long, then," I said, and asked him to read from the top.

"I'm sure you have some useful skills," Simmons said, which I thought was a little condescending. I mean, I'm a doctor, after all, so, yeah, I'd hope someone would want me on his team, if the time came to make teams. "Females have a tendency to self-deprecate," he went on, "but we'll all have a role to play in the new society."

I don't think he believed that. I think what he meant was "All who make it will have a role to play," and was only politely pretending that I'd make it.

"And, if nothing else," he added, "your eyesight is good."

When I gave him his new prescription, I almost apologized.

"Maybe next year," I said. He was so disappointed.

On his way out, he pointed at the framed poster I had hung by the door, a black-and-white version of the *Giant Steps* album cover.

"Didn't Coltrane beat his wife?" he asked me.

"Not that I know of, no," I said.

He didn't seem to believe me. He didn't seem to believe that beating one's wife was too different from any other personality trait, either. He'd asked in the same tone someone else might have asked, "Wasn't Coltrane the one who taught his cat to use the toilet?" (And, no, that was Mingus.)

At my mother's that Sunday—we did lunch every Sunday— I talked about Catapult's still-mysterious anger and the lock-smith's tragic childhood. My mother shared her general suspicion of locksmiths, who could open all doors. Certainly, she said, they entered homes when the owners were at work, to steal small items whose absence wouldn't be noticed for a while; worse, perhaps the locksmiths didn't steal anything, just took naps on beds that weren't theirs, drank out of people's favorite cups, shit in their toilets. Only other locksmiths ever had a clue.

"In your case, though, it's not a locksmith who did the deed," my mother said. "Obviously. We're looking at someone who knows about old optical equipment. Did you tell the police that?"

My mother was glad about the burglary, in a way. She got to use all the knowledge that she'd gleaned from reading crime novels for the past forty years.

"Maybe a former optometrist," she said, blowing her nose and folding the Kleenex neatly over the result. "Or a failed one."

Her building had implemented a new waste-sorting policy the previous month, and we'd mostly been talking about that, so my burglary provided a welcome change of topic, at least. Just as I was thinking this, though, my mother asked which bin used tissues should go in.

"I've been wondering for days," she said. "Can snot be recycled?"

"When in doubt, throw it in the gray bin," I said.

My mother doubted a lot. The gray bin was always full.

"I can put you in touch with my friend Rita for next week," she said.

"What's next week?"

"Well, like every Sunday, honey, there's the flea market on Palmer Square."

"And why would I go there with your friend Rita?" I'd never heard of Rita.

"Don't tell me you don't know about this!" my mother said. "Everyone who's been burglarized goes to Palmer Square to see if their things resurface. People call it the *Thieves'* Market. You never heard that? China, lamps, small furniture—lots of stolen property ends up there. I'm surprised the cop who filed your complaint didn't tell you to go there first thing."

"I guess I didn't look desperate enough to get my stuff back," I said.

And I wasn't. Insurance had me covered, and I'd been thinking about getting rid of the TV for a while anyway—I just wasn't sure how to dispose of it responsibly.

"Oh, you're getting that case back," my mother said. "It's all I have left from your grandfather."

"I thought the watch you're wearing was his. And the desk in the library."

She simply ignored this.

"Next Sunday," she said. "Nine A.M. sharp." She gave me Rita's number.

. . .

Rita, to my surprise, was young. I didn't know where my
mother made her friends these days. She'd had a bad fall a few
years earlier, and since then she'd decided to limit her outings to
what was strictly necessary, a category that didn't include social-
izing. Rita said that she was an "apartment therapist," which
didn't help me imagine how they might've met. My mother
didn't even believe in therapy for people.

Rita had told me to bring pictures of the stolen items, but I'd
never taken pictures of things, never really taken pictures in general, so I'd pulled images of similar objects from the internet and
printed them at the office.

"I guess these will work," Rita said, and she sat on the ground
to cut the images out and tape them (she carried scissors and
tape in her purse) into a notebook deformed by dozens of other
similar pasteups. My mother had told me that Rita had started
coming to the market after having been burglarized herself,
years before, and though she'd given up on finding her own
things, she'd realized she knew how to navigate the place, and
could be of help to the newly burglarized. She offered to look
for their stolen property on their behalf.

"How does it work?" I asked Rita. "Should I pay you for
every Sunday you spend looking, or only when you find something?"

"Didn't your mom tell you?" she said. "I do this for free!"

Free things made me suspicious.

"Now, you're probably thinking a free service can't possibly
be worth much," Rita said. "But I'm actually pretty selfish in
doing this. I just can't stand knowing that people are suffering
while I could help them. There's a lot of suffering here. Your
mother told me you were home when they did it? I was home,

too. You're lucky you weren't assaulted. I was. But, anyway, I can lighten the burden of others by showing them around, and that's payment enough. There're more than three hundred vendors here—it can be overwhelming at first—but most of the stolen stuff that enters the market actually ends up on the same twenty to twenty-five tables, so we'll start with those."

"You know which vendors are most likely to resell stolen property, and you don't tell the police about it?"

"The police know as much as I do," Rita said. "And it's not like the vendors are the actual burglars."

"Still, they could lead you to them."

"Arresting a couple of vendors will not make the number of burglaries drop, I can tell you that much. The guys would just find new ways to sell their stash, like on the internet, and good luck finding anything there. See, it has a sort of convenience, a thieves' market. People know where to go when they've been robbed. It gives them hope. It keeps things local. And I don't know if you've heard, but local is the future." She closed the notebook, where she'd taped the pictures of my almost-things under a dramatic "Missing" headline. "Globalization can only go so far before everything goes to shit. All civilizations go through the same stages before they collapse and break up into smaller groups, you know? I read a very interesting article about it."

"How many stages are there?" I asked.

"Nine," she said. "We're on the eighth."

We started looking. Rita introduced me to a dozen vendors. She gave them only my first name, because they didn't need to know my story—anyone who was there with Rita had the same story. She stopped on occasion to compare a picture in her notebook with something on a table. No match for me, or for anyone else.

I asked about her job, what it was that an apartment therapist did.

"It's just interior decoration," Rita explained. "Basically. Except not for people who just moved in and are all happy about it and have a vision, but for people who've come to hate their place, who feel trapped, who've lost all connection to it. I try to make them like it again, to find the right color for their walls, objects they can truly bond with."

"Would you say you're a good apartment therapist?"

She thought about it.

"Clients are usually satisfied," she said. "But some of them relapse after a while. Start accumulating shit and hating everything again. They can't help it. It's the eighth stage I was just telling you about. After abundance and apathy: dependency and bondage."

We weaved through the tables, talked about humanity's impending doom some more, and were offered coffee by a Malian national who sold mostly authentic West African masks and textiles. Akkram was his name. Akkram noticed I had cat hair on my sweater and asked many questions regarding Catapult. "How is she taking the burglary?" he asked, and I said that she complained a lot. "Poor baby," Akkram said. "It must be hard, not being able to speak, in moments like these."

Rita looked through her purse for a stevia packet for her coffee, and while doing so extracted a plastic whistle. She handed it to me.

"I almost forgot to give you this," she said. "Since I was attacked, I try to give one to every woman I meet. Especially around here—not the safest neighborhood, let's be honest."

When I asked what it was for, Rita said that it was a rape whistle.

"It's just a whistle," I said.

"Sometimes the simplest things," Rita said, and didn't finish her sentence, or didn't believe sentences needed verbs.

We didn't find my things, and no one raped us. Rita said not to worry, that it was rare for objects to resurface in the first couple of weeks after a robbery. I was a little annoyed at not having been told this before, at having set my alarm so early on a Sunday morning only to face such low odds.

When I entered my mother's apartment, she was in motion—a rare phenomenon. When not at work, she usually moved only from reading in bed to reading on the couch.

"Photographic paper," she said. "Can it be recycled as regular paper?" She held a large manila envelope bursting at the seams.

"I wouldn't think so," I said. "Isn't it full of chemicals?"

"Your father used to take so many landscape photos," she said, laying the envelope on top of the overflowing gray bin. "I don't get it. Some are nice, but it gets a bit tedious. Repetitive. I'm only keeping the pictures with people in them. And then I'll keep the best ones of you in a special envelope."

"Why would you do that?"

"I just want to know where they are. If there's a catastrophe and I have to flee. People never think to pack pictures in a catastrophe. I mean, except in the movies, of course, and even there they have to waste crucial time finding them in the family albums. They're just not part of the go-bag essentials."

"What's with everyone planning for a major catastrophe these days?"

"Don't you watch the news?"

"Of course I don't watch the news," I said.

"Well, that's smart," my mother conceded.

I asked what kind of catastrophe she was preparing for.

"I don't imagine anything in particular," she said. "Nuclear attack, pandemic, riots . . ."

"Where would you go?"

"Or it could just be that I have to go to the hospital in an emergency."

"Are you ill?"

"No," she said. "Not yet."

I tried to think of what I would put in a go bag, but blanked. All I could think of was underwear, pens, eye drops. A very sad bag.

"The thing is," I said, "you should probably take your go bag everywhere with you. Catastrophe might strike while you're out shopping. There might not be time for you to come home to pick up your stuff—there might not even be a home for you to come back to."

"I know that," she said. "Don't you think I know that? That's why my fanny pack is a reduced version of my go bag. Essence of the essential. Come to think, I'm going to have to pick a single picture of you and slide it in there."

The fanny pack my mother was referring to was a purple tartan monstrosity that my parents had given me to take on some science-class trip in middle school. It had rained the whole time and I'd never worn it. She'd found the fanny pack when sorting through my old stuff, during the couple of weeks she'd spent at home with a broken leg, after her fall. "Such a great invention," she'd said on the phone that day. "Do they still make them or was it just a nineties thing?" I told her that the only two people I'd seen wearing fanny packs in the past ten years had been jazz musicians. "Well, then jazzmen know what's up. It's perfect for a night about town. Could carry cigarettes, Mace . . . even a short novel, maybe? For the subway ride?" I told her she could keep the fanny pack, because that seemed to be the reason she'd brought the whole matter up, and she'd been wearing it ever since. She didn't walk around conspicuously sporting the fanny pack ("That's how you get mugged," she said) but concealed it under her sweaters. After her fall, she started wearing ample sweaters, not the lousy kind you see on depressive people but sweaters of well-shaped ampleness, made of pretty wools. The way they draped over her waist and hips, you would never suspect there was a purple fanny pack under them at all times.

"Is Dad okay with you tossing all the pictures he took?"

"Of course. He said to throw everything out, to just scan the ones I deemed essential and send them to him, for his own go bag."

I assumed my father had merely been polite. I couldn't imagine him packing a go bag. He already lived in the middle of nowhere, the exact sort of place that refugees would flood to in case of a major catastrophe. I guess maybe that's the one scenario, though, in which he'd feel the need to flee. He didn't like people much.

My parents divorced the year I went away to college. Not out of love for anybody else. Neither of them remarried or even dated afterward—not that I know of. They'd just had enough of living with each other, though not with *each other* so much as with *anyone,* I think. They're a pair of loners who became attached just long enough to raise a third one. I know people, grown men and women, whose parents worry that they still haven't found "the one," or even just "one." My parents never broach the topic with me. They know it's not for everybody.

"Can I take a look?" I asked, but I'd already retrieved the manila envelope from the gray bin.

After lunch, my mother went back to the novel she was reading, and I went through the photographs at the kitchen table. Lots of trees, indeed; lots of close-ups of flowers. The West, the Midwest, Mexico. I noticed that the room had gotten dark at some point, and I thought time had flown, the sun had set, but it was just clouds, nearly black clouds that wouldn't go away anytime soon. I turned the lights on, and the rain started. The light made me think of my father, how sad he'd made me on weekend nights, always working at that same table. He was a lawyer, but often he did all sorts of things for his clients that had nothing to do with the law, like their taxes, their correspondence. He helped out his friends and their friends, too, wrote recommendation letters for them, dealt with their DUIs. When I was a teenager, he made a big deal of setting up the attic with a state-of-the-art stereo system and a nice leather chair. He said that he needed a place to relax after work, but, because he was never done with work, he never went up there. There was always something extra he could do for someone. Maybe it was during one of those evenings, as he was solving a stranger's problems under the pasty kitchen lights, listening to his music on a lousy Discman, that he first devised his plan to become a hermit. I don't blame him. He had to do it. He was too nice to people. They would have eaten him alive if he'd stayed in a well-populated area. The stereo, the records, and the club chair were the only things he took in the divorce. It all seemed right to me now: him alone, finally listening to his records on the right speakers; my mother alone, reading; me alone, sorting through landscape photographs of trips I hadn't taken.

I selected two photos and threw the rest away again. In one, you can see my parents' shadows ending right at the edge of some orange canyon; in the other, there's that sequoia tree in the Giant Forest which has a hole in it the size of a house.

.   .   .

Rita would've kept looking for my things with or without me, but it felt wrong knowing that she was at the market alone, so I always accompanied her. Every week, we met at Akkram's table for coffee. Akkram always inquired about Catapult. He's the one who said that what she missed was TV.

"I fully sympathize with your cat here," he told me. "I don't know what I would do without my shows. And, mind you, I see actual people every day, lots of them, and I still need the fake stories. Your Catapult is home alone most of the time. The people on TV were a big part of her social life."

"But I leave the radio on for her when I go to work," I said.

"Not the same," Akkram said. "Can't see the faces. For all your cat knows, the voices are in her head, and she thinks she's going crazy."

After three months of going there every Sunday, I was starting to know all the vendors. I noticed, also, the freshly burglarized, carrying pictures of their missing property. Some came to Rita, some preferred to look on their own. Since I'd met her, Rita had found nine stolen items, negotiated their prices, and delivered them back to their original owners. They reimbursed her, of course, but also often offered extra compensation and invited her in for coffee (sometimes champagne), which she systematically refused. She didn't do this for a reward—or, rather, her reward was to have found the item. There was a flap at the back of her notebook where she kept a stack of white stickers that said "Found!" in red letters. Her favorite thing was to peel off a sticker and paste it above the picture of the object in question, obliterating the "Missing." It was hard to tell when Rita was happiest, looking or finding. It was obvious that she would still be doing this in forty years (assuming the world didn't end first), rummaging through piles of objects that didn't yet exist, that hadn't yet been invented.

One morning, I saw a vase that my father had brought home

from a trip to Mexico. A woman was holding it up in the sun-light for inspection. Her T-shirt said "Best Mom Ever." I won-dered how other mothers felt when they saw such a T-shirt. I could've asked Rita (she had a daughter) but didn't. I pointed at the vase instead.

"That vase was my father's," I said.

"Are you sure?" Rita said. "I didn't know your dad had been burglarized."

"He wasn't. We just gave all his stuff to charity after he left. About twenty years ago."

"I'm so sorry. Your mother never mentioned it."

"Oh, he hasn't vanished or anything," I said. "He has a phone and everything, somewhere in the woods. My mother still talks to him."

I knew by then that my mother and Rita had met at the hospital—my mother's fall having occurred the same day Rita had been assaulted by her burglars. They didn't see much of each other, but they spoke on the phone regularly, according to my mother, and I found it strange that she had never mentioned my father to her.

"My dad's not big on owning stuff anymore," I told Rita. "It's strange to see something of his."

I saw Simmons then, my state-of-nature patient, looking at a display of knives, two tables up. I was wearing my prescription glasses and didn't want the secret of my bad eyesight revealed, but our eyes met before I could take them off. I can't tell for sure what happened then—I'm not the best at reading people, and it all went too fast for deep analysis anyway—but I think he pan-icked. He disappeared into the crowd immediately.

"Do you want to get it?" Rita asked me, her thoughts still on my father's vase.

I said I didn't, and Rita bought it herself.

"Just in case you change your mind," she said. "You'll know where to find it."

The woman in the "Best Mom Ever" T-shirt, who'd previously coveted the vase, was now wondering if she'd made a mistake in discarding it.

"Why doesn't your daughter ever come here?" I asked Rita.

"She's better at home with her dad," Rita said. "This place is too depressing. You can't bring a kid here."

It felt rude to note that there were tons of families walking around.

"And I don't want her to see me as this loser," she added.

"What loser? You're not a loser."

"Honey, of course I'm a loser. You're a loser, too, by the way. We're all here looking to pay *a second time* for stuff we already owned. I mean, we can't let go of things—things!—that it took a stranger a minute to take away from us and profit from. *They're* the winners. The market was nicknamed for them, not us. If someone was writing an essay on the Thieves' Market, *they* would be the thrill. We'd be interviewed, maybe, for color, for laughs. But we're the losers here. Losers A to Z."

She was smiling while saying this, but her eyes still teared up.

"I thought you'd given up on finding your things," I said. "I thought you weren't really looking anymore."

"Well, I'm not," she said. "Not really. But it's always somewhere in the back of my head. You never know when things will resurface."

I thought about buying my father's vase back from her immediately, so she could at least feel, in that moment, that we shared the burden of loserdom, but then I didn't. I didn't even want my own things back.

.   .   .

On Mondays that winter, I had been taking shifts at the ER, for ocular emergencies. After my shift, I'd gotten in the habit of heading to the Cave, a jazz club a few blocks from the hospital. The music wasn't great there (they rarely saved the best lineups for Mondays), but the pours were generous. Simmons was at the bar when I came in that Monday, and at first I thought it was a weird coincidence—two chance encounters in just two days— but he'd been waiting for me, he said. I couldn't remember mentioning working at the ER to him, or going to the jazz club afterward, but maybe stalking was part of the training he'd devised to ensure his survival. Or maybe he'd called my office. Maybe my secretary had given him my schedule.

"I owe you an explanation," he said. "About what happened yesterday. I shouldn't have run away like that. That was cowardly. Let me buy you a drink."

What had caused Simmons to run away from me at the market hadn't been my wearing glasses but his not wearing his. He thought that I'd noticed, even though, in the course of examining patients, I end up seeing them without their glasses more often than with.

"I went to see another ophthalmologist," Simmons explained, "and he said it was okay to get LASIK, even though my vision hadn't been stable for twelve months, and you know that's what I always wanted to hear, so I went for it. I felt wrong proceeding against your advice, and I'm sorry. But, well, not that sorry, because it worked! I have perfect vision now. I mean, near-perfect."

"Congratulations," I said. I didn't tell him to enjoy it while it lasted.

"You're not mad that I didn't follow your medical opinion?" Simmons said. "I felt really guilty—"

"I'm happy for you," I said. "Now you can just relax and wait for the world to collapse."

"Thank you," he said. "In the meantime, though—and don't tell my girlfriend this—I feel like getting the surgery is the best decision I've ever made. I shot six ducks in a day last week. Personal best."

He'd confessed to having gotten LASIK and to having a girlfriend before I'd even ordered a drink. I didn't really see a reason for us to hang out anymore, but I still pounded my scotch, and ordered a second one.

We talked about the different ways he was preparing for the state of nature (he knew how to build a fire with just sticks, and not only how to shoot but also how to make his own bow and arrows), and over the third drink I mentioned my father, and his self-sufficient life in the woods. Simmons asked me for his email. I asked him if his girlfriend, whom he'd referred to as K., was looking forward to the state of nature as much as he was.

"She says she has to get laser hair removal on her legs before it happens, and then she'll be all set," he said.

"She doesn't think pants will still be easy to come by?"

"I think it's for her own comfort."

"What's her name again?"

"K.," Simmons said.

"I mean her whole name."

"Katie."

"What's Katie short for?"

"Probably Katherine, don't you think? Or Kaitlin?"

"Don't ask *me*."

"I guess her mother is Russian, though. Could be Katia."

"Or Ekaterina," I said.

"Wow! You think?"

He had to pee, and while he was in the bathroom I thought about how K. would probably not become his wife—not until death did them part, at least—and about how no one ever stayed together forever and how unsad that was.

The jazz trio that had been playing since we'd come in wrapped up its first set. The bass player grabbed a mic and said, "Guys, we'll take five, be back in fifteen," which was a joke you could tell he'd made every night of his performing life. It still got a couple of laughs. The drummer stood up from behind his toms, and, sure enough, he was wearing a fanny pack. I was drunk enough that I flirted with him when he stood by me at the bar. One thing I know about jazz musicians is that they can never believe it when someone who's not a jazz musician talks to them.

"Where do you buy a fanny pack these days?" I asked the drummer.

"Well, this one has a very special history," he said.

Before he could launch into it, I told him that I wasn't too interested in the history of things, in general. He said something about how objects ended up saying a lot about our souls, actually, how our relationship to them was also part of our humanity, etc. The sentimentality of his speech might not have disturbed me so much if he'd been less earnest, if he'd just assumed that cheap psychology was how one picked up women at bars, but he seemed to believe every word he spoke.

"Like," he said, his ponytail brushing against his cheek as he leaned forward, "it's no accident that the first thing you wanted to talk to me about was my fanny pack. Fanny packs must mean something special to you. Mine made you think we might have a connection."

"My mother wears one," I said, and I understood something then, all at once. Why my mother wore a fanny pack. The real reason she'd become friends with Rita, what had brought them close, at the hospital. There had been clues—her shutting herself up in her apartment, the can of Mace, the silent quotation marks she seemed, more and more, to place around the word "fall," when she mentioned her "fall."

The drummer kept talking while I tried to write a message to my mother, apologizing for having only now come to understand what had happened to her. Letting her know that we could talk about it, if she wanted, or that we could also never talk about it, but that, in a way, her sending me to Rita might've meant that, deep down, she was ready to talk about it now, with me, or so it seemed. It couldn't be that she just wanted a stranger to give me a rape whistle, could it? Well, actually . . . maybe it could? Maybe I was overstepping? Probably, I thought. Probably overstepping. If my mother had wanted me to know she'd been assaulted, she would've said something, she would've been direct. I couldn't just send her a text about this in the middle of the night. Actually, I could, but I shouldn't. Or maybe I should? And, in fact, no, I couldn't, either. There wasn't any cell reception in the club. I'd tried to send the message, but the delivery had failed. If that wasn't a sign that I shouldn't send it, it was at least a guarantee that I wouldn't send it until later.

"That guy's creepy," Simmons said. He'd gotten rid of the drummer while I'd been typing. "Did he bother you? Are you all right?"

"Let's get out of here," I said.

We went to the CVS across the street to buy some Alka-Seltzer, in anticipation of our separate hangovers, and because we were drunk we looked at every item in the store that was more than three different colors at once. Simmons tried some juggling balls and I compared two different fanny packs. He told me just to go with my gut. I chose the one that had the most pockets, and he offered to buy it for me. "Could come in handy one day," he said.

At the register, I picked up a DVD of the third season of *The Walking Dead* to watch on my computer with Catapult. We hadn't seen the first two seasons, but I didn't think she'd care. Simmons said that it wasn't the most realistic, as far as survivalist works of fiction went, that it was still too bathed in American puritanism, too shy in coming to terms with the speed at which morality would disappear in the event of a zombie apocalypse, but that there was still some useful information to pick up from the show.

"If anything, it teaches you to do exactly the opposite of what the characters do."

On the sidewalk, we divided the contents of the Alka-Seltzer box and I put my twenty-four packets in my new fanny pack.

Simmons hailed a cab for me, but I said I preferred to walk.

"You're not walking home drunk in the middle of the night," he said. "Not on my watch."

I told him that I'd done it before, that I was a responsible adult, that I had a whistle.

"Nonetheless," he said, "you should be more careful."

"I *am* careful," I said.

"Well, you should be more afraid, then."

I accepted the cab, and before he closed the door on me Simmons said he would see me next year, for his checkup, if I still wanted him as a patient. I didn't tell him that his eyesight would likely start deteriorating again before then.

I was so dizzy in the car that I told the driver to drop me off a couple of blocks before my building. I needed to walk the rest of the way, no matter what Simmons thought. It was freezing out, and it hurt to breathe, but everything stopped spinning, at least, and I had more balance now, and being aware of my balance made me aware of the stillness all around me, and the silence. I don't love silence much. It's too easy to break. It's one of the reasons I don't visit my father in the woods too often. I can't fall asleep there.

I can't tell you why I blew the whistle. Nothing was threatening, only the possibility that the silence might be broken, and I guess that I may have had this idea that if I was the one to break it, it would be all right, or not as bad. What would be all right, though? What would be not as bad? I don't know. I didn't blow the whistle to get attention, or at least I don't think I did. I didn't really think about it. All I know is that I blew it, and nothing changed. No one came.

The Presentation on Egypt

IT WASN'T HIS JOB TO EXPLAIN IT OVER AND OVER, TO SIT THE families down and say, "The husband/the brother/the son you knew is no more, it's only machines breathing for him now, and you wouldn't be letting him go, because he's already gone." He was the surgeon, not the organ-donation person, not the social worker, not a friend. His job was to say it once. Once was often enough—families would unplug a loved one within a few hours. But certain people required extra attention. TV shows he'd heard of (TV shows his own wife watched) had led some to believe that desperate cases were never that desperate, that all you had to do, really, was to keep asking the surgeon, and the surgeon, because you kept him focused and engaged in the case, would suddenly light up, go to the lab for half a day, find a solution to reverse your loved one's vegetative state, and hug you warmly at the end of it all.

"But he just looks so peaceful," the wife of one of his patients told him that night. She'd been delaying the unplugging for a few days.

"He's gone," Paul said.

"How can you be so sure?"

He listed again the signs of brain death.

"But we all know the stories about people waking from comas after years," the wife said. "Or communicating with blinks. What if he just needs a few more days to figure out how to blink?"

"He's not in a coma. He's not in a vegetative state," Paul said. "He is brain dead."

The wife said again that her husband looked peaceful. "Like he's dreaming," she said. How cruel would it be to just unplug him in the middle of a dream?

"And what if he is dreaming?" Paul said, instead of repeating the brain-dead part. "How many of our dreams are pleasant, would you say? How many do you wish would go on forever?"

The wife thought about it. She hadn't had a dream about flying in a very long time.

"Aren't most of your dreams horrifying?" Paul insisted.

He was talking about himself now, of course, the dreadful dreams he had, and the boring ones, the ones about packing endlessly for a trip he never finished packing in time to take, the ones about looking through every single drawer he'd ever seen in his life for his tax return. The boring dreams that he woke up exhausted from, as if he'd gone through a day instead of having recovered from one.

"What if your husband is stuck in a bad one?" Paul asked. "What if you could free him from that?"

The wife started crying—not for attention, not to get Paul to change his tone. She was very tired. She hadn't gone home since her husband's accident. Her fourth-grade students had come to see her, to give her the "We miss you" drawings they'd made, but she hadn't gone to meet them in the waiting area, so they'd left their art at reception. She hadn't showered or slept or combed her hair in days, and hadn't wanted to scare them.

"I guess Clark spoke of bad dreams," she said, trying to look at her husband and giving up instantly, to cry harder. "He never liked sleeping very much, either. He thought it was a waste of time."

They let Clark go later that night. The wife asked Paul to attend, and instead of pleading a prior commitment, as was his habit, he sat next to her the whole time. He would even have taken her hand, had she expressed the need. Twenty-six minutes after they unplugged Clark, his heart stopped for good, and, once Paul had recorded the time of death, he checked on one more patient (that one would make it), sent out a recommendation letter for one of his interns (something he'd kept putting off), drove home, smoked a last cigarette, and hanged himself.

Anna didn't make much of Paul's empty side of the bed—she was used to waking up alone.

Danielle was already up and watching the Discovery Channel, pretending to know more about sharks than the voiceover was willing to divulge, improvising facts as she went along, to make the ocean more interesting.

"After they shit them out, sharks actually keep the bones of all the humans they eat, and they use them to build houses with," she told her mother, as she came down the stairs.

"I don't want to learn anything before breakfast, honey. We've been over this."

Danielle joined Anna at the kitchen table and asked her to eat her breakfast quickly, for she had a lot to tell her about Egypt.

"Your presentation is going to be great," Anna said. "You shouldn't even think about rehearsing it now. The most important part, on the day of, is to relax."

The word "relax" made Danielle tense. Lately, everybody seemed to want her to make it a part of her life. Her piano teacher had spent her most recent lesson pressing down on Danielle's shoulders as she played, urging her to loosen up, drop her shoulders, think of them as goo, or cotton, or rubber (the teacher couldn't make up his mind), telling her that she'd never play beautifully if she kept her shoulders so stiff, and even though Danielle wanted to play beautifully there had been nothing she could do. If anything, an hour of pressing down on her shoulders had turned them to stone. She'd pretended to be sick so that she could skip the following lesson.

"I want to wear my sweatshirt with the pyramids on it," Danielle said. "For my presentation."

"Your sweatshirt has *Mayan* pyramids on it."

"That's part of my lecture," Danielle said. "To talk about the differences. Don't you think I can tell the difference?"

Danielle was nine years old.

Anna almost suggested that, if Danielle knew so much about places like Egypt and the Gulf of Mexico, she could probably locate the laundry room and retrieve her pyramid sweatshirt from the dryer herself, but something she would later think of as higher-order maternal instinct locked the words at the base of her throat and made her stick out her tongue at her daughter instead. Danielle told her how childish that was.

Danielle never went into the laundry room, which must have factored into Paul's decision to hang himself there. Anna, when she saw him, didn't scream. She didn't believe what she saw, and yet made an instant decision to keep it from her daughter, send her off to school, deal with the situation after that.

A cold plan, she realized as she devised it. She was not yet losing her mind. The seconds she was in would repeat themselves forever, haunt her at odd moments, flash through her head in the checkout line, when the girl asked if she wanted the PayDay with her or in the bag, and maybe Anna knew this already, that she'd never be done with the seconds, and so there was no actual need to be fully in them as they slid into the past.

She took Danielle's sweatshirt out of the dryer, shut the door behind her, and walked back into the kitchen, her heart beating in her ears, her hands cold and clumsy around the embroidered drawings of Chichén Itzá. She tried to fold the sweatshirt on the kitchen table, gave up, draped it over a chair instead. She ran hot water on her hands and forearms as if it could stop the wave of cold she felt going through her body—the hands seemed to be the point of entry. Paul's body was going to be refrigerated, she thought, and Danielle would have to know about that part, eventually—she'd ask questions—but not the suicide, she thought, no, she would never have to find out about that. Anna wanted to go back to the laundry room, make sure she'd seen what she'd seen, but she knew what she'd seen, she even knew that Paul hadn't pissed or shit himself—there had been no smell, no stain on his pants, no puddle under him. He must've prepared for that possibility, emptied his bladder and bowels before hanging himself. *Emptied his bladder,* Anna said to herself. *Why am I thinking these words?* She went back to the sweatshirt, tried folding it again.

"Hey, don't fold that, I want to wear it!" Danielle said, and Anna sent her up to her bedroom to get dressed. Before it was time to leave for school, she asked Danielle to make sure to empty her bladder, and Danielle thought it was funny, because Anna usually said "one last piss for the road," and Danielle made up a song about emptying her bladder while she did so, purple panties at her knees, a song that was also about water in all its different states.

It was getting cold outside, coats had been taken out of storage, time had to be spent sliding them on in the hallway, dangerously close to the laundry-room door.

"Did I tell you why the Egyptians built all the pyramids on the same bank of the Nile?"

There was no reason for Danielle to open the laundry-room door, but Anna still wondered what she should do if such a thing happened. Should she pretend she was seeing the scene for the first time?

"Come over here, sweetheart, we're late. Busy day today."

They didn't think to turn the TV off, or the lights, and the house stayed like that for the fifteen minutes it took Anna to drive Danielle to school and come back, the Discovery Channel lining up facts about marine life in one room, her dead husband hanging in another.

She would never know this—the paramedics wouldn't tell her—but Paul, in addition to emptying his bladder before kicking the chair, had put on an adult diaper he'd taken from the supply closet at the hospital, to be on the safe side.

Danielle's fist remained in her coat pocket, clenched around the lighter, until her mother had not only dropped her off at school but turned the corner toward home, out of sight. Her father had left the lighter on the kitchen counter. He wasn't supposed to smoke anymore, and Danielle, the first to get up that morning, and the first to see the lighter and the ashtray by the sink, had thought she'd do him a solid—empty the ashtray outside, secure and hide the lighter, give it back to her father while no one was watching, the next time she saw him (at dinner that night, she hoped: she couldn't wait to let him know that, while he wasn't suspecting it, she'd been his ally all day). She loved keeping people's secrets. She assumed that the more she kept, the faster she'd grow up. The problem was that she'd mainly kept fellow children's secrets so far, and she couldn't imagine that those truly counted. Still. They might've been a test on the road to keeping bigger secrets, *actual* secrets. (Her neighbor Susie seemed to believe that any thought she had was a secret—she'd sworn Danielle to secrecy in advance of confessing such things as hating blueberries or Julia, her twin.) Danielle must have passed the test, because this *was* grown-up stuff, this was important, her father not having really quit smoking, her father lying to her mother. Looking down from her bedroom window a few nights earlier, to investigate an owl sound she thought she'd heard, Danielle had seen her father smoke a cigarette a floor below, elbows on the kitchen sill, upper body leaning out of the window frame. He'd seen her seeing him, had trusted her not to say anything. He hadn't even mentioned the possibility of buying her silence, just asked for it with the simplest gesture of a hand. She would slip him the lighter later that evening, when her mother wasn't looking. Maybe she wouldn't even say a word, just wink at him. But maybe a wink was too childish.

In the meantime, she planned to use the lighter. Either set something on fire or just show it off at school. She toyed with it all through first period, flicking it the second the teacher turned to the board, trying to melt different things (her eraser, a pen). When the teacher mentioned that something smelled like burnt plastic, no one told on Danielle, even though they'd been observing her experiments, even though some of them were scared of Danielle, unsure what she was capable of.

At recess, she explained the physics of the lighter to her boyfriend—the flint, the spark wheel.

"It's so small," Cesar said, weighing the lighter in his palm. "It looks like a kidney bean."

"It's actually called a split-pea lighter," Danielle said. She knew that it didn't make much sense to have a boyfriend at her age, but Cesar had asked politely, and people were usually intimidated by her, so she'd drawn the conclusion that at least he was brave. She took the lighter back.

"My father's into miniatures," she explained. "He has a lot of very small things." She realized that this might make her father sound immature. "He's a brain surgeon," she added.

"I know," Cesar said.

Danielle said they should try to set the school on fire, and Cesar said no, that they would go to prison if they did.

"Children don't go to prison," Danielle said. "Grown-ups think that everything stupid or horrible we do we either didn't mean to do or happened accidentally. We can do anything."

As they were making plans to set the school on fire, Mr. Schull, the recess monitor, came up behind Danielle.

"Are you guys playing with matches?" he said. "Give them to me immediately."

Danielle knew that if she put the lighter back in her coat pocket Mr. Schull would see, so she stuck it into her mouth instead, tucked it between her gums and the inside of her cheek. Cesar took a step back from Danielle and showed his palms to Mr. Schull.

"Danielle, let me see your hands."

She still had her back to him. If she turned around, he'd probably see the bump in her cheek and ask her to open her mouth. She moved the lighter right below her palate. Mr. Schull grabbed her shoulder and made her face him. "You're awfully quiet, Danielle," he said. "I've come to expect elaborate pleas from you."

"We weren't doing anything wrong," Cesar said. "She was just melting the plastic on her windbreaker cord."

Danielle knew that Mr. Schull's attention would be trained on Cesar for only another second or two. There was no time to think. She swallowed the lighter.

"What did you just do?" Mr. Schull asked. "Open your mouth."

She opened wide. The lighter had gone beyond the uvula, no problem, but she still felt it down her throat, struggling to get past the point where her collarbones dipped. She thought that Mr. Schull would be able to see it if he looked into her mouth at the right angle. He didn't. He let go of her face.

"What did she just swallow?" he asked Cesar.

"I think what you just did was an invasion of privacy," Danielle said to Mr. Schull.

"I think it was just gum," Cesar told him. "She always swallows her gum."

The bell rang. Danielle was punished for chewing gum.

Punishment, at Peters Elementary, meant going to the school library during lunch break and reflecting on your behavior. Danielle had her habits at the library, a favorite spot. At this point, she knew where everything was, so she went straight for the wildlife section and picked out a book about sharks. She wanted to know if they built houses, like she'd told her mother they did. She was pretty sure they didn't, but maybe they did something else that was impressive. She also wondered how she would explain to her father that she'd swallowed his lighter. She could feel it in her stomach now, or thought she could. She assumed that her father would have to cut her open in the bathroom to retrieve it, and that he would be mad at having to do more work at home. She wasn't looking forward to dinner anymore.

At noon, the headmaster walked into the library, followed by Danielle's aunt Esther.

"Danielle," the headmaster said, squatting down to be at her level. "Your aunt came to pick you up. There's been an accident. Your father is at the hospital."

"My father is always at the hospital," Danielle said, though she knew the headmaster hadn't meant it that way.

"Something happened to him," he said.

"Well, I can't just *leave*," Danielle said. "I have a presentation in the afternoon. A presentation on Egypt."

"I think Miss Jenny will agree to reschedule."

The night Paul died, Anna won twelve grand in the lottery. She found out only days later, after Paul was buried, on one of those evenings when she'd catch herself wishing for another funeral to plan. She didn't want anyone else to die, of course, but picking a last tie, nice songs to play during the service—it had all kept her from thinking too hard about the meaning of life. Plus, no one (or so she thought) had ever died while planning a funeral. She assumed that funeral planning was akin to hitting a Pause button on any other shitty thing that could happen to you. But now that there was no script left to follow, now that the body was gone, meaning was all there was to ponder. She'd been happy with Paul. He'd managed to make her happy while having only a vague notion of the word himself. Was that noble or stupid? Had she taken too much from him? Would he have enjoyed life more had he not had her to please or pretend for? Why hadn't he left a note? She knew why he hadn't left a note. Paul hated repeating himself. The circularity of a depressive frame of mind, combined with the way he talked, a high-speed mumbling, had already forced him to repeat himself more than he could stand. Also: the repetitiveness of life itself.

Since the funeral, she'd been playing the radio real loud, to focus on other people's thoughts, and it wasn't until someone on *All Things Considered* mentioned something about the Caribbean that she was reminded of the lottery ticket in her purse. She'd never dreamed of the Caribbean herself, but she assumed that other lottery players had a uniform fantasy of a white yacht anchored there. She played the lottery every week, even though Paul made a good living and she had a job of her own (real estate). When he'd tell her it was a scam, a waste of money, she'd say, *I need the possibility, however minor, of being surprised.* She regretted ever having said those words to him.

Twelve thousand dollars. It was roughly what burying Paul had come to. She thought of buying Danielle something nice, like an aboveground pool or a dog, but then she knew it could never be that nice, that it would always be associated with this time in Danielle's life, her father's "heart attack." She slid the winning ticket under a Chicago magnet on the fridge. Chicago—the city she was from, not the band. Someone on the radio was talking about the way ducks had sex. Danielle came into the kitchen with blood dripping from her chin.

When they opened up Danielle, they retrieved not only the miniature lighter but three Lego pieces, a marble, and a key-chain flashlight. The Legos were dull and discolored by her stomach fluids, but the lighter retained most of its shine. The flashlight still worked. The surgeon asked Anna if she wanted to keep the "items," as he called them, and she said yes, she thought Danielle might like to have them when she woke up. She assumed that Danielle had swallowed the lighter after learning that Paul had died, as a way to express her grief. Anna didn't give the Legos and the marble and the flashlight much thought. She asked the surgeon if she should worry about the fact that her daughter swallowed things.

"I mean, I know it's not *normal*," she said, "but how abnormal is it? Is it a cry for help? She's very sad, I know this, but do you think she's depressed?"

"Well, I'm not an expert on mental health," the surgeon said, "but I've been retrieving foreign objects from people's insides for the past twenty-eight years. More often than not, they seem oddly mentally stable. As far as I can tell, they just think it's fun."

Anna held on to that diagnosis for many years.

Danielle moved out young, but not to go to college. Anna considered selling the house, didn't, retired early, took up weaving and pottery, never remarried. Danielle moved back in with her after every breakup, sometimes for a few days, sometimes for weeks. When she broke up with Armand, her mother knew that she would stay longer, Armand having been not only her boyfriend and her roommate but her employer—she left him and her job, as a desk clerk at his hotel, in one fell swoop. Two months into her renewed cohabitation with her mother, Danielle still hadn't found a new job, and, as far as Anna could tell, she wasn't looking too hard. She'd taken to journaling, which worried Anna. Wasn't keeping a diary for depressive people? Were all depressives suicidal? She thought about reading the diary while Danielle was out, but Danielle didn't go out much, and, when she did, Anna would talk herself out of spying on her daughter's interiority. It wasn't as if being aware of Paul's had ever helped much.

Danielle had thought of suicide a handful of times, of

course—who hadn't—but mainly as a distraction from the boredom of her hotel-lobby work. *If I killed myself right now, in this elevator, what would that do to the business?*—things like that. On many a slow afternoon, she'd wished she hadn't been born, but that was different. That wasn't a suicidal thought; it mostly sprang from laziness, or an unfulfillable desire to nap. She was wishing she hadn't been born, one morning, when her mother came home from the store. She'd been on the couch reading about diluted Buddhism instead of looking for work.

"What are you reading?" her mother asked.

"I don't know," Danielle said, and half closed the book to look at its cover. "Something about finding inner peace and pure joy through Buddhism. It was right there on the coffee table."

"Oh! That's my book about inner peace!" Anna said.

"Makes sense."

"What does?"

"Well, it's not *my* book about inner peace, and you're the only other person living here."

"Ah," Anna said. "Got you." She was silent for a few seconds. "I thought you meant something else. Like it made total sense that I would read about inner peace because I'm such a bore."

"I don't think you're a bore," Danielle said. "And Buddhists are pretty good, I think. As far as spiritual people go."

"I think so, too," Anna said. "I'm glad we agree on something."

Danielle asked her mother why she was reading about inner peace. Anna wasn't actually reading about inner peace, she explained—not yet, at least. She'd found the book on the bus a few days earlier and had asked the other riders if it belonged to anyone, but nobody had so much as vaguely looked in her direction to acknowledge that she'd spoken.

"People are just so rude," she said.

Mother and daughter agreed on that, too, but Danielle didn't say so. A conversation wasn't really worth having when you agreed with the other person.

Rude people were a mystery to Danielle, because being polite was just about the easiest thing she could think of. All you had to do was to know when and when not to look at someone, and the distinction between the two circumstances seemed pretty easy to make. Politeness was a quality you could acquire quickly when you felt you were a little lacking in the positive-traits department, Danielle thought, and so whenever she encountered rude people, she took it to mean that they believed they had enough virtues as it was, that they didn't see a need to make the little extra effort.

"Is it interesting?" Anna asked her daughter, of the inner-peace book.

"You could've left it where it was."

Danielle realized that she'd adopted an annoyed tone of voice, even though her mother, in that moment, didn't particularly annoy her. She saw Anna getting ready to leave her alone, and understood that when her mother died, no matter how long from now that was, she'd remember this very second of having been dismissive toward her out of sheer habit, and feel horrible about it until she died in her turn.

"It's just that if I were an actual Buddhist," Danielle said, stopping her mother on her way out of the room, "I would be pissed that people now seem to believe that the Buddha was primarily seeking *happiness* and not *nonexistence*."

"Happiness is certainly overrated," Anna said. She knew that that was the kind of thing you had to tell a depressive person so that she wouldn't feel too alienated from the rest of the world.

"And nonexistence underrated," Danielle said.

"I don't think nonexistence *can* be rated," Anna said. "By definition."

"I'm pretty sure it's under-," Danielle said.

"Are you all right, honey? You were with Armand a long time, and I get that it's hard, but you worry me a little these days."

"I'm fine, Mom. Definitely not planning on slitting my wrists over Armand's picture."

"Who said anything about slitting wrists?"

"I was joking," Danielle said, "saying 'nonexistence' sounded nice—like, if I didn't exist, I wouldn't have to look for a stupid job right now, et cetera."

"It doesn't have to be a stupid job, honey. You're still so very young, you still have time to find something you're passionate about."

Anna regretted using the word "passionate." There was so much pressure in it. She saw Danielle wince. Danielle had been spending a lot of time thinking about lines of work lately, and how people ended up modeling their worldview on whatever it was that they did for a living—how mathematicians thought everything was numbers, how writers thought everything was fiction. Even Armand had tried to convince her that checking strangers in and out of identical rooms mattered. "Life is a hotel lobby," he'd say. She wondered whether garbagemen went around telling people that everything was waste.

Danielle had never wanted to *be* or *do* anything in particular. She'd always enjoyed learning about things, but the knowledge had never transformed into a calling. Always ahead of the learning curve, she'd ended up taking it full circle, had trapped herself in the circle, even, while her slower, not-as-curious classmates had used the curve as an on-ramp to all kinds of careers. Some of them, like Cesar's wife, had even invented their own professions. She'd been one of the very first app designers, had come up with a pet-dating app that had made her and Cesar rich.

"Was Dad passionate about his job? I know you weren't too happy with yours," Danielle said. She didn't talk about her father much, but she did ask questions, which Anna always tried to answer as honestly as possible, to make up for the big lie about his death.

"He liked his job, I think, for the most part. The nurses annoyed him, of course, and the patients . . . He wasn't crazy about dealing with the families. But he liked fixing people, I think. I don't know."

"Sometimes when you talk about him," Danielle said, "it sounds like maybe he was a little bit of an asshole."

"All I mean is, he had doubts, like every sensible human being. No one is always satisfied a hundred percent of the time."

That was putting it diplomatically. Paul hadn't been satisfied even 20 percent of the time, not on his wedding day, not when he mended a broken person, not when his research got funded, not even when Danielle was born. Every day, even a good one, was an annoyance or a challenge on the way to eventual fulfillment, which he believed—or at least seemed to believe—he'd receive. The little moments of joy were not for him. He wanted all the joy, all at once, at the end of his life.

"Was he a polite man?" Danielle asked.

"Very," Anna said. "Very polite."

Danielle sneezed and her heart tightened, or so it felt. She pressed the heel of her hand hard and high on her chest, over her left breast, where she believed her heart to be.

"Are you all right, honey?"

"It's nothing. I should probably make an appointment with the cardio again, see if that mitral-valve-regurgitation thing has evolved."

"He didn't seem worried about it last time. Didn't he just say that maybe it would become a problem in, like, twenty years? You probably just pulled a muscle sneezing."

"Surely," Danielle said.

She wasn't a hypochondriac, but she did have her heart checked more often than she admitted to her mother—as far as she knew, a bad heart was what had killed her father. "Anyway," she said, after whatever had tightened in her chest loosened a bit. "Jobs. Cesar offered to have me help him and his wife work on their pet-hotel project, with my experience and all."

Anna felt guilty about the heart scares, of course—she'd instilled the fear—but it was better that her child worried about a nonexistent genetic condition than about the real one, was how she comforted herself. She knew that some people didn't consider suicide a genetic condition, but she also knew that there had been five suicides in four generations of Hemingways. What kept her up at night was the question of whether there would've been as many had the first one remained a secret.

"That's wonderful!" Anna said. "Pets. Pets are wonderful. They're a real emotional help."

"What does that have to do with anything? Cesar and Steph just want to treat them like your regular American consumers, as far as I understand the plan."

"Nonetheless, I think it would be wonderful for you to work around animals. You've always liked animals."

Danielle wasn't entirely sure of that. She'd never met one she'd built a relationship with, mostly knew them from books and TV. She was lying about the job opportunity anyway. Steph didn't need help with her project. She and Cesar weren't doing great, actually, last Danielle had heard.

She called Cesar that afternoon, while her mother was out, to prepare him to lie in case he ran into her.

"Sure," Cesar said. "I'll lie to the nicest woman on earth. Again."

Cesar had broken up with Danielle at age ten. He'd told her that she was too sad for him, which she'd understood, and had even admired him for daring to say. He'd told her she wasn't too sad, though, for them to remain friends. She'd thought that he was letting her down easy, but he'd meant it. They'd been close all through junior high and high school, had even stayed in touch during Cesar's college years in Glasgow. He'd gone there to study literature but had become a carpenter somewhere along the way. That's how he presented it: he'd *become* that, not *decided* to switch career tracks. One day he'd been a scholar with an interest in building, the next a carpenter with an interest in Victorian literature. He'd still graduated before moving back to the U.S., to open a woodworking business.

"You know who else I lied to about you recently?" Cesar said. "Fucking Armand! He *called* me on my birthday. Didn't text me. *Called*."

"What did you tell him?"

"I told him you were doing great."

"I *am* doing great."

Cesar had built floor-to-ceiling bookshelves in Armand's lobby that Armand had filled with books bought in bulk and arranged according to color.

"Are you guys going to be friends now?" Danielle asked.

"I don't see that in the cards for us, no."

"Good. He would only just constantly break your balls about how negative you are, how life is a glass half full or whatever. God knows he broke *my* balls about it."

"Well, it's true you're not exactly a ray of sunshine," Cesar said.

"And fuck you, too."

"I just find it funny that you always go for the super-happy-go-lucky guys, when you're about the darkest person I know."

"You need balance in life," Danielle said. "Also, am I that dark? Don't I just see the world as it is?"

"You *like* feeling shitty," Cesar said. "You go the extra mile."

Danielle tested her theory on Cesar, about lines of work, how she believed that a person had to convince herself that the one path she'd chosen was the most meaningful, and how maybe that was why nobody ever got along. Cesar thought about it, but not for very long.

"Yeah," he said, "I don't think you're right—that a mathematician sees everything through a math prism, or whatever. I read some literary criticism about that, actually. It talked about how farmers never thought in farming metaphors, for example, how only writers thought they did."

"Armand spoke almost *exclusively* in hotel metaphors," Danielle said.

"Speaking is different than thinking."

"You mean you never *think* in carpentry metaphors?"

"Like what?"

"I don't know. Like you never tell yourself, 'Well, that was a waste of wood,' instead of 'a waste of time'? Or 'That guy only knows to cut along the grain,' or whatever?"

"You just made these up?"

"'You have to wait for the sawdust to settle' . . . I don't know. Didn't Jesus rock the carpentry metaphors?"

"Maybe he rocks them in the book, I don't remember, but I'm telling you: if that's the case, the writers made him do it. Jesus himself never thought in carpentry metaphors."

Danielle had a fleeting thought about Egypt, not about pyramids but about something she'd read in the Egyptian Dream Book. Her father had told her about it eighteen years earlier, when she'd been gathering materials for her presentation—how Egyptian sleep temples were also healing temples, hospitals, sort of. They'd looked it up in the encyclopedia. The Dream Book was a long list of dreams that were believed to be either auspicious or bad omens, and they'd gotten a kick out of reading examples, one of which Danielle remembered: "Auspicious—if a man sees himself sawing wood in a dream, it is a sign that his enemies are dead." They'd laughed at the dream descriptions, she and her father, because the dreams were so specific, so unlike any dream they themselves had ever had or would ever have (dreams of measuring barley, dreams of slaying hippopotamuses, dreams of seeing yourself in a mirror) that they'd felt protected from the world, from both the good and the bad that could befall them.

It surprised her sometimes how much she remembered from the few days before her father died, as if maybe her brain had known to pay extra attention. It was all the more eerie that everything that had happened in the weeks after was a blur. She knew she'd gone back to school after the funeral, and that she'd gone to the hospital at some point, for the lighter removal, but she had no recollection of these things. She couldn't even remember if she'd ended up giving her presentation or not. She remembered taking the time to borrow the book about sharks that she'd been browsing when the headmaster interrupted her with the news, but she couldn't recall actually reading it. She'd never returned the book. It was still right there, on her old bedroom shelf. There must've been reminders from the library, letters and calls, and Anna must've inquired about the book at least once before writing the school a check for the book's replacement. What had Danielle said? Had she pretended the book was lost? Important to her? Had it been?

"Do you remember if I ever gave a presentation on Egypt at school?" she asked Cesar.

She could picture herself researching mummification, and looking up the word "desiccated," but not standing in front of a room to share her findings.

Cesar said that she had, but maintained that they hadn't started dating yet, at that time—that her presentation on Egypt was one of the little things that had made him fall for her. She didn't correct him on that. He had to be thinking of another talk she'd given. She used to always volunteer for show and tell.

After she hung up with Cesar, she lay in bed and read about sharks. Sharks didn't build homes, of course. They had to be in constant motion to keep breathing through their gills. Some of them never slept. It was possible for a shark to drown. She thought she would've remembered that fact, had she read the book before.

Danielle knew that her mother was lying about her father's death. She'd never heard of a young person dying peacefully in his sleep, the way her mother said it had happened. Anna insisted the heart attack hadn't woken him, but that didn't make any sense to Danielle, who could be woken up by the smell of toast. He had woken and he had suffered. She was convinced of that.

She heard Anna come back and open all the windows on the first floor. Anna was obsessed with air circulation, but also worried about burglary, so she opened and closed windows several times a day. She liked doors to be open, too. In a few minutes, she would knock on Danielle's bedroom door and share with her some random information about the outside world. This was only ever an excuse to check on her and to "forget" to close the door on her way out. The "forgetting" used to drive Danielle crazy. As a teenager, she'd often slam her door in response, but that only had the effect of bringing Anna's head back between the door and the doorframe to ask, "Did you say something, honey?"—after which Danielle would yell at her to close the door once and for all, and Anna would ask why she needed the door to be closed so badly. Danielle never had a satisfying answer to that. She was never doing anything private or embarrassing. Always reading, doing homework, thinking in bed. She sometimes thought now that maybe, if her door had been closed all those years, she would've had a more exciting life. Or developed a more interesting personality, at least. Operating as if she could be walked in on at any moment had made her dull. Probably. She thought of the phrase "That ship has sailed" as she heard Anna open the kitchen window downstairs, and wondered if any sailor had ever thought it. The kitchen was right below her bedroom. Many years before, she'd looked out her window and seen her father smoking down there, elbows on the sill. She'd called to him, and he'd looked left and right to see where it had come from. She'd had to say "Up here!" for him to look up. He'd seemed surprised to see his daughter there, in her bedroom, surprised that the interior layout of their house should have direct consequences on the outside world, on whose window looked out on what. He'd looked at her and crossed his lips with his index finger, and Danielle had nodded and pretended to zip her own lips, to assure her father that his secret was safe with her. She thought about this gesture often, how he might have just been asking her to shut up and go to bed, not to keep a secret.

She closed her eyes now, hoping to fall asleep before her mother came up to let her know what was for dinner, or what she'd learned in weaving class. She listened to her heart—not to her metaphorical heart but to the actual murmur, the leaky valve through which blood regurgitated backward at a volume that wasn't yet cause for concern.

When Anna walked in, Danielle was either sleeping or pretending to. Anna stood on the threshold for a minute, giving her eyes time to get used to the darkness of the room, to discern different gray masses, the bookshelves, the desk, the hamper, to make sure that her daughter's chest was still rising and falling under the blankets at regular intervals.

Only Orange

ALL I SAID WAS THAT SHE MUST LIKE BEIGE A LOT. I WAS TRYING
to put my finger on why I disliked her so much. Audrey. My
little brother's new girlfriend. I thought maybe it was the different shades of beige she'd been wearing all week.

"You must really like beige," I said, and she said: "What do
you mean?"

"Your pants," I said, "your shirts—all beige. Or . . . oatmeal,
maybe." "Oatmeal" sounded less aggressive. I'd been told I was a
little mean at times, in my choice of words.

"My pants are green," Audrey said.

"Jeanne is right," my brother said, and it was the first time
he'd agreed with me all year. "Your pants aren't green, babe."

Just like that, Audrey found out that she was color blind.

She spent the rest of our family vacation (a ten-day biennial
endeavor in the south of Spain) pointing at different things.
"And what color is that?" she'd ask.

My parents thought it was so interesting. Especially because they could give Audrey clear answers, present themselves as experts on something they'd never really thought twice about.

"Why, Audrey, this is orange," my father would say, and he'd describe orange, trapped between yellow and red—he'd talk about sunsets, the fruit, quote Henri Bergson, tell her that maybe orange was the only color there was, in the end. "There's just so much to say about orange. I'd never really thought about it."

"The things you take for granted," my mother added.

I thought Audrey was faking it. How could you make it to twenty-six and not notice that you were color blind? She needed to be the center of attention, is what I thought. My brother was a painter. Had they never talked about color?

"No, Jeanne, we never talked about color," he said. "Why would we talk about color? Did you and Matt talk about color?"

"Matt teaches geography."

Lino hadn't liked my ex much, though I'm not even sure he was aware of that. For the past five years, during my whole relationship with Matt, my brother had only ever uttered Matt's name to isolate the qualities of an average human being, for the purpose of illustrating a point he was making about culture, or policy, or cultural policy. "People like Matt don't care about contemporary theater," he'd say. "They work hard, they come home, they just want a beer in front of the TV." I'd told him once how condescending that was, using Matt as the gold standard for the random and the small, but he had pretended to admire him, us—*Don't throw me into this,* I'd thought, and not said—for our pragmatism, our ability to focus on the day-to-day. He'd also said that there was no shame in normalcy, that I was right to be drawn to it, especially after my previous boyfriend.

. . .

Audrey and Lino had been dating for more than a year, but they lived in the United States and I in Paris, so I was meeting her for the first time. All I knew about her was what my brother had told us over Christmas dinner, eight months earlier, when their relationship was new enough that she'd spent the holidays with her own family.

"Where did she go to school?" I asked.

"Lewis & Clark."

"What's that? Where the *Daily Planet* gets its interns?"

"*Lewis* & Clark," Lino said. "Not Lois."

I thought he was making this up. I had to look it up on my phone. I knew he must have had the same thought. Watching *Lois & Clark: The New Adventures of Superman* every Tuesday night in the mid-nineties was one of the only good moments we'd shared.

Matt, whom I was still engaged to at the time, then told me everything he knew—which happened to be a lot—about the Lewis and Clark expedition. So I knew a bit about Audrey's education, and I knew that she'd been adopted, of course, which made me envious. To be able to look at the people who love you the most and not have to worry that you'll turn out exactly like them must be amazing, I thought. An endlessly renewable source of relief.

"Now I wonder if one of my biological parents was color blind," Audrey said one evening, a day or two after finding out that she'd been wearing beige all along. We were having dinner on the boardwalk—seafood, tapas. It was about ten o'clock and people were still going into the sea.

I hated having to pretend that it was tragic that Audrey would never get to know what kind of eye problems her real parents had had. What she truly didn't know was how lucky she was. In fact, there was a part of me that believed that Audrey knew *exactly* how lucky she was, but that she also knew that, as an orphan, there were all these strings she could pull to induce sympathy, love, and guilt, to buy excuses, to explain herself; and that she intended to pull those strings until they broke, which they never would, because when you were a born orphan—that is, when you'd actually spent your first few months or years in an orphanage—you got to be an orphan for life. You're expected to get over losing your parents if you knew them, but not if you never met them. Even when Audrey was in her eighties, it would be one of the first things people said about her: "She didn't have it easy. She was an orphan."

"That must be hard," my mother said, "not knowing anything about them."

Audrey smiled and took a sip of wine.

One thing I didn't understand was how my mother could've read so many novels and still take anything anyone ever said at face value. As if deception and complications were only tricks that fiction had invented to compensate for the lack of duplicity in actual people.

"It comes in waves," Audrey explained, "the wondering about them."

I wondered how I could prove that Audrey was faking color blindness. There had to be tests, I thought. But they would probably be easy to flunk. It's easy to pretend you can't see certain things.

I got a whiff of cigarette smoke from the next table. I inhaled as deeply as I could. Audrey coughed dramatically.

"I'll ask them to put it out," Lino said. Her savior.

"We're outside," I said. "You can't ask the locals to put their cigarettes out. We're guests in their country."

"I'm sure they're not even Spanish," my brother said. "People who actually live here don't go to the beach or on the board-walk. It's all tourists in this area."

"What are you talking about? Everyone's speaking Spanish."

(We were speaking French, by the way. Our language. Au-drey was fluent in it.)

We'd been coming to Almería for more than ten years; my parents had visited one summer and fallen in love with the place. I'd met countless locals on the boardwalk.

"Your brother is right," my father said. "People here live with their backs to the sea. Just look at Joaquín." Joaquín was a chess partner my father had befriended in town. "Doesn't even own a bathing suit."

"It's quite natural, if you think about it, to not take advantage of your own city the way a tourist would," Audrey said.

"I'm sure they swim early in the morning," I said. "Or in the off-season."

"Yeah," my brother said. "Like you go to the Eiffel Tower in the off-season?"

"It's not the same," I said.

"How often do you go to the Eiffel Tower?" Audrey asked me.

"There's no such thing as the off-season for the Eiffel Tower," I said.

"She's never been," my brother said.

I often felt a little betrayed by Lino, which probably stemmed from the initial lie that had accompanied his birth. When my mother was pregnant with him, she'd decided to assuage a jeal-ousy I don't remember feeling by telling me that the baby would come out of the womb carrying a present for me. For a whole year, I believed that Lino had been born carrying my doll Polly. For a whole year, I expected random toys to fall out of my mother's vagina. When I realized that the doll had come from the same shop that all my other toys had come from, I became a bit wary of Lino. It wasn't fair—he hadn't been the one to lie to me—but it was hard not to look at him and my parents as a group plotting against me, not to wonder what else they were hiding. When Lino decided to become a painter and my parents were supportive, I'd felt excluded from their group again. Because my parents were both teachers (history for him, French for her), I'd grown up under the impression that people matured only in order to teach what they'd been best at in school to the next generation, and so on and so forth until the species died off. (I teach algebra.) But Lino deciding to pursue a career in doing instead of teaching, encountering success in the doing— that had opened a gate to possibilities I hadn't been aware of. I had no talent whatsoever and couldn't have taken advantage of the gate if I'd wanted to, but still. I felt like an idiot for not having seen it.

"I can't wait to see the Eiffel Tower again," Audrey said. She'd been to Paris once, as a teen. "I'll take you. It'll be fun."

Back at the apartment we were renting, I googled color blindness. I learned that color-blind people could sometimes see things that those who saw all colors couldn't. They could see hidden patterns formed by black-and-white dots swimming among other black-and-white dots. I looked at a series of Ishihara plates, but the hidden figures for the color blind were actually quite distinguishable to me. I could pass the test that proved I was color blind, as well as the one that proved I wasn't. Online, at least.

According to how Audrey described seeing things, she seemed

to be the "protanopia" type of color blind. Most things, to her, were a little green. I googled "how do color-blind people see rainbows," and found a page that showed how people with different types of color blindness saw different things. Had Audrey truly believed her whole life that the stripes on the American flag were forest green? Had she never wondered why almost everything was green? Protanopia was extremely rare in women, the internet said. Like, 0.03 percent of women had it. I guess Audrey was very special.

I knew why I disliked Audrey. I'd quit smoking the week before the vacation, thinking that maybe I could be spared my mother's remarks about how she couldn't bear the thought of her child dying before her. "Of cancer," she always added, in case I hadn't gotten it. Being in withdrawal from nicotine, I knew that I wasn't in the best state of mind to meet new people, or to give anyone a chance. What I did not know, however, was that no one was going to notice that I wasn't smoking. And that, of course, made me want to smoke. People make such a big deal of it when you smoke, but then no one registers it when you quit, or, if anyone does, it's the quickest pat on the back—you're doing something good for yourself, after all, how hard can it be? Whereas being color blind? That must be tough.

The next day, I went out to have breakfast on the boardwalk, like I always do. Audrey had risen early and gone swimming. I could see her in the distance from the terrace of the Delfín Verde, the café just downstairs from our apartment. I ordered my coffee and orange juice in Spanish from the same waiter who'd taught me how to, years before. He'd noticed right away that I'd quit smoking. He'd made a big show, since then, of taking the ashtray off my table every morning.

"I saw you and your family last night," he told me, slowing his Spanish as much as he could. "Your brother, he has a new girlfriend!"

He hadn't commented on Matt's absence this year, though Matt had come on our family vacation the past two times.

"Yes," I said. "Her name is Audrey. She cannot see colors."

I didn't know the Spanish word for "color blind." He thought that I meant she wasn't racially prejudiced.

"No," I said, and then I showed him an Ishihara color plate on my phone.

"Ah! *Daltónica*," he said.

"*Sí,*" I said. "*Daltónica*."

He thought that was interesting, but I forgave him, because waiters have to pretend that everything is interesting.

"They make glasses for the color blind now," he told me, pointing at his own frames to illustrate the Spanish word "gafas." "They put the glasses on, and they can see colors."

I knew what he was talking about. My internet search had turned up those glasses, but I hadn't bothered reading about how they worked. I'd taken it for granted that such a thing would exist, as I took most scientific progress for granted, the vaccines and the high-speed internet. It seemed normal to me that someone would come up with these ideas and solutions, fix every one of our physical problems, try to abolish space and time, until we were left to deal with the truth of life (once everything else was solved, we would know what that was), but my waiter, and the way he mimed putting the glasses on, the joy that a color-blind person would experience, apparently, seeing my half-empty glass of orange juice (it was, in fact, a pretty color)—it all reminded me of how science used to feel magical.

My parents came out of our building then, my father dressed to go play chess in town, my mother holding her goggles, swim cap, and flotation belt. She knew how to swim, but sometimes, she said, she didn't feel like making the effort.

I waved at them, and they took it as encouragement to sit with me.

"Have you had breakfast yet?" my mother asked. "I know it's useless to try talking to you if you haven't had breakfast yet."

My father nodded gravely. I pointed at my glass of orange juice and empty coffee cup.

"That's not breakfast," my mother said. "You need solids in the morning."

My father silently agreed with that, too.

"Tall glass of water first, sure, to get rid of the toxins, but then you have to have a nice assortment of food groups," my mother added. "Your digestive system needs variety. It's like anything else: routine kills it."

These were the people who'd told me that if I swallowed chewing gum it would make bubbles in my stomach and I would explode.

"Is Lino up yet?" I asked.

I wanted to change the topic to one that pricked her instead of me. It was only a little past nine, and Lino never got up before noon—he could even go until three P.M., if he'd worked late, and he never skipped his nap in the afternoon, either. This sleeping pattern was the only habit of his that my mother couldn't fully get behind. Of course, he was an artist, and artists had a different relationship to time, but fourteen hours a day? Was he ill? Was he depressed? Could his too many hours of sleep be a cry for help? She'd gone over all these theories through the years, but her son was perfectly fine. A high-functioning artist. I, on the other hand, had had two nervous breakdowns in the

past four years and, since the second one, had been taking cita-
lopram steadily and Xanax as needed, but, my sleeping schedule
being what it was (i.e., that of a person who had an actual job to
go to, a job she relied on for food and shelter), my mother never
worried. I'm not saying that she should have, mind you, or that
she was a bad mother for not doing so. I don't tell her everything.

"Have you heard from Matt lately?" she asked me.

I guess she was learning to counter my low blows with some
of her own.

"I almost called him the other day," my father said. "I had a
question about sinkholes."

"Matt's a geographer, not a geologist," I said.

"I'm sure he still knows about sinkholes. He knows everything."

"But he hates it when people just assume he does," I said.
"Take his knowledge for granted. He wants to surprise you with
it, to be admired, not be used like a search engine."

"Did you stop admiring him?" my mother asked. "Did he
stop surprising you? Is that what happened?"

What had happened was that I had found out Matt had been
sleeping with another teacher at our high school for months, but
I couldn't bring myself to tell my parents. I didn't want them to
think less of him. He'd been what they liked best about me the
past few years.

"I think Audrey and Lino still surprise each other," my
mother said.

My father agreed, and they both scanned the beach ahead of
us for Audrey and her pink towel, which she thought was baby
blue. They really liked her, I guess. They wanted her to stay in
the picture. Audrey was done swimming and now looked out at
the Mediterranean like she was the only person who really un-

derstood it, the only one who'd ever had deep thoughts about the sea. What shade of green did she see the water as?

My parents went on with their day, my father to his chess game, my mother to lay her towel next to Audrey's, and I stayed at the Delfín and looked at the horizon. I'd always been good at doing nothing, but, since I'd quit smoking, staring emptily into the distance had become the only thing I could do without wanting a cigarette too badly. I watched the ferry that left for Morocco cross paths with the one that was arriving. I tried not to have any deep thoughts about paths crossing, people never meeting, or the refugee crisis. Deep thoughts made me want to smoke. Pure boredom did, too, though, so there was a balance to find. I thought about how I could look at the sea for hours without ever feeling the need to go in, no matter how hot it got. I loved looking at the waves the way I loved looking at the Eiffel Tower when it showed up on my commute. Never occurred to me to go visit it.

My mother floated on her back, a little way from shore. Audrey was on her stomach now, tanning and being accosted by a teenager selling friendship bracelets. He sat in the sand next to her and they chatted for a while, pointing at different bracelets he had pinned on his cardboard panel. I assumed that she was telling him about her recently discovered color blindness, and how she would need his help to pick out bracelets, since she couldn't trust her taste anymore. (Audrey spoke a little Spanish, too.) Back at the apartment, over lunch, she gave me one.

"To thank you for making me realize I was color blind," she said.

She'd thanked me about a hundred times already. It was now the only thing she could think of to talk to me about, as if I didn't have any other purpose in life than to discuss her disability.

"I also got one for Marion," she said, handing me a second bracelet.

Marion is my daughter. Not with Matt but with the man before—him, my parents never ask about. Like me, all they know is what they see on TV, or used to see on TV, when he was a participant in, and nearly won, a *Big Brother*–type reality show, years after vanishing from our lives.

"That is so thoughtful," I said. "I'm sure she'll love it."

"I remember you saying that she loved purple, that her whole room was the color of eggplant, so that's why I got her this one."

"How did you know it was purple?" I said.

"Well . . . I asked the boy who sold the bracelets if he had anything purple. I think that's the one he told me to get . . . Wait, is it not purple?"

"Oh, it's purple," I said.

"Purple as it gets," Lino added.

She sighed in relief.

"I'm looking forward to meeting Marion at Christmas," she said.

"She's a trip," my father said, politely. He loved his granddaughter—he just didn't like her much. Few people did. The reason Marion was at camp and not with us was officially that she needed to learn to make friends—and I hoped that's what she was doing—but mostly that I wanted to avoid quarrels between her and my father. Marion, who was twelve years old, was the reason he'd started taking chess lessons, and practicing with Joaquín when in Spain and with some other old man when in France. The previous winter, Marion had thrown a chessboard at him and called him a fool, for castling when he had—for castling stupidly, in general, just to show that he knew what castling was. After he asked for an apology, she'd declared that he was the one who should apologize, for all the scholar's-mate openings he'd inflicted upon her over the years, all of them repeated insults to her intelligence. My father wasn't going anywhere anymore without his two chess bibles: one about openings, the other called *The Art of Sacrifice in Chess*, two recommendations he'd gotten from Marion. Through me.

"I really hope I have a daughter one day," Audrey said. She didn't look at my brother while she said this but at her plate of goat cheese and tomato jam. "But I don't know that I'll ever be able to."

"Why not?" my mother asked.

"I just read this book that said that a woman couldn't have a daughter as long as she hadn't resolved all her issues with her own mother."

"That can't possibly be true," I said.

"It makes a lot of sense, actually," my mother said.

I wondered how she'd ever been trusted to teach anyone anything.

"And since I'll never know who my real mother was," Audrey went on, in case we hadn't figured out that that was where she was heading, "I'll never be able to resolve our issues and have my own daughter."

I stared at Lino to get him to acknowledge that his girl-friend's reading list was a little embarrassing.

"Maybe the fact that you have a good relationship with your adoptive mother will help?" he said.

While they all napped, I watched videos of color-blind people trying on their color glasses for the first time. In none of the videos was the reaction subdued. Seeing in full color for the first time was apparently akin to having an orgasm. Some people shouted, some people cried. Some people couldn't keep the glasses on—or off—for more than a few seconds at a time; they needed to contrast the colorful and the bland. I tried imagining it: never having seen the color of beer, the colors of a Matisse painting. Maybe I'd cry, too. I'd cried at less beautiful things.

Before I knew it, the glasses were in my cart, and I was considering shipping options. I entered my brother's address in Brooklyn, then backpedaled and checked the box for expedited international shipping. I wanted to witness it. I would witness it in forty-eight hours or less: Audrey seeing her first real sunset. I owed her a gift, what with the thoughtful, ugly bracelets she'd bought from that teen on the beach.

I believed that having seen all these videos of color-blind people discovering color made me something of an expert; I'd be able to tell if Audrey was faking it. I knew she would ham it up, but I'd see through her bullshit, if bullshit there was, and I planned to be an adult about it—not to call her on it and expose her but just to derive satisfaction from knowing that I'd given her something she had no use for.

Lino woke from his nap. I told him about ordering the glasses and regretted it immediately—he would tell Audrey, who would have plenty of time to prepare her act, by watching the same videos I had.

"I want it to be a surprise," I said. "Please don't tell her the glasses are coming."

"You hate surprises," he said.

"Well, this one won't be for me," I said. "And I get the feeling that Audrey might like surprises."

My brother wasn't stupid.

"You don't have to pretend you like her when it's just me," he said. "But do try making an effort when she's in the room, okay? That's all I ask. I think she likes you. She always wished she had a sister. She thinks maybe she had one and they were separated in the adoption."

"Come on," I said. "We all wish we'd had different childhoods, all right? I'm not going to feel sorry for her. I wish I'd had a sister, too, did you know that? Do you find me more interesting as a result of finding this out?"

"Actually, yes, maybe," Lino said. "I guess I wished I'd had a brother. Or been an only child."

"Who wishes they were an only child?"

"I'm joking. Just trying to point out that whatever we fantasized about as children doesn't hold a candle to what an orphan wished for. It's just not the same. We knew where we came from, our fantasies were for fun, they never really hurt. We always went to the kitchen for dinner when Mommy called. We could experience both the fantasy of being someone else and the reality of knowing our biological family. We had more options."

"But why would more necessarily be better? I mean, the orphan who doesn't know anything about his birth parents—who is he to claim that knowing is better? He's never experienced the knowing, after all, the way we haven't experienced orphanhood, so how can he say it's superior? Why not let us who've had that experience decide?"

"You're insane."

That was a bit of a compliment, coming from him, so I went on.

"Many people wish they'd grown up orphans, for the perks—we just don't say it out loud."

"The *perks*?"

"Are you sure she's even an orphan?"

We'd been whispering this whole time, but Lino went back to his full voice to say the next thing.

"Maybe you should start smoking again" was what he said, at which moment Audrey walked into the living room.

"Jeanne!" she said. "I had no idea you'd been a smoker— your skin is so radiant! Congratulations on quitting! Isn't it so hard? My father, when he quit, he was a real mess."

"She *is* a real mess," Lino said. "Jeanne is usually much nicer than what you've seen so far."

I was actually touched by that. I wasn't sure if Lino believed it, or if he was just making excuses for me, but still. Making excuses for someone was proof you cared about them.

"It is very hard," I told Audrey. "Thank you for asking. I'm sorry I'm a little on edge these days."

"One day at a time," she said.

I clicked on Track My Package a dozen times in the next few hours, then again the following morning. The glasses had made it to Madrid overnight. They would be Audrey's by tomorrow. At the Delfín, I asked the waiter how things were, and he said that he was *constipado,* which I thought was a little more than I needed to know, until he explained that being *constipado,* in Spanish, meant having a cold. I told him that I had ordered the glasses for my brother's *daltónica* girlfriend, and he thought that this was very thoughtful. Said that he would love to see it when she wore them for the first time.

"We could have a show right here on the terrace," he offered. "A party."

I said that would be nice.

My phone rang, and it was a certain Clara, from the director's office at summer camp. I was told that Marion had beaten up another girl, a fourteen-year-old.

"Why?" I asked.

"It doesn't matter why," Clara said. "The kid's in the hospital, with a broken nose and a concussion. They're going to keep her under observation for the day."

It wasn't the first time that Marion had hit someone (she'd slapped a boy the previous winter, hard, for calling her "boxy"), but she'd never broken bones before.

"Did they fight this morning or last night?" I asked, somehow thinking that it made a difference. I guess it did, or I guess I thought it did—that hitting someone first thing in the morning was perhaps worse, a sign of terminal anger, one that eight hours of sleep hadn't been able to tamp down to allow the new day a chance not to suck.

"It was this morning at breakfast," Clara said. "You have to come pick her up as soon as possible. We cannot keep her here with us."

I said I understood.

Hanging up, I realized that my main takeaway from the phone call was surprise at not having been called sooner about something that Marion had done. It meant that she'd been trying hard to behave. She'd promised me she'd try, and Marion didn't promise things lightly, just to defuse or prevent arguments. She loved arguing. I knew that she'd tried, and also that I could never congratulate her for trying, because she had to learn that trying was not enough.

I decided to lie to my parents and tell them that Marion was the one who'd ended up in the hospital, with a tonsil infection. They didn't need to know. Rather, I didn't need to interpret their silent judgment of the man I'd picked to be Marion's father. That I was twenty-three at the time didn't sound like a good excuse anymore, now that Audrey had entered our lives, a trilingual professional young woman in her twenties with a good head on her shoulders and excellent taste in men. Of course she and Lino would have a daughter. She would have a name like Célestine, or Zoya. Audrey would worry for a while that the girl was color blind, but she would turn out to have perfect eyesight.

I watched Audrey shake the sand off her towel. She didn't know it yet, but she would go back to America with sand in her luggage that would never leave her. Even I brought some home with me every time. Books I never took to the beach still managed to trap sand in their spines; the sand then found its way to our couch; Marion then complained about it irritating her sensitive skin. I wondered if Audrey ever thought about all the kids in the orphanage who hadn't been picked. That's what I would've obsessed about in her place, not my biological parents.

An hour later, I was at the airport, too early for my flight. I kept forgetting that, when you didn't smoke, you didn't have to build time around meetings and train rides for a final cigarette, or stand in front of bars and doctors' offices while you took your last puffs. You could just go in.

At Orly, everyone looked disappointed. Or mad. Even the lovers who'd just been reunited looked mad—mad at the weight of the suitcase, mad that he hadn't brought flowers, mad at an underwhelming reality. Marion's camp was in Normandy, so I still had a bus and a train to catch. I bought a pack of cigarettes at Gare Montparnasse. No one was going to care if I started smoking again, except maybe Audrey. I was the only customer, and the cashier resented me for disturbing her phone conversation.

"I'm very sorry that you lack privacy in your place of work," I said.

"What's that?" she said, away from the receiver.

I said I hoped she was having a nice day.

She was framed by trashy magazines, and the cover of one informed me that Marion's father was single again. Who could possibly care? I wondered. Who still cared? It had to stop, at some point. The reality-TV show he'd starred on had been off the air for three years. Other shows had taken its place, even more shocking and even more boring ones, with hotter and dumber participants, but Marion's father was still interesting to some people. They wanted to know if he was happy. He'd seemed so troubled—a bit dickish, yes, but so vulnerable, and honest about his past mistakes . . . the audience had loved that.

God, that cigarette was good. If all cigarettes tasted the way one did after two weeks of abstinence, no one would consider quitting, I thought. *Oh, really?* I berated myself immediately. *Things are better when you don't have them all the time? What a discovery! You should write that down for posterity! Print it on a mug!* I smoked a second one. Not as good. Not nearly.

Marion apologized for punching the girl, but she didn't mean it. She was glad about the punch, only sorry that it had had consequences.

"What are we going to do with you?" I said.

Marion didn't do rhetorical questions. "I guess you'll send me to another shrink," she said.

She could have made excuses, her father being a loser who'd abandoned her before she could even say a word, but she never played that card. She vaguely knew about the show—that her father had confessed to another cast member, on camera, that he hadn't seen his daughter in years and felt lousy about it. I'd received several calls from production after that, asking if I would consider bringing Marion to the set for a reunion on live TV, and I'd said no. When they insisted, I talked to Marion about it, and she confirmed that she wasn't interested. She thought he was an idiot. I said, "Yes, he's an idiot for not having spent the past nine years with you," and she said, "No, he's an idiot because he thinks that Lebanon and Libya are the same country," which indicated that she'd actually watched a few episodes. When production insisted some more, I told them to feel free to pass our number on to Marion's father, if he wanted to reconnect off camera. He never got in touch.

We rode back to Paris in silence, Marion reading her comics, me looking at her reflection in the train window. On the Métro back to the apartment, I received a video from Lino. The glasses had arrived in Almería an hour before, and they were all having a party at the Delfín to celebrate. Audrey had insisted that my brother film her putting the glasses on for the first time so that I could share this moment with them.

Night was falling in Paris, and men and women on the Métro looked concerned, or angry at themselves for not accomplishing what they'd hoped to accomplish before sunset. Almería, the video reminded me, though in the same time zone, still had a good hour of daylight ahead, and that seemed enough to keep all hopes up. Audrey didn't want to wait for the sunset or anything special to try on the glasses: she wanted her first moment in full color to be a random one, and to measure all beauty from there. The first thing she looked at was my brother, and she couldn't believe it—she kept touching his shirt, his skin, his face. Then she looked at her tapas, the beach, the sea. Faking it or not—it seemed like she wasn't—she looked more joyful than I'd ever been. Or than I'd ever seen Marion be. I showed her the video.

"That's Lino's girlfriend," I said. "She's color blind."

To my surprise, Marion found the news worthy of attention. To my surprise and relief, I should say. You don't always want to see yourself in your children. Children notice what you passed on to them, too, and they resent you for making them in your image.

She watched the video with a focus she usually reserved for scientific experiments. "She looks too happy to be interesting" was her conclusion. She handed back the phone.

"She was adopted," I said. "She's not happy."

Marion looked at the video again and shrugged. "Maybe now that she sees colors she'll dress a little better," she said.

Now was perhaps not the moment to give her the purple friendship bracelet Audrey had bought for her. She would deem it ugly, I knew, ugly as the Eiffel Tower.

"Has my grandfather gotten any better at chess?" she asked.

I just smiled. I didn't know what to say. I didn't know anything about chess, and so little about my father, in the end.

I'd been in transit all day, in the sky and now underground, alone and now with her. Our suitcases stood upright on their wheels and swayed in front of us, threatened to tip over with every stop and turn of the Métro, but Marion didn't seem to worry that hers might fall, hit someone's knees, break open. She didn't pretend to attempt to steady it by resting a hand on the handle, so I put one hand on each suitcase.

What was so stupid about castling? I wondered. Why couldn't she have given my father a break about it? Why couldn't she give anyone a break, not hit them, hold her own suitcase? I realized I hadn't asked her what the girl had done to deserve the blow.

When we got home, there was a message from Clara, and I feared that the girl had taken a turn for the worse, that the broken bone in her nose had perforated an eye, dug into her brain, or paralyzed her, but the message was from earlier that morning, before Clara had reached me on my cellphone, when my main concern had been to expose Audrey's lie in front of those who loved her.

I texted my brother to see how life in color was treating his girlfriend.

"We're watching *Grease* in Spanish," he answered. "She says she's never taking the glasses off."

"*Grease*?" I texted back.

"Her favorite movie."

I wondered how one could like the movie *Grease* if one didn't know the color pink.

"Thank you," my brother added.

I started writing a response, but decided against it. I could stand to rest on a small victory.

Audrey ended up taking the glasses off, of course. At Christmas, when my mother insisted that she take a "real" look at the assortment of pastries she'd spent too much money on, Audrey only flashed the glasses before her eyes. Marion made an effort and wore the purple bracelet. She told Audrey, when Audrey arrived, that it was nice to meet her, and for a moment it seemed as if she'd never hated anybody.

In the kitchen, I joked to my brother that Audrey had renounced access to the full color spectrum after seeing his paintings—too much to bear, she preferred the beiges and the greens. He said the glasses gave her a headache.

"I can't remember *not* having a headache," I said. "Maybe before Marion was born?"

"You shouldn't talk like that," my mother said. She was making coffee for all, decaf for Audrey. "Marion could hear you."

I hadn't meant that Marion's existence had made me sick, only that I was in pain all the time, that it was what women had on their plate, the headaches, that they were not an excuse not to fuck or not to wear glasses, that we just had them, for real, all the time, did we not?

"I haven't had a headache in years," my mother said.

I said that was because she wasn't of childbearing age anymore.

When we came back to the living room, my father had taken his chessboard out and was showing Marion the move-by-move sequence of a game he'd committed to memory, the Levitsky–Marshall. She was enthralled. My father had figured out that the best way to communicate with her was to present only facts, other people's plays. Audrey watched the game and knew better than to ask questions—she wasn't a chess player, but she could tell when her ignorance would not be perceived as cute. My mother brought her a cup of decaf and sat in the club chair closest to her. It was all very Christmassy, the whole family in knit sweaters, blowing on steaming cups, some of us playing, others content to simply be there digesting among loved ones.

My brother started sketching the scene on one of the drawing pads my mother kept around the house because he could be inspired at any time. I don't think Lino was ever inspired, he just liked drawing, and he drew when he was bored, drew what was in front of him. He'd tried teaching me a bit, long ago, said I should try to picture spaces and people as shapes, that this would help me see order in chaos and build balanced compositions. He never drew self-portraits. Sometimes he drew me. I'd even made it into a painting he sold to a collector in Switzerland, a pool-party scene in which everyone looked murderous and I wore a turtleneck. Now I sat beside him on the couch, to ensure that he wouldn't include me in the Christmas sketch, and also to allow myself to glance at his progress. He started by drawing intersecting lines, separating the paper into clear sections. I guess he thought that the way the family had arranged itself made for an elegant composition, triangles overlapping, or something.

Beyond

USE OF THE WORD "FAT" IS NOT PERMITTED AT BEYOND. THE kids here are *overweight,* Walter explains, although "overweight," too, might be considered problematic, and should only be used in case of absolute necessity. It is still a hurtful word. It still implies the existence of a norm.

Maisie doesn't understand why Walter gathered all camp personnel half a day early to tell them that. She hadn't planned on calling the children fat.

Eugene knows he's fat. He expects to be called it. Of course, though, he didn't get the memo about the word "fat," its being verboten. Kids sacrificing their summer to weight-loss camp were only sent colorful pamphlets, popping with inspirational quotes and grateful testimonies: it would all be fun at Camp Beyond, so much fun—"*beyond* fun," in fact. Eugene tries to imagine what lies *beyond* fun. Whenever he hears the word "beyond," what he pictures is a man walking off a cliff, or through a space portal into another dimension: no more of the same for the man, but radical change. Privately, he renames the camp "Beyond Fat."

When the kids arrive, there's a welcome speech, and immediate apologies for the weather. The man in charge, Walter, speaks from a small stage: "We'd planned to spend the afternoon outside, but—" He pauses there to point at the ceiling, indicating the sky beyond the ceiling, the storm that dims the bright lightbulbs for seconds at a time. Eugene wishes for the lights to go off for good, for the day to somehow be canceled, the whole camp thing.

"We'd planned an outdoor cookie hunt," Walter says. "You were supposed to put in some effort for these!"

Each kid has been given a Ziploc containing a single sugarfree cookie.

"But I guess you can just have your cookie now, and we'll all go on the treadmill in a little while instead. Running *post*-cookies instead of running *for* cookies, what's the difference? In the end? Cookies are eaten, miles are run."

A girl to Eugene's left looks at her cookie and turns to him.

"I would never run for *that*," she whispers.

Her name tag says "Alice."

"I know," Eugene says.

"If in a week you see me ready to run for *that*," Alice insists, "please stab me in the heart."

"I know," Eugene repeats. "I hate raisins."

"It's all so de*gra*ding."

Something follows about mutual respect, about Beyond being a safe haven where hurtful words, behaviors, and even thoughts have no rightful place.

"Same goes for yourself," Walter says. "For your own personal thoughts about yourselves. Self-deprecation is not allowed here—"

I'm fat and ugly, Eugene thinks immediately. *Even my parents think so.*

"Except, of course, when you're in session with our therapist here, Sabina. To Sabina, you can say absolutely anything you want. She will not judge you."

Sabina waves at the children.

"Does that mean that everyone else will judge us?" asks a kid Eugene and Alice cannot see.

"Of course not," Walter says, and for a moment it seems he is going to add something generic about the absence of judgment at Beyond, but after a few seconds, he only repeats the words "Of course not," a little slower.

The speech ends. The boys go one way and the girls another. Each group is then split in two according to age. Eugene hears a boy comment on the non-coedness of the dorms. "Like we'd want to hit *that*" is the comment. Eugene is sent to line up with the boys thirteen and older. He'll only turn thirteen during his third week at Beyond, and wasn't sure whether they'd put him with the ten-to-twelve or the thirteen-to-fifteen group. He looks at the younger kids. They seem nicer.

Fights for top bunks quickly break out. Eugene, seeing an opportunity to display maturity, sits on a bottom bunk (the one nearest to the door), and starts to unpack. He thinks that not taking part in the argument will demonstrate his coolness, that he is above silly quarrels. He's also ashamed to think this. He wouldn't even accept a top bunk if it was offered to him. They make him scared he'll roll over the rail in his sleep and wake up in the middle of his fall. He unpacks clothes, toiletries, and the empty notebook that the camp has required each participant to bring. He decides to wait and see what the others elect to display on their nightstands before taking out the books (Stanislavsky, Brando's autobiography), the photographs, the bundle of postcards his little brother, Max, has written for him in advance of camp (one card for each day Eugene will spend at Beyond). The others are still arguing. Eugene, his backpack on his knees, pulls Max's first envelope from the bundle, the one Max has written today's date on.

Gene!

It's your first day! I bet it sucks. I wish you didn't have to go but I know that you'll feel better when you're thinner.

Eugene often thinks of Max as the child his parents had to taunt him: joyful and thin. Everyone loves Max. Eugene maybe more than anyone else.

If you have trouble falling asleep tonight, think about the penguin on this postcard. How comfortable does he look?

I love you, brother. I wish I was fat and I'd gone with you!

Max

Eugene fans through the twenty-eight envelopes and notices one that Max has decorated with glitter and confetti—it's the one Eugene will open on his birthday. He keeps fantasizing that he'll look good that day. His goal is to have lost eight pounds by then. When he pictures it, though, he's lost way more than that.

"Well, you're definitely up there," Eugene hears one of the

boys tell him. They've settled the matter of top-bunk distribution.

"What?"

"We're talking about who's fattest here. Assessing the playing field," another boy explains. "You're definitely up there."

"We're not supposed to judge," Eugene says.

"It's not a judgment. It's an observation. We're all fat here, dude."

"Yeah, Aaron was just saying he might be the fattest here, right, Aaron?"

"I'm two hundred and two pounds," comes Aaron's confirmation.

They've bonded while fighting. Sized one another up, learned one another's names.

"Well, I'm only a hundred and eighty," Eugene says, and regrets it right away. He never knows when defending himself will sound badass or whiny.

"That's it? You must have very light bones."

"Maybe it's just the fat distribution around your neck," Aaron says. "Gives that impression you're heavier."

Eugene repeats that they're not supposed to judge.

"Jesus, will you relax? Double chin's the first thing to go once you start losing weight."

"I heard tits were the first things out," Eugene says.

His talk of tits makes everyone self-conscious—silence sets, arms cross over chests.

"Anyway, sorry I hurt your feelings," the first kid ends up saying. "I assumed you knew you were one of the fattest here. I assumed that's why you'd picked a bottom bunk. But I'm guessing these top bunks are specially designed for big guys like us."

"I fucking hope so," Aaron says.

"Would be stupid otherwise."

"Humiliating."

"Maybe we're supposed to lose weight through humiliation."

"Doubt it. I'm guessing we've all been humiliated before, and yet here we are," Aaron says. "Fatter than ever. At least as far as I'm concerned."

"But we've never been humiliated *as a group*. Maybe we're supposed to look at each other and think, *Is* that *what I look like?*"

They look at each other.

That first night, Eugene can't sleep. He wanders around the building and winds up in the kitchen to refill his water bottle. They've been told not to go into the kitchen, but Eugene assumes the food will be shut away, so what could he be accused of? He still ducks under a vinyl-clothed table when he hears footsteps coming his way. Four or five adults. A key turning, bags of chips popping open.

"So here it is," a male voice says, "the adult pantry."

"And do we each get our own key?"

"Tequila?" A different male voice.

"Sure!"

"Oh . . . you too, Maisie? I didn't think you drank."

"Why would you think that?"

"I mean, you teach yoga. Aren't you supposed to be super healthy and content or something?"

"Is it ever going to stop raining?"

"My phone says no."

For a minute, Eugene wishes he could tell the different counselors' voices apart, but then nothing interesting gets said, and he can't wait for them to leave. After a while, the only voice he recognizes, Walter's, interrupts the group. "We've just had our first crier!" Walter announces. You can hear he's beaming.

"Who was it?" someone asks. "Was it Eugene? I bet Cassie that Eugene would be our first crier."

"You bet wrong," Walter says. "It was Alice. Who had his money on Alice?"

Sound of bills leaving pockets.

During their first therapy session, Sabina asks Eugene who at home does the cooking, like it might mean something.

"My mom," Eugene says. "On special occasions, my father will make duck, or rabbit."

"Do you like duck or rabbit?"

"Not really, no."

"They aren't very popular foods among children," Sabina confirms. Eugene says nothing. "Do you ever think that the meals your father chooses to cook for you . . . that there's something a little passive-aggressive about his choices?"

"I don't," Eugene says. "*He* likes duck and rabbit."

Eugene has never seen a therapist before, but because he's a fan of *The Sopranos,* he's familiar with the concept. He wishes he had a familial puzzle for the therapist to solve, that his mother was as horrible as Tony Soprano's, but his parents are okay. They even let him watch *The Sopranos,* with all the cursing and the violence and the sexual innuendos.

After teaching the kids their first yoga class, Maisie finds Eugene crying alone in the changing room. She's been told all the kids would cry at some point, whether right away, like Alice, or after the litany of insipid meals got to them—the halibut and the steamed zucchini, the roasted tomatoes or the thumb-size cheese portions, all potential breaking points—but she still doesn't know how to handle it. People have told her she wasn't a good shoulder before. She's not even sure she's a good yoga teacher.

"I'm sorry," she tells Eugene. "I thought everyone was gone."

Eugene looks up at her but doesn't stop crying. She sits next to him on the bench.

"Yoga can really stir up some deep emotions," Maisie says. "Do you want me to get Sabina?"

It's the first time Eugene has managed to cry on demand, for no other reason than acting practice. He's overjoyed that Maisie is buying it. He can't exit the scene, though, not in the middle of such rousing success.

"It's my grandfather," he says. "He died last month, and sometimes it really hits me. The reality of it."

That part is not exactly a lie. His grandfather died the year before and not last month, but Eugene still relies on old memories of him to work on his crying.

"Do you want to talk about him?" Maisie asks.

"He used to be an astronaut," Eugene says. That's not true, of course, and he regrets mixing Method acting with improv. He's not ready for that. He got carried away. Deflection is needed. "He never went to the moon or anything like that," he says.

"Did he go out in space at all?"

Eugene shakes his head and his crying intensifies.

"He was never selected."

"It's the hardest part," Maisie says, "when someone dies, to think of all the things they didn't get to do."

She seems to know what she's talking about, and Eugene suddenly feels bad for fooling her. His crying becomes real, at least he thinks it does, but it's hard to tell.

. . .

During a cigarette break on the covered porch, Sabina discovers a bird's nest on a beam, between two rafters. The babies were just born: they're all pink and blind and their beaks stick out and cry whenever Sabina comes near. She thinks the kids are going to love it, that they're going to love seeing the baby birds grow while they're at Beyond. She thinks the birds are a beautiful metaphor for the transformation the kids are undergoing.

Alice tells Eugene the metaphor could've worked with butterflies, maybe, with something sluggish and ugly becoming light and beautiful, but she can't quite see what's nice about baby birds. All they do is feed. Wait for their mother to come and spit out worms into their mouths. Birds creep her out.

Eugene opens a new postcard from Max every morning and rereads it at night. In each card, which he has predated, Max imagines what they'll both be doing on the actual day.

> Today is the 12th, which means we're on our way to the cabin. I am probably singing in the car a lot, and we're probably stopping at Rodeo Diner for lunch. You probably long for Rodeo Diner now that I wrote Rodeo Diner, and you're going to think about it all day, but don't! Food is boring! We're not supposed to think about it much. It's just energy to do fun things throughout the day!

When he reads these cards, Eugene gets a feeling his family won't come back for him at the end of camp, that their lives are unfolding far away, both in time and space, and that it is how they want it. He feels they are forgetting about him.

Today is the 13th and we must've arrived at the cabin. I hope to see a lot of eagles this year, and to catch good fish on the boat. It won't be the same without Grandpa, but maybe it will also be good to miss him there rather than at home. Does that make sense?

Eugene doesn't think it does.

It rains constantly. The kids spend a lot of time on the treadmill. An afternoon yoga class is added. They do occasionally go out on the covered porch to look at the baby birds. The birds are growing fast.

After a week of rain and canceled outdoor activities, kids and counselors decide to put together a talent show. Aaron's talent is juggling. Alice says anyone can juggle. Many kids undermine her by saying they can't juggle. Only seven kids sign up to be part of the talent show. They will perform at the end of camp.

Eugene has never been onstage. He wants to be an actor, but only in movies. He doesn't want a live audience. He doesn't sign up.

Walter takes Maisie aside to tell her that he's heard children complain about yoga being harder than they thought.

"You're challenging them quite a bit," he says.

Maisie tells Walter that she's mostly working on the standing postures, building up the kids' sense of balance.

"I mean, I'm not asking you to lay out your pedagogy or anything," Walter says. "I'm sure you know what you're doing, in general, but the context here . . . our kids are a little challenged in the flexibility department, is what I'm trying to say."

"Flexibility and balance have nothing to do with weight," Maisie says.

Walter doesn't seem to find the fact relevant to their conversation.

"Has anyone complained?" Maisie asks.

"Not directly, but I heard kids say yoga was way harder than they thought."

"That's not necessarily a bad thing."

Walter disagrees.

"We want to build confidence here," he says. "I was thinking about yoga more as a way for the kids to relax. An easy class. They're in a fragile state already. Vulnerable. We don't want them to think, 'Oh man, I can't even do *yoga*.'"

He says this like doing yoga is akin to taking a nap.

During his session with Sabina, Eugene asks if she's seen *The Sopranos,* and what she thinks of Lorraine Bracco's portrayal of Tony's doctor, if it feels true to life as a psychiatrist. Sabina tells him she's not a psychiatrist, and what does *he* think of the therapy sessions in *The Sopranos*?

"They don't really seem to help," Eugene says. "But I like Dr. Melfi as a character."

They go on talking about *The Sopranos,* what it is that Eugene likes so much about the show. Eugene says first of all it's so funny, but then when Sabina asks if he has a favorite joke from the show, his mind goes blank. Or rather, all he can think of is jokes about how fat the characters are ("Get off my car before you flip it over, you fat fuck," "She's so fat, her blood type's ragù," "She's so fat, when she goes camping, the bears have to hide *their* food"), and he knows Sabina will make too much of it if he tells her any of them.

"I think one thing I love about the show is that I used to watch it with my grandfather," Eugene says. "He's dead now."

"I'm so sorry to hear that," Sabina says. She asks Eugene if he and his grandfather were close. He tells her his grandfather was a brain surgeon and that surgeons are extremely hard to be close with, because they only see bodies as machines.

"And how do *you* see your body?" Sabina asks him.

It rains and rains and rains.

One afternoon, Eugene finds Alice on the porch, juggling with tennis balls. She wants to prove to everyone participating in the talent show that their talent isn't an actual talent, that anybody can do what they do. She's confident her voice is better than Margaret's, that she's a better speller than John, and that the one magic trick she knows will surpass Lisa's.

"But I'm shit at juggling," she says. "So I need to practice if I want Aaron to feel bad. I need to practice *a lot*."

"Why do you want Aaron to feel bad?"

"It's nothing against him in particular," Alice says. "It's just everyone. Everyone needs to understand that there's nothing special about them."

Eugene is better at juggling than Alice, and offers technical advice. She loses patience quickly and throws her balls in frustration, as far away from the porch as she can. She is surprisingly strong. One of the balls lands in a puddle of mud. Another, which she throws with even more anger than the first, hits something in midair—a bird. Eugene hopes it's not the mother bird coming back to feed her babies, but of course it is. No other bird would be flying in the rain. Both bird and juggling ball fall to the wet ground in mirroring arcs.

Alice brings her hands to her mouth as if to muffle a scream, but there's no scream.

Eugene walks to the fallen bird to assess the damage.

"It's just stunned, right?" Alice ends up asking from the porch. She doesn't want to look.

The bird's eyes are open but the neck is broken.

"Don't worry," Eugene says. "I'm sure it happens all the time."

He has no idea what he means by this.

The bird landed on a patch of grass near some bushes. Alice watches Eugene shuffle through leaves, opening up a space for the body.

"Oh my god, it's dead," she says.

"I'll just put it in there and give it some time to gather its spirits," Eugene says. "We can't leave it in the rain."

He looks like he's done this before, hidden a body. Alice can't help but think how ugly Eugene is, especially knelt down like that, the peeking butt crack seemingly endless.

In Eugene's hands, the dead bird feels flimsy, all fragile angles, like an improvised Lego structure. Even though it's already dead, he's afraid the bird might break further and disintegrate. He lays it down delicately on the ground and releases the bush branches he'd been holding away. They bounce back into place and hide the bird almost completely.

Today is the 19th and who's to say what's going on with you or me? I'm writing all these letters weeks in advance for you to open at camp. It's the kind of thing you're not supposed to do, I think. It feels a bit dangerous. What if I die during our camping trip, and then you have letters signed by me that are dated from days after I'm dead? That would be so creepy! It feels like I shouldn't play with the space-time continuum this way. But it's also a bit exciting.

Eugene wishes Max hadn't mentioned it. He's been uneasy with the idea of his brother predating postcards since the beginning. He wishes he could call his family and make sure they're all okay, but phone calls are prohibited for the duration of camp. Unless there's an emergency, of course. *If something had happened to Max,* Eugene thinks, *or Mom or Dad, there would've been a call.* This sets his mind at ease for a minute. *Unless they all died together in a car accident and no one has yet been able to identify the bodies.* Maybe Eugene himself is already dead, Eugene thinks, a ghost. Maybe everyone here is dead and that's why it's called Beyond.

That night, it is hard to fall asleep again. He thinks about his grandfather, the last few weeks of his life. His mother had wanted him to come live with them. Eugene doesn't want to think about his grandfather. He listens to the rain and tries to forget about death. After an hour of this, maybe two, he hears blankets shuffling a couple of bunks down, and Aaron whisper, "Is anybody awake?" Eugene doesn't answer. The question feels like a trap. Aaron repeats it.

It is assumed that the bird episode will remain a secret between them, but as a guarantee that he won't use it against her, Alice still asks Eugene to tell her something he's never told anyone before. He tells her his biggest secret, which is that he wants to be an actor. Not even Max knows this.

"I tell everyone I want to direct movies," he says to Alice, "but really, I want to act."

He only tells Alice his secret because he's pretty sure he'll never see her again after camp.

Alice isn't as surprised by his ambition as he thought she would be. She immediately tries to think of fat actors. Actors who've started out fat, that is, not actors struck by fatness mid-career.

"I guess men are luckier in that they don't *have* to be good-looking to be actors," she says. It is unclear whether she intends to be mean or is just thinking out loud.

"Thanks," Eugene says.

"Oh, grow up. We're *both* repulsive."

"You shouldn't say that word."

"You mean because 'self-deprecation is not allowed here'?" Alice asks. She believes constant judgment of oneself is the only way to betterment.

"But wait," she says, suddenly computing. "If no one knows you want to be an actor, does that mean you never actually performed with anybody?"

"You don't really need others to know that you're acting in order to act," Eugene says.

"Yes, you do," Alice says. "Otherwise, it's not called acting, it's called being an asshole."

She forbids him to ever use her as an acting partner without her knowledge.

"I can't always be wondering if you're lying to me or not."

She speaks as if she intends to be friends with him forever. Before he even has time to gauge how he feels about this, Alice is on to her next idea.

"We should do a scene together," she says.

"For the talent show?"

Alice rolls her eyes.

"Who cares about the stupid talent show! I mean let's work on something just for yourself. Just to know where you stand. Is there a monologue you know by heart? A scene?"

The only scenes Eugene knows by heart are from *The Sopranos*.

Every time they reach the portion of yoga class devoted to inverted postures, Maisie tells the girls currently on their "moon time" to skip them and relax in child's pose instead. Something about energies flowing the wrong way. Alice has been bleeding for days, but she doesn't think anyone needs to know about her cycle. She does the inverted poses: bridge, candle, plow. Plow's her favorite anyway. She doesn't see why she should skip yoga's only rewarding posture just because she's a girl. She pictures the thick blood traveling to her head.

That afternoon, though, Alice is quite tired, and asks Maisie if she may do the whole class in dead child's pose. Maisie tells her there's no such thing as dead child's pose.

"It's either child's pose or corpse pose," she explains, "and either way, no, Alice, you may not do the whole class in either."

"But why not?" Alice asks. "Maybe, instead of doing one pose after another like we've been doing, we could just focus on a single pose and try to really *master* it. Isn't that in line with yogic thinking? Do less, but do better?"

Another girl tells Alice her idea is bullshit. "I mean, not entirely bullshit, but I feel like your argument might have more power if you hadn't suggested we start with mastering corpse, which is basically, like, not a pose. All you have to do is *lie* there."

"Well, actually," Maisie says before Alice gets a chance to stand up for herself, "corpse is the pose that took me the longest time to really understand. It's a little more complicated than just *ly*ing there—it's about trying to be both here and not at the same time."

"What do you mean, *not* be here?" Eugene asks.

"I mean that there's a balance to find, in corpse pose, between consciousness and unconsciousness, and once you find it, it's truly intense. Not really comparable to anything else your body is used to."

"Like an orgasm?" Alice asks.

"Yeah, like you would know," the other girl says.

"Kind of, I guess," Maisie says.

"Well, let's all do corpse, then. I mean, if it really is the hardest pose."

"Except there's no real pleasure in corpse," Maisie says. She feels maybe she's promised the kids too much. "It's just similar to an orgasm in that it's a new state your body can be in that you didn't know it could be in before it suddenly was. And then you want to find that again and again any chance you get."

Maisie has everyone lie on their mats, eyes closed, palms up, feet slowly falling left and right, the opening between them a hand-fan shape—everything abandoned to gravity.

She gives her usual list of instructions as she walks between the mats, names different body parts that the children should visualize, relax entirely, and let sink into the mat: eyeballs, tongue, brain.

Walking among the kids, Maisie finds it hard not to think about beached whales. When she gets to Eugene's mat, she notices that he's still unable to close his eyes. Corpse is the only pose that demands people close their eyes, but some simply cannot do it. She places a little cushion on Eugene's eyes, as she was taught to do in such cases. The cushion is ultrasoft cotton, filled with lavender bits. Eugene can still see some blue light hustle through it. He falls asleep.

He falls asleep for a second or a minute and either snores or farts—farts, in fact, as becomes obvious after a few seconds.

"Shhh," Maisie says, to quiet the ensuing laughter, but there is no way to restore a child's focus once someone has farted.

"Well, at least you were trying," Alice tells Eugene as they roll up their mats. "We were supposed to not pay attention to anything around us. By laughing, we were the ones who failed."

"I'm pretty sure I wasn't supposed to fart either," Eugene says.

"Whatever. We would all have farted if we'd really let go. Because we're fat and putting our bodies through this whole ordeal. There's a lot of air in there. Soon we won't be so disgusting, though. Skinny people don't fart."

Eugene doesn't want to ruin her faith in that. Max farts a lot. He wonders if everyone in Alice's family is fat.

Everyone wonders about the birds. No one has heard a peep from them in a few days.

"They must've left the nest," Sabina says. "I looked it up—these kinds of birds actually grow very fast."

Eugene assumes the baby birds are starved, dead at the bottom of the nest.

Walter takes Maisie aside. He heard she tried to teach the kids how to orgasm in her class. Maisie starts laughing. Walter asks what's so funny.

"It's just the idea that I could teach them that . . . I mean, it's a class a lot of women would want to take."

"What are you teaching them, then, that they think is an orgasm?"

"We were just studying corpse pose," Maisie says. "Letting go. They must have renamed it that."

"They renamed a pose called corpse *orgasm*? Sick little fucks."

He thinks about it for a few seconds.

"Why is there a corpse pose to begin with? I thought yoga was all good energy and life affirming."

Maisie laughs again, but this time when Walter asks what's funny, she doesn't give an explanation.

I've been doing this for so many postcards/days now, and every time I write down a date, I really try to imagine what that day will be like for you and me. I can almost see it sometimes, just a glimpse of the cabin, of breakfast, of you opening an envelope. I think seeing the future might just be a question of practice. If you spend enough time actually trying to visualize a certain day, a specific hour, you'll get to see it.

If you're bored today, try to see tomorrow!

Your brother Max

Aaron juggles by the window while Eugene reads his morning card. Aaron can juggle three balls with only one hand. He can also talk while he does it.

"This is called a reverse cascade," he says.

Then he asks Eugene if he has a thing for Alice.

"A thing?"

"I think she likes me," Aaron says.

Eugene tries to see the future, zooms in on the talent show. Aaron's juggling bit, a triumph. He can't picture Alice.

The next morning, after a mile on the treadmill, Alice faints from anemia. She tells the camp nurse that she's been bleeding for more than a week, "since the bird," she says. She hates birds, she adds. Their eyes are so round and black, you never know what they're looking at.

"She's confused" is the nurse's professional opinion.

She recommends iron supplements and red meat.

Alice lies in bed for the rest of the day. Eugene goes to check in on her a couple of times.

"That bird cursed me," she tells him.

"I think it might just be your body that's confused by the change in diet," Eugene says.

"Maybe *your* body's confused by the change in diet."

She apologizes immediately for her childishness.

"I'm losing my mind," she says.

It's the first time Eugene sets foot in the girls' dorm. No bunk beds there, only singles, lined up along the walls. There are posters of famous, good-looking women over some beds, to give the girls who pinned them courage, Eugene assumes. They go to sleep telling themselves they'll look like this one day, maybe at the end of camp. In Eugene's dorm, some boys have taped pictures of the same famous, good-looking women over *their* beds, and they fall asleep thinking maybe one day they'll look good enough that a similar girl will like them. It strikes Eugene that no one dreams of boys.

Over Alice's bed, there's a handwritten alphabetical list of foods with associated calorie counts per hundred grams. She catches Eugene looking at it, and confesses her shame that food is so important to her. "I know it's stupid," she says. "I know I should be happy to get healthier, but the thought of never eating pizza again . . . it just makes me sad."

"I don't think you have to swear off pizza entirely," Eugene says. "More like you have to keep it for special occasions."

"Right. I guess all that's required of us is to plan our fun in advance, at regular, well-spaced intervals."

Eugene tries to see the future again, like Max suggested. He picks a random day, ten years from now. He sees the lake where he and his grandfather used to fish.

"I think other things are going to become enjoyable to us as we grow older," he says.

Alice says they should rehearse their *Sopranos* scene. Eugene wrote one down from memory. It's mostly a monologue, in which Tony Soprano (Eugene) tells his therapist that he's passed on his depression to his son, but Dr. Melfi (Alice) still has a few short lines.

"*It's in his blood,*" Eugene says, as Tony. "*My rotten fucking putrid genes have infected my kid's soul.*"

"You're not very good at this," Alice tells him, as herself, after they go through the scene a couple of times.

"I know," Eugene says. "I think I'd be better at comedy."

"People say comedy's the hardest."

Eugene gets up early on his birthday. Breakfast won't be for an hour. He brushes his teeth and goes downstairs to sit on the porch and watches the rain fall at two speeds, fast and steady in the clearing, in slow drips from the awning right in front of him. He reads again the card Max wrote for his birthday.

Today is a great day! It is the day you were born, 13 years ago. Sometimes I wish I could see into the past and see that day for myself, like you remember the day I was born and you say Mom and Dad were so happy and you were too, and I would like to see them so happy on the day *you* were born, because they must have felt at least as happy as they were for me, and probably more. Because you were the first, and things are just always so much more and so much better the first time.

Eugene hopes Max is wrong, that first times are no better than others. He thinks back to the day his mother came home from the hospital with Max. All he wanted was to look at the new baby, but his parents were nervous whenever he came too close.

Eugene's shape on the porch makes Maisie jump—she's ready for her run, music is leaking from her earphones.

"Happy birthday!" she tells Eugene. She commends herself for remembering. "Are you excited for the field trip?"

The field trip has nothing to do with his birthday: the kids are all going into town to eat at a restaurant. They are to put into practice what they learned so far about nutrition and self-control in a real-life setting. Eugene is not excited about it. He and his family never go to restaurants. There's nothing real life about them.

"You run in the rain?" he asks Maisie.

"I've been running every morning here, yes," she says. "I'd never run before. It was my challenge for the summer."

Eugene says he doesn't understand why a person would challenge herself. Isn't life itself challenging enough as it is?

"You're quite the sage," Maisie says. She says that challenging yourself on a regular basis makes it easier to deal with unforeseen difficulties when they arise. Eugene is pretty sure she's wrong about that, but doesn't say so.

. . .

The children bake a cake for Eugene, replacing sugar with al-
lulose, and butter with mashed bananas. It turns out rubbery, of
course, but they still have it for dessert at lunch. Four ounces
each. They wait an hour before going on the treadmill. Eugene
has read in Stanislavsky that the most important thing for an
actor is to think of scenes in terms of verbs before going into
them. Verbs are more important than adjectives and nouns and
personal memories. Verbs are action. *I'm losing weight,* he thinks
as he runs in place, and wonders if losing weight is an action. He
wonders the same thing about running in place.

The bus parks a few blocks away from the restaurant so that the
kids get some exercise before dinner. It is still raining, but only
lightly. Eugene steps in dog shit and finds a big puddle to wash
off his shoe. Alice stays by his side and watches the dog shit
break free from the rubber sole.

"Do dogs ever step in dog shit, you think?"

Eugene thinks about it.

"If *I* were a dog, I'd definitely step in dog shit," he says.

They were not hungry before, and they're even less hungry
now. At the restaurant, they order the right things and barely
touch them.

In yoga class, they work on pigeon pose. Maisie says pigeon
helps with sciatica, as if she expects the kids to develop the condition soon. She asks them to picture their hip bones as chicken
wings, and Eugene thinks of the dead bird, the angles he felt.

In the shower, he tries to imagine his bones under the flesh, not just the hips but all of them, which ones he'll get a glimpse of first, once he starts getting thinner. Even his elbows are padded in fat for now. Will it hurt when the cushions are gone? When he puts his elbows on a hard surface?

Alice comes over to his dorm after her own shower, to work on their scene. Both her and Eugene's hair is still wet and sticking to their scalps, and she jokes that they look brilliantined and they should be rehearsing a scene from *Grease* instead.

"From before Sandy looks good, obviously."

Eugene doesn't take the bait. He thinks if he stops responding to Alice's self-hating remarks, she'll stop making them, will maybe even stop believing she's ugly.

She is still critical of his acting and wants to write down directions for him. She grabs the notebook on his nightstand.

"Don't write in this," Eugene tells her. "It's the notebook they told us to bring to camp."

"So what?"

"So I think they're going to want us to use it for something at some point."

"I've been using mine as a food journal," Alice says.

"What's a food journal?"

"You write down everything you eat."

"Is that what we're supposed to do? No one told me."

"I just kind of assumed," Alice says.

Eugene asks for more details about the food journal, what the point of it is.

"I think the idea is to get to a point where you're so disgusted with yourself, you stop eating. Helps you lose touch with your body. Or something."

"My grandfather was a surgeon," Eugene says. "He saw the body as a machine."

"You're so full of shit. I told you not to lie to me."

She winces then, bends over in pain, splashing her stomach against her thighs.

"Are you still bleeding?" Eugene asks.

"Are you my gynecologist now?"

"Maybe you should see one."

"I'm fine," Alice says. "I'm taking my iron pills."

She's getting used to the bleeding at this point and almost wants it to go on. She assumes the more she bleeds, the more weight will exit her body.

After the spasm of pain is gone, she asks Eugene what his grandfather's job actually was.

"He was retired," Eugene says.

"Sure, but before that?"

"I don't know," Eugene says. "He was already old when I was born."

Alice gets another spasm of pain.

"Maybe we should try corpse pose," Eugene says. "It helps relax the muscles, it might help with the pain."

They try corpse on the dorm floor, and after perhaps a minute, when Alice's pain starts to retreat, Aaron comes in and laughs at them and rushes out to tell everyone that Alice and Eugene were trying to have an orgasm together without touching, like Maisie taught them in yoga class.

During his session with Sabina, Eugene wants to talk about Tony Soprano.

"I'm working on a scene, and I don't really know how to go about it. Maybe we can psychoanalyze the character I'm playing? In the scene, he thinks he's given his son the depression gene."

"It's interesting that you would decide to play a father role," Sabina says, but Eugene doesn't see why.

"Children characters are just too boring," he says. "They're always so precocious and cute, like what happens to them doesn't matter because they immediately become wise about it. Or the opposite: they're so clueless they just lash out and they're super mean to their parents."

"I see you've given this a lot of thought," Sabina says. "Which category do you think you fit in?"

"Neither. It's what I just said: this is how kids are in movies. It's unrealistic."

"And you think adults in movies are more true to life? How would you know, having not yet been an adult yourself?"

He doesn't know how to explain it. Sabina asks if one of his parents is depressed, if he's worried that something has been passed down to him.

"You don't understand," Eugene says. "I just want to talk about the scene."

Sabina tells him she remembers someone saying that acting was living truthfully under imaginary circumstances.

"What does that mean?" Eugene says.

"What do you think it means?"

"What's imaginary and what's not?"

"Exactly," Sabina says.

Eugene is getting tired of this.

"Can *I* take notes during our sessions?" he asks. "I want to write down what you said, about imaginary circumstances. Maybe I'll understand it later."

Sabina tears a page from her pad for him, but she's not sure she should allow the taking of notes by patients. It's the first time anyone has asked.

"Let me write it down for you," she says.

A good compromise. While she writes down the quote, Eugene asks about the notebook they were required to bring.

"No one told us what to do with it," he says. "There's only a week of camp left."

Sabina has no idea what he's talking about.

"A notebook?" she says.

"Are we supposed to use it as a food journal?" Eugene asks.

"I don't know," Sabina says. "What would *you* want to use it for?"

When Alice finds out Eugene has a page from Sabina's notepad, she wants to cover it in pencil and see what Sabina wrote on the previous page. They shade the page gray, but no white letters appear, only white lines and curves, little doodles.

"This pisses me off," Alice says.

"Looks like she's learning to draw."

The shapes are naïve drawings of animals, a cow, a sheep.

"Everyone thinks they're an artist," Alice complains, and it's hard for Eugene not to take it personally. "Why is Sabina *drawing* during our sessions? She's supposed to help us get better."

"You said yourself you don't want to get better. Only thinner."

"It doesn't matter what I want," Alice says. "*She* should want me to get better."

Eugene thinks about imaginary circumstances. He imagines he's thin, that he's a great actor, he imagines that the dead bird's remains aren't in the bush, that the babies survived and left the nest. It's all so easy to believe for a few seconds, but never much beyond that.

. . .

A few days before the end of camp, Alice is gone. The counselors are not supposed to give details, but Maisie tells Eugene they had to call a doctor in the middle of the night because Alice was in too much pain. Something ruptured within her, Maisie says. A cyst. She's going to be fine, but they still had to take her to the hospital.

Aaron starts a rumor that Alice died and the adults are trying to hide it from them. He says he saw dirt under Walter's nails, that they must've buried Alice's body under the cover of night.

Out of boredom, some kids start believing it. Or at least spreading it.

Alice's imagined death goes from accidental to suspicious, and everyone has a different idea who murdered her, and why. Their guessing game is so engrossing that the children don't notice the clouds parting, the sun shining through the windows for the first time in weeks.

The weather clears for the remainder of camp. A theory solidifies around Alice's death: the children think, or pretend to think, that Eugene did it. They circle through potential motives as they laze in the sun, walk in the woods. Was it jealousy? they wonder. Did Alice just not like him that way?

Eugene decides to act unaware of the stories. He's enjoying the setup, the imaginary circumstances. What would the real murderer do? What would an innocent? He doesn't forget that Alice is in fact alive and well (Maisie gives him reports on her health every morning and night). Several times a day, he pictures her eating orange Jell-O in the hospital.

But if his audience wants him to be a murderer, a scorned lover, a budding psychopath, he can accommodate their desires.

Fuck the talent show, as Alice would say. Fuck the planned and rehearsed bits. He can act whenever he wants.

He dives in the lake and swims farther than he's allowed to, because that's what a dangerous man would do. When he turns around to see the others stare at him from the shore, he tries to guess what they might be saying about him.

It gets to Walter's ears that the kids believe Alice has died. He blames Maisie and her teaching them about playing corpse.

"Because of you, we're sending them home with morbid and twisted fantasies," he tells her. Maisie objects that she didn't come up with the names.

"You said to teach them yoga," she says.

"And they think *Eugene* killed her?"

Tomorrow is your last day. You must be excited to come home, but honestly, I hope you're a little sad, too, because I hope you made friends. I know you were friends with Grandpa, but we all need friends our own age!

Had he really been friends with his grandfather? Eugene wonders. Or was it just something he'd said after he died, to get extra sympathy? Half of the time, he didn't even understand what his grandfather said to him. Like, for instance, the last few weeks of his life, when Eugene would look at him all sorry, the old man would tell him not to be so doom and gloom, that he wouldn't switch positions with him for anything in the world. "I'd rather be bedridden than a child again," he'd say. What did that even mean?

He skips the talent show and goes for a swim again, assuming no one will notice he's not in the audience. He tires quickly and decides to just float for a while, his belly up in front of him, concealing the horizon. He can tell he's lost some weight, and wonders just how much. Soon he will know. They will all be weighed tomorrow, like they were upon arrival. He assumes the camp counselors have bets running on which kid lost the most. He doubts anyone put their money on him.

Chicago on the Seine

I USED TO TELL MYSELF STORIES ON THE JOB, TO MAKE IT FEEL exciting—spy stories, exfiltration stories, war stories. I used to come up with poignant little details that turned the repatriation cases I worked on into *Saving Private Ryan,* into *Johnny Got His Gun.* "Repatriation"—there's such a ring to it, such drama. I imagined maimed bodies in dirty tents, nurses changing brown, bloodied gauze, bending over beds to tell the wounded, "The call came in—you're going home." Yet I worked in Special Consular Services at our embassy in Paris. The Americans I helped repatriate mostly broke legs in Pigalle or crashed rental cars in Normandy. Miracles didn't happen to them in Lourdes— people don't talk about it, but those for whom miracles don't happen in Lourdes tend to leave France in worse shape than they arrived.

Occasionally, I had to send a body home. What I'd noticed was that death abroad was more common on package tours. It appeared that, contrary to popular belief, the group didn't lift you up but in fact granted you permission to go soft and fall ill. A group needed a weakest link, demanded it, and there was always a chance that you could be that link.

Eva Glasper exemplified this. She'd died the night before, collapsing after a three-course dinner on the Right Bank. She'd been in Paris for an engineering conference, not on vacation, but the idea was the same: for three days, she'd been part of a group, followed the group's every move, and she'd died in a foreign land, alone among strangers.

I'd talked to her daughter Lisa twice already. Lisa wanted the repatriation process started right away, her mother's body back in Boston ASAP. I skipped lunch to make arrangements with the shipping and receiving funeral homes, with De Gaulle and Logan airports, and, when I called Lisa again to let her know that her mother would be on a cargo plane to Boston first thing in the morning, I expected gratitude for my fast and efficient work. She was, however, disappointed. She'd hoped repatriation would happen that day.

"I don't like the idea of Mom spending another night alone at the morgue," she said. "So far away from home."

"I know it's difficult," I said.

"Is there someone you can recommend to keep watch over her?"

I knew what she meant, I believe, but still I played dumb. I asked if she meant a priest.

"Not a priest," she said. "Someone who could stay with Mom all night, someone nice, preferably, who will explain to her what happened."

"Right," I said.

"I'm not crazy," Lisa said before telling me that the hours after death were critical: bodies should not be left alone and uncared for. If the dead were alone for too long before burial, they could be driven to disquiet, volatility, and eternal roaming. She used the phrase "spectral invasion."

"My mother wasn't ill," she went on. "She wasn't preparing for this to happen, so her spirit is probably very confused right now. Confused and angry. That's the worst combination. That's a recipe for spectral invasion."

I perceived no hint of shame in her voice as she admitted to believing in ghosts.

The TV was on in front of me, covering Hurricane Jared's progress toward Florida, four thousand miles away. U.S. news played in the background nonstop at the embassy now. We used to watch it only during political crises and human catastrophes, but I guess someone had failed to turn it off at some point, weeks or months before, and we'd all tacitly agreed to wait for the next disaster to come to us live.

"We can't let my mother become a ghost," Lisa said. Then she added that I sounded like a nice guy, that maybe *I* could go sit with her mother's corpse. She would pay me for my troubles, she said. I didn't want to spend the night with a dead body, but I was curious to hear how much she'd pay, so I pretended to think about it. I let a little bit of silence take hold. I looked around our open space, then up at the TV again—silent images of planes grounded in Tampa, men nailing plywood to windows in Naples, women praying in Fort Myers.

"Mr. White? Are you still there?"

I googled Eva Glasper while her daughter spoke. I'd seen her passport photo in her file, but a person never looks less herself than in a passport photo. I wanted to see snapshots from real life. I wanted to see whether Eva Glasper had the makings of a ghost, whether she'd been handed a raw deal and might feel cheated, justified in her "eternal roaming," in her anger and her demands. If I believed what movies said about ghosts (and movies were, as far as the topic went, all I had to go on), something every ghost wanted was reparation. According to her posts on Facebook, though, Eva Glasper seemed to have had a happy life, to have lacked for nothing. No rants, only gratitude for her family and for her colleagues at MIT, appreciation posts for her favorite TV show, *For All Mankind,* despite most of the science in it being "off." When it came to fiction, I knew that some people were able to engage only with material they had the capacity to correct. My mother had been that way. As a nurse, she'd loved to spot all the errors in *ER,* but it was still her favorite show. She said that the writers had gotten something right about the emergency room that made you look past all the fuckups.

I told Lisa I would find someone to sit by her mother.

Minutes after I hung up, Marianne came over to my desk for a chat. I wondered if it was something she felt obliged to do now that we'd broken up, come over for chats, to prove to herself that we were over each other, that there was nothing left there. Maybe she thought she was being nice. She reminded me that today was my father's birthday.

"You don't have to do this anymore," I said. "Remind me of things."

"Have you talked to him yet?"

"It's only six A.M. in Chicago."

"When you do, tell him I said hi. And happy birthday."

I still hadn't told my dad about the breakup. Not that it would've pained him, or caused him to worry; we just didn't talk about these things. My father and I mostly talked about movies, to be honest. Sometimes TV. But mostly movies. Marianne had

found it sad when we visited him in Chicago the previous summer. Our dynamic. She'd said that I should let my father in on
the details of my days, that, if I never had a conversation with
him about my life, I would regret it when he was gone. "Movies
are part of my life," I'd told her. "I watch them."

"How are you otherwise?" she asked now.

I told her about my phone call with Lisa Glasper, her request
that I keep her mother's body company at the morgue so that
she wouldn't become a ghost.

"How much money did she offer?"

"Five hundred dollars," I said.

"I can't tell if that's stingy or not. Five hundred? To sit with
her mom's dead body all night?"

"And lead her spirit into the good place," I said.

"Are you going to do it?"

I couldn't accept the money, of course, Marianne and I both
knew it, but it was still fun to consider it, to turn that sum at
different angles against the light and ponder its meaning.

"I wonder what she heard in your voice that made her think
you'd be a good fit for the job," Marianne added. "You could be
a total creep, for all she knows."

"I told her my mother was also from Boston," I said. "I think
that created a bond."

"But your mother wasn't from Boston," Marianne said.

"When you're dealing with bereaved families, you have to
establish trust," I said. "A bond. The veracity of the bond is ir-
relevant."

"You establish trust by lying to them?"

"It's not like I'm dating this girl," I said. I studied Marianne's
reaction to the word "dating." Something was bothering her,
but it wasn't the idea that I could (and would, in all likelihood)
date another woman in the future.

"I can't believe you told this stranger anything about your mother," she said.

"I didn't. You said so yourself—my mother wasn't actually from Boston."

"You know what I mean. You never talked to *me* about your mother."

There it was. Marianne was jealous, but not romantically so. She'd always wanted me to talk more, to open up to her. For the past two years, she'd tried to get to the bottom of my childhood trauma (my mother's death when I was ten), to understand how it had shaped my worldview, and I'd resisted, valiantly, assuring her that my worldview was not to linger on the past.

"Do you want me to tell you something about my mother?" I asked. Now that we wouldn't grow old together, it didn't seem so appalling to let her know more about myself.

"Of course!" Marianne said. "What was she like?"

"She believed in ghosts, actually. My mother. Just like Lisa Glasper."

"Really?"

Marianne's "Really?" made me doubt myself. That was the problem with talking about the dead. Even when you were pretty sure you were telling the truth, you could never feel a hundred percent like you were. How could you be sure the person hadn't changed her mind before dying, or wouldn't have, if given a little more information, a little more time? You had too much power, when speaking of the dead. They had the double disadvantage of not being able to fight you if you said something false about them, and of not having had access to any of the new knowledge the world had amassed since they'd died. I often thought that that was the worst thing about dying: that all your last positions and opinions became fixed forever, that you couldn't change your mind anymore. It made you look stupid.

I didn't know whether my mother really believed in ghosts. She might've been serious when she'd said it, she might've been joking. What I knew for sure was that I'd grown up afraid of everything—the dark, gusts of wind, falling ice. My mother had started showing me horror movies and ghost movies way too early, as an attempt, I believe, to make me less of a wimp. I admired those guys who went down unlit basement stairs after hearing strange sounds in the middle of the night, but her efforts didn't really work, no matter how many times she told me that ghosts were scary, yes, but ultimately harmless. "Like Dad," she once said. "A little gruff on the outside, but truly kindhearted. They just want our help!" I didn't tell her that the idea that my father could need our help was the scariest thing of all. We kept watching ghost movies. We spent a lot of Sundays discussing what we would do if we became ghosts ourselves, who we would mess with. She told me that, if she ever died, she would come haunt me, but not in a scary way, just to hang out, to watch ghost movies with me on Sundays and explain what the movies had gotten right and wrong about the afterlife. It had sounded fun, the idea of watching ghost movies with a ghost, but then my mother fell ill, and, on top of fearing that she'd die, I became scared that she'd die and follow up on her haunting plans. I spent the last weeks of her life wanting to ask her not to come back after her death, but stopping myself for fear of hurting her feelings. What ten-year-old didn't want his mother to come back from the dead to watch movies with him on Sundays?

On the TV, over Marianne's shoulder, the same weatherman I'd been glancing at since morning was gesturing over an animation of Hurricane Jared, like he was trying to wipe it. I wondered if he actually knew anything about meteorology, or if he was just an actor saying his lines. Behind his hand movements, the hurricane was all the colors of the rainbow, like a pinwheel, a swirl lollipop.

"Do you know anything about the color code?" I asked Marianne.

"What? Are we still talking about your mother?"

"No. Do you know anything about the color code, in hurricane graphics?"

"I think it has to do with wind speeds," Marianne said, without turning around to look. "Different colors for different wind speeds."

I said I didn't understand how there could be different wind speeds within the same hurricane and the hurricane could still move along as one, at one single speed.

My father called me at work around four P.M. It was only nine A.M. in Chicago, but I knew he'd already been up for hours, scanning national and local news for things to get furious about.

"Did you see about the horses?" he said.

Two horses had died on a movie set in California. My father couldn't bear the thought of animals being used for entertainment.

"Happy birthday!"

"There'd better be consequences," my father said, about the horses.

I imagined the apartment around him, our too-thick-and-too-long curtains, all that extra fabric at the bottom bunched up on the floor like dirty laundry. As a kid, I'd had fantasies about chopping it off.

"Any special plans for the day?"

"Define 'special,'" my dad said.

I said, "Lunch, maybe? Bowling? A beer with a friend?"

"Barra's coming over later," he said. "We're watching *The Hustler* tonight. Maybe we'll have a beer."

My father had this friend he watched movies with once a week. Another widower, not especially bright. When I'd first met Barra, as a teen, I'd been embarrassed that my dad had made friends with such a dimwit, but then Barra had had us over for dinner, and, seeing how clean and bright his apartment was, meeting his own son and being introduced to his DVD collection, I'd become embarrassed about us, our apartment with the curtains, the grime on the laminated counters, the ugly VHS shelf. My father had resisted DVDs for way too long. He still had our tapes, in fact, the ones with real titles that he'd bought and the blank ones we'd recorded a million movies over, the labels on their spines a geological record of my childhood, movie and show titles crossed out every time we taped new movies and new shows over them, layers upon layers:

~~Miami Vice~~ ~~Churchill documentary~~ ~~Quantum Leap~~
~~Duel/Night Court~~ *Blade Runner* DO NOT ERASE

Either we reached that *Blade Runner* stage—something worth keeping forever—or we kept going, erasing and erasing until we couldn't, in all conscience, ask more of the tape, until random split seconds from *Knight Rider* emerged in the middle of *Stand by Me,* until it looked like the ghosts of previously recorded movies had come to haunt the new ones. Sometimes I pictured the tape thinning and thinning, scenes pressing on other scenes, fighting for space. At some point, we retired the tape. It always felt bad retiring a tape on an insignificant note, a just-okay movie, but it was better, I thought, than insisting on finding the tape's ideal content and risking having the strip snap.

"Marianne says hi," I said.

"Okay," my dad said.

I considered telling him about the breakup, or about Eva Glasper, but he wanted to talk about the dead horses in Hollywood.

"I don't buy that they died of food poisoning," he said. "I think someone poisoned them deliberately."

Our unit's secretary came to my desk and handed me a padded envelope.

"A courier left this for you at reception," she said, and I was glad to have my father on the phone as she said it. He probably got a kick out of hearing that line—he probably imagined himself involved in glamorous international intrigue simply for overhearing it. *A courier left this for you at reception.* He loved spy movies. I think that he (like I once had) still wanted to daydream, or perhaps actually believe, that my work at the embassy was cover for something better.

"You have to go?" he said to me on the phone. "Sounds important."

I had no idea what my father imagined about my life. Did he think my work was risky? Did he think I was a brave man, fighting evil in the shadows?

"It's nothing," I said, before deciding to give him a little thrill, to play along with his fantasy. It was his birthday, after all. "I just need to help get someone out of the country."

"Someone important?"

"You know I can't disclose that kind of information."

The padded envelope contained Eva Glasper's personal items, found at the restaurant where her heart had stopped. Her packed suitcase, and everything she'd had at the hotel, had been sent straight to De Gaulle for her transport the next day, and what she'd had on her person at the hospital was now with her at the morgue, but the restaurant hadn't known where to send the thin notebook she'd put by her plate, along with the complimentary pen she'd received from the Paris Aerospace Conference. I leafed through the notebook. She'd taken a lot of notes, sketched many cryptic diagrams, made a handful of quick yet precise technical drawings. This notebook was the kind of object a prop master would've wanted for a movie about industrial espionage, either to cut to quickly in a mad-scientist scene (scientist up all night, surrounded by her notes and open textbooks) or to place at the center of the plot (a notebook with calculations holding the answer to global warming, the key to humanity's survival). I'd always wondered who made these things, the crazy notebooks in movies—if one guy in Hollywood was known for them and filled three or four a year with equations, drawings, and maps, and whether his work was led by scientific truth or by aesthetics. I knew that Eva Glasper's notebook was real, that it contained real science, but it still looked fake to me.

"I'll let you go, then," my father said, and did.

Eva Glasper's body was on the Left Bank. I took a bus there, and as it crossed the Seine, my brain glitched for a second. Instead of registering the Eiffel Tower ahead, it supplied a Chicago insert, the Whirlpool building. This had happened to me before on buses over rivers. Crossing a bridge on foot never did it, but something about the specific speed of a bus got my brain reaching for old images, giving me temporary access to a nonupdated version of me. The former version of me had taken the LaSalle bus every week, to see an allergist downtown. After the bridge was the Whirlpool building, and, since then, that was apparently what my lizard brain expected and prepared my eyes for when I crossed a bridge on a bus. The same thing had happened in my previous postings, at our embassy in Cairo and at our consulate in Seville. The Whirlpool building over every river. Chicago on the Nile, Chicago on the Guadalquivir.

The morgue used to be a public place in Paris. Back in the nineteenth century, I'd read, you could just go in to see who'd been stabbed the night before, who'd jumped into the river. People showed up every day for entertainment. Thousands of them. I guessed some also went in fear, because their husbands hadn't come home, or their children were missing, but for the most part Parisians went there for fun. Access to the morgue is of course restricted nowadays, but a diplomatic ID gets you in almost anywhere, and I was prepared to show mine at reception. There was no one at reception, though. No reception to speak of, really—the door to the small stone building simply opened onto a hallway, off of which branched other hallways. I didn't want to accidentally stumble on a dead body—I'd come to see Eva Glasper's, to make sure Eva Glasper's ghost didn't leave Eva Glasper's body, and seeing any other body would've felt wrong, like stealing—so I kept my eyes down as I walked the hallways. After a minute I heard something, other footfalls, and followed the sound.

"May I help you?"

I assumed she was a mortician. She wore scrubs and purple Crocs.

I said I was looking for Mrs. Glasper.

"Are you family?"

"I'm from the American embassy. I talked to your colleague on the phone earlier."

She asked for identification and led me to the body.

"I was just finishing working on her," she said. "I haven't seen anything suspicious so far."

"Why would you have?"

She figured that, if the embassy had sent me, it meant Eva Glasper had been more than a simple engineer, or that we suspected some kind of foul play.

"I've just come to pay my respects," I said.

I didn't think she believed me.

She offered to leave me alone with the body, but once she left the room it became hard to remember why I'd come. Was I supposed to talk to Eva Glasper? Her daughter had wished for someone to explain the "situation" to her, but could I communicate it telepathically, or did I have to utter actual words? I dragged a stool closer and sat for a while. What *was* the situation? I wondered. What remained unclear to Eva Glasper's soul or spirit or ghost, if it was still floating somewhere over us in the room?

"There's been an accident," I said. "You died."

And then: "I brought you your notebook."

After a minute, it didn't feel as uncomfortable as I'd thought it would, sitting there talking to her. It did feel like she was still with us in some way, in some unthreatening way. Maybe her daughter was right, maybe something of the deceased did linger in the hours following death, and you had to guide it somehow, or let it know you were there while it figured out where to go.

I told Eva Glasper about the horses in California, which had died almost exactly when she had. She might meet their spirits where she was headed, perhaps even ride them all the way there. It sounded corny, but it was freeing to be corny, to let out clichés and comforting words. I knew they had no truth, but for generations they'd made death bearable. At least for a little while. I remembered reading somewhere that death was easy to understand at first, that it was only the amount of time it lasted that was incomprehensible.

After about twenty minutes, I heard a sound, like someone clicking a pen through a loudspeaker. I asked Eva Glasper what she thought it was, and immediately regretted doing so. You could always pretend that the dead were good listeners, but asking them a question broke the spell. I assumed that Eva Glasper's ghost had ideas about what the sound had been (something to do with the cooling system, most likely), but, because she couldn't voice responses anymore, my asking her a question might have been humiliating. Maybe Eva Glasper was angry right now, which was the exact situation her daughter had feared, an angry ghost refusing her new quarters. I imagined her ghost exploding in silent rage above my head, a breach in the fabric of life, a reversal, spectral invasion. I imagined Eva Glasper trading places with me, taking over my life while I took her spot in the cargo plane tomorrow, the grave in Boston. A change in narration—Eva Glasper narrating my life from now on, starting right now, this very evening. Would I even notice? Would she have to be me, or would she bring herself and all her knowledge about aeronautical engineering into my body with her? Would she love the same people I loved, or dismiss them and pick new ones, men and women I had never noticed? We heard the clicking sound again.

I've always wanted to try, came a thought (mine or hers?)
a different body.

I picked up the notebook I'd left by her side, worried but also oddly thrilled by the possibility that its contents might suddenly make sense to me. Because I had become her, or she had become me. But it was all still gibberish.

The mortician knocked, and let me know she'd soon have to put Eva Glasper's body back in the cold. She saw the notebook in my hands and said, "I read to them sometimes, too."

She was holding a magazine in her right hand and gave it a shake, as if to prove her assertion.

"I wasn't reading to her, I—" I looked down at the notebook and closed it. "Here, will you add this to her personal items?"

The mortician came closer, but didn't grab the notebook. She looked like she'd been crying.

"I can't add anything," she said. "All her stuff is in a sealed bag. I can't mess with it. You'll have to send it to the family yourself."

Perhaps she was still crying.

"Or keep it," she added. "She's not going to need it."

"Are you all right?" I asked.

She said she could give me five more minutes, and I assumed she would leave the room again, but she sat across from me, on the other side of Eva Glasper, and started reading her magazine. The way she'd folded it, I could make out that she was reading an article about Thomas Pesquet, the French astronaut. The famous photograph of Pesquet reading *The Little Prince* in the International Space Station illustrated it. He was going to space again in a few weeks. The mortician sniffled softly.

"I hate Thomas Pesquet," I said, trying to cheer her up. "He's smart and good-looking, and, what, he gets to leave Earth whenever he wants, too? How lucky can a person be?"

For some reason, this made the mortician cry harder. Her name was Romy.

"I'm sure he worked very hard to get where he is," she said, about Thomas Pesquet.

"I'm sorry," I said, not sure exactly what I was apologizing for. "You're right."

I looked at Eva Glasper's face, the eyes so still under their lids. She'd had an opinion on Thomas Pesquet, I assumed, just yesterday. An opinion on the whole space program. Now fixed. Now unchangeable.

"It must be difficult, working here," I said to Romy, who'd gotten up from her chair to blow her nose. "It must get lonely."

Romy said she loved being alone. Her boyfriend had just broken up with her, and that was tough on her ego, of course, that was why she was fragile right now, but really, the idea of being on her own again was alluring, *badass,* even, she said—she used the English word.

"I'm sorry you had to see this, though," she added. "I don't usually cry in front of strangers."

"No need to apologize."

"I like to think I'm prepared for the bad stuff," she said. "I mean, I work here. I've seen it all. But, you know, life can still surprise you. I guess that's a good thing?"

She said she'd seen many people come here over the years, to see family members one last time, and that most of them didn't talk to her, but that some did, and either said things like *I always knew something like this would happen* or *I didn't even know anything like this could happen,* and it was hard to know who was better off, those who'd always known and to some extent prepared for the bad thing to happen, or the unprepared.

"The bad thing happens regardless," she said.

She put her magazine down and offered me a KitKat bar.

"I think the unprepared are better off," I said, declining the KitKat.

"All that tells me about you is that you're the preparing kind."

She chewed her KitKat for a while. I admired people who chewed their food extensively; I found them patient and serious. I often swallowed things whole. I'd scratched my throat on pointy breadcrumbs many times—my pharynx had to be all scar tissue. I wondered if Romy would ever work on someone she knew, a friend's body, an acquaintance. Perhaps she'd work on me when I died, if I died in Paris.

"You said you read," I said, "but do you ever talk to them?"

"The bodies? Of course I do. I talked to her all afternoon."

She put a hand on Eva Glasper's hair.

"Do you ever take photos of them?"

It was something I'd wanted to do when my mother had died. I'd had the thought that it would help me down the line, to remember that she was truly gone, but I'd known not to ask my father.

"Sometimes I have to, for legal," Romy said. "But mostly no. I don't do weird shit. I don't even tell them jokes. You have to act as if someone's always watching."

"Like God?"

"More like cameras," she said.

"Are there? Cameras?"

I must've looked alarmed, because she burst out laughing and said, "I knew it! I knew you were going to do some weird shit. You left something on her body, didn't you? Did you hide some state secret? A microchip in her mouth?"

On my way home, I passed a movie theater that occasionally went all night on Fridays, for Horror Night, New Hollywood Night, Rom-Com Night, whatever they had on hand. For eighteen euros, they played three or four films back to back and served you breakfast in the morning. Today, because it was late September and the universities were again in session, the theme was "Back to School," a triple feature for students and the nostalgia ridden: *The Graduate, Wonder Boys,* and *The Social Network.* I went in. There were short breaks between the movies, for people to go to the bathroom or step out for a cigarette, but I stayed in my seat. I wanted the movies to blend together.

I didn't stay for breakfast. I didn't want to discuss the movies with strangers. I'd discussed them all with my father already, long ago. My opinions of them hadn't changed. I went to a nearby café, sat on the terrace. Reading the *Times* on my phone, I learned that, at some point while I was watching *Wonder Boys,* Hurricane Jared had made landfall in Florida. They were starting to tally the damage.

An American couple and their daughter sat a few tables away, and I listened to their conversation. They were loud enough for that. They'd been in Paris for two days, they knew how to order coffee now—she wanted a *grand crème* and he an *allongé.* They'd seen the Rodin Museum and the Orsay. They would shop across the street at Le Bon Marché after breakfast and take a cruise on the Seine in the afternoon. It sounded nice to be in Paris on vacation.

I watched a plane fly a few thousand feet above us and pondered this discrepancy, that there was little in life more stressful than being on an airplane, and little so soothing as watching one at cruising altitude from below—the possibilities! The miracle of human engineering! Where could the plane be going? It was too early for it to be the one that carried Eva Glasper's body.

The café was relatively empty, and the waiter, perhaps envisioning a tip of American proportions, asked the family if they were enjoying Paris so far. The father said he was learning a lot. The Arenas of Lutetia had left quite an impression on him. To think that the Roman Empire had spread all the way up here, that maybe he'd been walking the same ground as Julius Caesar . . . how *wild,* he said. It now made sense to him that Europeans and Americans should have such different approaches to life and time. How could they not?

It used to embarrass me when Americans in Europe said out loud what everyone else had noticed or thought about before but deemed too obvious to share. I thought Europeans were already convinced we were idiots—there was no need to give them more ammunition. Over time, though, I'd realized that it wasn't so much that Europeans thought we were idiots as that they understood us to be simply less ashamed than they were, and, in the end, I've concluded they're jealous of our confidence. Our belief that, maybe, we were the first to have thought of something, that we might ever say something new. The confidence could play against us, too. It grated on people. Bar fights could erupt in the Latin Quarter because an American had talked too much. (I'd repatriated many victims of bar fights over the years.) I hoped the American family would keep enjoying their Paris trip and nothing would happen to them. Perhaps it was to make sure of that that, after they'd settled the bill, I waited a few minutes and followed them into Le Bon Marché. I kept my distance, but I followed.

I followed them first to the toy section, which looked more like an art installation, plush toys hanging from the ceiling, exploded Lego structures under glass cases. The daughter was afraid to touch anything.

"Do they actually sell sets here?" I heard the father say.

The for-sale Lego boxes were indeed quite concealed, piled deep under the display tables.

"It's like they're ashamed to admit they want our money," the mother said.

I followed them through the shoe section after that, through purses, through cosmetics. I heard the lady at the Chanel counter ask the mother, in English, if she and her daughter would like to have their makeup done. The mother looked hurt to have been recognized as so obviously American, but she said,

"Why not?" The Chanel lady sat the girl and her mother in high chairs, and started working on their faces simultaneously, like a chess grand master.

The father, knowing he was in for a twenty-minute wait at least, started looking around for ways to pass the time. He noticed me. "You were next to us at the café!" he said. He didn't seem to find that odd. Not for a second did he think that a stranger could've followed his family around. It was all a fun coincidence to him, probably meaningful. I felt guilty for following them. If he asked what I was doing in Paris, I was ready to answer that I was here for the aerospace conference, to show him Eva Glasper's pen and notebook as proof, but he asked what I was doing in the department store instead. I was shopping for my own wife and daughter, I told him. I was going home tomorrow, had been here on business—the girls would want something from France. He asked how old my daughter was. With all the lies I'd told so far, I can't explain why this one gave me a hard time, but I froze. I couldn't come up with a made-up age for my invented daughter. The man seemed to understand reasons for my silence that I couldn't possibly have hinted at, and he patted me on the shoulder. We worried so much about our girls, he said, that we simply forgot to watch them grow. My daughter was probably two years older than I thought she was, he joked, before taking me around the jewelry section. I shouldn't try to be too creative, according to him, I should just get her a simple necklace, a gold chain with a charm, the first letter of her name, perhaps? A timeless piece. I got out of Le Bon Marché five hundred euros lighter—just a touch more than what Lisa Glasper would've paid me had I accepted her money. A necklace for my daughter, a leather clutch for my wife.

I parted ways with the Americans on the sidewalk. The lady at the Chanel counter had made the girl look much older and her mother years younger, enhancing a feeling I'd had before, after staying too long in department stores, that these places were like busted time portals, that time moved differently there. Only the father had come out unchanged. We shook hands and wished each other a safe trip home, tomorrow for me, next Wednesday for his family. They should enjoy their time in Paris, I said, and he didn't seem to have any doubt that they would. Nothing bad would happen to them, and they wouldn't do anything stupid, either—nothing they wouldn't be able to fix. I waited until they disappeared into the Métro to return my purchases.

Offside Constantly

I READ A LOT ABOUT FAMOUS PEOPLE AND HOW THEY DIED. OR just what diseases they had. I started with actors and writers, but now I'm down to congressmen. Painters, too, I read a lot about, but only because my brother has so many books about them. (Is it "has" or "had"? The brother is gone, but the books are still here.) My brother loved painters, paintings. Me, I don't really know what to do with a painting, how long I'm supposed to look at it. I prefer movies. Before I watch a movie, I check how long it will last.

My brother was always going to die young (he had cystic fibrosis), but still he thought maybe he'd last long enough to study art history at the Sorbonne, and then some more at the École du Louvre after that, and then maybe have his own gallery in Paris one day. He painted a little bit himself, Thomas, but he wasn't very good at it. That's what he said, at least. I liked his stuff, I think, but mostly because I liked him a lot. When it comes to art, I can't really tell what's good and what isn't. What's easier to tell apart than Good Art and Bad Art, though, is a prestige illness from a regular one. It's not up for debate that mental illnesses have had the most cachet, historically. Manic depression, schizophrenia, anorexia nervosa—anyone who was anyone had one of those. Then come certain STDs, like syphilis, or AIDS, but it seems odd to me that STDs should have cachet, and I wonder why some of them do and others don't (herpes doesn't get you any points, for instance, even though you can die from it), but I guess it's not worth thinking about STDs too much, since there's zero chance I have one of those.

We're trying to figure out what's wrong with me. Everyone says probably narcolepsy, but they can't really confirm unless they do a spinal tap, and my mother is against that. She's scared a spinal tap will be too painful or leave me paralyzed. What frightens me about it isn't so much that it will hurt as that it might confirm narcolepsy. I don't want narcolepsy. Narcolepsy is one that people make fun of. It isn't even mental. It doesn't matter that Nastassja Kinski and Churchill had it. It'll be forever stuck at funny-disease level. Unless someone very hip gets it soon.

I went to a third neurologist on Monday. He gave me a sheet of paper with a perfect circle in the middle. He asked me to draw a clock inside it, showing the time of my choosing. These things, you always think there's a trick, so I asked if there was a trick, but he said no, no trick, just draw a clock. I wondered what time would make me the most interesting case. I made a mark for every minute and drew a clock that said eight-twenty-five, but then I realized that both hands hanging down in the lower half of the circle might be interpreted by the doctor as indicating depression, so I added a third hand, for the seconds, and I pointed it all the way up to twelve, for hope. Depression is not one of the mental illnesses that get you a lot of cred. The doctor barely glanced at the drawing.

Later, in the parking lot, I asked my mother what she thought the clock test was about.

"I don't know," she said. "I'll look it up online when we get home. Do you remember what time you drew?"

I nodded, then she nodded. Whenever possible, she liked to double-check my results against the internet.

"The first two neurologists didn't ask me to draw any clocks," I said.

My mother seemed to believe that this meant the one we'd just seen was a better physician, that he'd know what was wrong with me.

She always came with me to these appointments. I was fourteen, still a child, sort of, so I thought that it had to be that way, that she had to come to ask the doctors the right questions, but when she'd sent me to the first shrink, and then the second, they'd both asked to see me alone, and she'd seemed to understand.

I was afraid sometimes that there was nothing wrong with me. Something was going on, for sure, what with the absences at dinner and the sleeping fits during the day, but sometimes the body does weird things, and doctors don't have a name for the behavior, or they can't find it in their books, and, because the symptoms aren't too worrisome, they just send you home to keep on living, telling you only to come back if things get worse. That's what they'd been doing with me.

I thought I might have a fake disease, one I'd developed only to get my parents' minds off my brother. That would've been shitty of me, worrying them for nothing, but I couldn't ignore the possibility. I'd read on the internet that sometimes when a child died, a sibling became mysteriously ill, in order to give the parents a goal, a reason to live. (Save the remaining child!) I didn't want to be that kind of person. I wanted what I had to be real but treatable. Or manageable, at least. I wanted something with some cachet. Like, nothing intestinal.

Heart conditions have cachet. Marfan syndrome is respectable, because they think Lincoln had it. Lupus has cachet, too, but I don't know if that has to do with who had it (though people like Flannery O'Connor had it, and maybe J Dilla) as much as with what it evokes. It's hard to argue against a disease that has so much metaphorical weight, what with the idea of your own body attacking itself. If you're not terrified by that, then you're not alive. Also, the name itself. *Lupus*. Whoever named lupus "lupus" knew what they were doing.

I'm not interested only in old diseases. Every Tuesday, I read the obituaries Francine Eliot writes for *Inventaire*. It's important to stay in touch with what your contemporaries die of, I think, and to keep up with new illnesses, too. Medical mysteries. A few months ago, for example, on the radio, I heard about a wave of babies born without arms in the Southeast. They were just starting to look into it. I wondered what had spurred the investigation—when exactly one armless newborn had become one armless newborn too many. But that's neither here nor there. One thing we know for sure is that I have all my limbs.

My father gets *Inventaire* in the mail every week, has since forever, for the international-politics section. Every time we move (we move every year or so, for his job), it's a conversation,

a worry: Will the mail be forwarded to our new address seamlessly? Will there be a lag in his delivery of *Inventaire*? My mother
reads it after him. Her favorite part is the books section. Thomas
only ever looked at the last page, the obituary of someone who'd
"left us" that week. He's the one who got me hooked on it.
Growing up, because of that page, I'd believed that only one
person died per week, that a paper shrine in *Inventaire* was what
awaited us all at the end of this. It was only when Debbie Reyn-
olds died just one day after her daughter during Christmas Blues
2016 (Christmas Blues = deaths occurring right after Christmas)
that I'd realized people died all the time, everywhere, every second. After that, I started seeing death everywhere. It was like
when you're taught what "offside" means in soccer: once you
understand the rule, you see it nonstop and call offside constantly. That January, John Hurt and Emmanuelle Riva died a
couple of days apart. Same thing happened the following summer, with Sam Shepard and Jeanne Moreau. (Jeanne Moreau
made it to *Inventaire*'s last page that week, not Shepard, which
was at the root of an explosive argument between my parents.)
A guy named Eric Schweblin used to write the page, but he
died, too, and the lady who wrote his obituary got his job. Francine Eliot was younger, more in touch with the times. She
started writing more and more obituaries for nobodies, for the
regular people who died in terrorist attacks, for example, or for
early victims of the Covid pandemic. Thomas liked when it was
a nobody week in *Inventaire*'s obit, but I didn't see the point in
learning facts about people who would be remembered only for
dying tragically, not for something they'd accomplished during
their lifetime. It was too depressing.

When Thomas died, though, I sent his photo and a few details to Francine Eliot, to see if she would write about him. She
never responded, and it's been seven months now, almost, so I

know it's not going to happen, but I still cross my fingers every week that it will be him on the last page of the magazine.

My mom explained later what the clock drawing was all about: "It's to see if you have dementia. It's routine, but they still have to check."

She said that it didn't matter where I'd drawn the hands of the clock, because all that the doctors were interested in was whether I'd drawn them and the numbers they pointed at within the circle.

"So at least I don't have that," I said. "I don't have dementia."

We'd ruled out a number of things by now. MRIs were clear. I wasn't having mini strokes. It wasn't epilepsy. I was sad, yes, but not depressed, the psychiatrists had concluded. Blood tests showed nothing other than a little anemia.

"Maybe I'm transgender," I told my mother.

It was something I'd been thinking about. Maybe the reason I slept so much during the day was that I couldn't stand being in my body.

"Why would you say that?" my mother said. "Do you feel you're a boy? A man?"

"I wouldn't mind being one sometimes."

She seemed relieved to hear this. She took a deep breath and said that wishing to be a man was just a normal part of being a woman.

"Wanting to be a man is different from feeling like you are a man," she added.

"Is it? How do you tell the difference between a feeling and something else?"

She took a shortcut then. She'd been taking these more and

more, lately, but they were always shortcuts to what she wanted to say, not to where I'd been going.

"We don't want another boy," she said. "We don't want to replace your brother. We're very happy with our little Johanna."

The next day, *Inventaire* came in the mail. Francine Eliot had written a nobody obit, the first one since Thomas died. I read it over breakfast, before school. The nobody had been blue eyed. He'd done nothing with his life; he was being celebrated only for having lived, for having had dreams. The biggest of these dreams had been to publish poetry, but, because life had denied him that satisfaction, Francine Eliot was giving it to him in death, by publishing a sonnet he'd written in his old age.

Fuck that, I thought.

Why did he deserve the space? Thomas hadn't gotten what he wanted from life, either. I wrote an email to Francine Eliot right away, via the magazine's contact page. My first impulse was to let it all out, the anger, the disappointment, to tell her every-thing that was wrong with the nobody's poem (rhyming *amour* with *toujours*), how much more interesting my brother had been, but then I became sleepy and took a short nap on the desk. When I woke up, I was in a completely different frame of mind, bordering on suicidal, and I deleted what I'd written. I replaced it with a lie. I told Francine Eliot that I was myself dying, and that my only wish before I died was to read my big brother's obituary as written by her. I didn't want her to write mine when the time came, I just wanted to "see him alive again in [her] words."

.   .   .

At school, they didn't mind the sleep attacks anymore. By "they," I mean the teachers, of course—who the hell knows what the kids were thinking. As I said, we moved every year, so, in general, there was no sense trying to make friends, but particularly not here. Big brother dying three weeks into the school year, and now the sleeping—who wants to hang out with the new girl? Anyway, the teachers were nice. They'd all liked Thomas, the little they'd gotten to know him, so they were keen to give me a break. I'm assuming they'd all read the first few results of a narcolepsy search on Google by now, too, and had been reassured by the following statement: "While scary, the episodes are not dangerous as long as the individual finds a safe place in which to collapse." In their classrooms, there was always a table my head could fall onto.

I averaged three attacks a day. Most of them lasted between ten and twelve minutes, but they'd been getting longer lately, and I was waking up more and more slowly. Even once I was awake, it had begun to take a minute or two before I could start moving my body again. I'm guessing that everyone has had those nightmares in which they're conscious of an imminent danger but can't save themselves because they can't move. I'd always thought that the scary part was the specific danger of the nightmare—the killers coming for you, the monsters, whatever—but it turns out it's the paralysis that gives you the cold sweats. You could see your happiest memory play again and again, or a young Paul Newman walking toward you with a bunch of roses: if you can't move, you'll want to scream. Which was what I wanted to do now, when I woke up and couldn't move. The thing was, though, I couldn't really scream, either, so I made these embarrassing sounds instead, throaty *mm-m-m*s that were a bit sexual, I guess, and made everyone laugh.

I tried not to attempt screaming that day, in French class,

when I woke up to the sight of my neighbor, Victoria, writing a list of people to invite to her birthday party. (I wasn't on it.)

There was a column for girls and one for boys, and her issue seemed to lie with the girls. She kept going over the girl column like she was composing a poem and there was a perfect rhyme she wasn't seeing, her right hand running her pencil eraser along her neck.

By the end of class, I could move freely again, but Victoria was still stuck with her list. Everyone left the room but us. I always stayed in classrooms during breaks and recesses. People thought I did that because of the narcolepsy, and I think they felt sorry for me, but really, I liked the silence, the empty rooms, looking at what everyone had left behind.

"Is it your first time throwing a party or what?" I asked Victoria.

"What?"

"It shouldn't be that hard to know who you want to have at your party."

Victoria looked surprised that I could speak. Surprised and suspicious.

"I know how to throw a party, thank you very much," she said. "I've seen movies."

"So?"

"So, there's always a party."

We hadn't seen the same movies. My favorite ones were *Léon: The Professional* and *My Girl,* with Anna Chlumsky.

I asked Victoria if she didn't have a class to get to.

"It's PE now," she said. "You don't need to be on time for that."

That was the silver lining of my mysterious illness: I hadn't had to suffer the indignities of phys ed in about six months. I'd jumped at the chance to get a medical dispensation. The people

I understand the least in life are those who insist on participating in phys ed even when they have a good reason not to. There was a girl like that in my previous school—she had six million ulcers or something, a rare condition, but she still went every week, and we had to watch her pain, the contortions in her face when she ran, and we had to pretend it was all right, admire her strength, pass her the ball if she asked for it. She threw up after every class. The film she had to be playing in her head to endure this, I can't relate to at all. I don't want to be the freak that I am, but there are still limits to what I'll do to fit in.

"I think it's going to go away," Victoria said to me, out of nowhere. "Your falling asleep like that. I think it's just the way your body goes through the trauma for now, but then it will all fall into place. One day it will stop, and you won't even realize it. It will be like the last hiccup in a hiccupping fit. You never know it's the last."

"I think I'll know," I said, but she went on with more examples. "It's like how your parents don't remember the last time they tucked you in, or read you a bedtime story. Ask them, you'll see. They don't remember the last story they read you. One day, they just stopped doing it."

She coughed twice after she said all this, turned away from her list to face me as she did, like she thought it was worth seeing. Her eyes didn't narrow as she coughed.

"The list I'm making," she said, "it's not for a party. It's just a list of people I've had violent thoughts toward."

"How violent?"

"I have an anger issue," she said. "I'm working on it."

I'd thought it was short for a birthday-party guest list, but now, knowing what it was, it seemed rather extensive.

"How violent are the thoughts?" I asked again.

"Pretty violent. And it's not just thoughts. Sometimes I have dreams so violent and gory I have to close my eyes in them. You ever closed your eyes in a dream?"

I had, in fact, twice. The two times I'd dreamed of Thomas since he'd died.

"Last week," Victoria said, "I dreamed I was crushing Miss Barbette's skull against a kitchen counter, over and over and over again. I couldn't watch, and I told myself, in my dream, even though I knew I was dreaming, to close my eyes. The sounds were spot on, though. It's really fucked up, what your brain can come up with, in terms of sensory details."

"What did Miss Barbette ever do to you?"

"Nothing, really. That's why dreams don't count as much. The people you see in them, they're stand-ins for other people."

"Who was she a stand-in for?"

Victoria shrugged.

She'd never actually been violent, she explained. She only ever had the thoughts, but the thoughts were becoming bothersome. They encroached on her concentration, messed with her grades.

"That's why I'm making the list," she said, tapping the eraser against the piece of paper. "I need to get to the bottom of what it is that makes me think violent thoughts about these people in particular, so I can fix it."

I looked at the list. The only thing the people on it had in common was that they were idiots, but then some other idiots hadn't made it to the list, so that couldn't be the only criterion. I'd never had thoughts or fantasies about committing violence. I wondered if I would ever have to resort to violence in my life, physical violence. I wondered if not preparing myself for the option would make me more or less likely to succeed at it. Maybe you have to surprise yourself with your violence, I thought, if you want it to work.

"When did it start?" I asked. "When did you start having the violent thoughts?"

She couldn't tell exactly.

"It was progressive," she said. "Unlike your condition. It's not like one day I was fine and the next I started daydreaming about murdering people."

"My thing was progressive, too."

"Well, not really. I was there when it started. That German class? You didn't *half* fall asleep."

"Fair enough."

I think she was trying to convince me that what she had was worse than what I had, which I guess is what teenagers do. When it comes to suffering, they always want the upper hand. Me, I know it's not a contest, because Thomas always said "It's not a contest" when I tried to rank Francine Eliot's obituaries from best to worst life lived. I kept all of *Inventaire*'s last pages and organized them from best to worst in a binder. My favorite life Francine Eliot had written about so far was Tom Petty's. Michel Serres's was second. Favorite didn't mean I thought these men hadn't suffered (I know everyone suffers), just that they'd had a lot of good times. The worst life in the binder so far—I won't name names, because I don't want to cause more pain to the family, but it's a woman, though the person just above her is a guy, and I keep hesitating between the two, and I keep the woman last only because of her gender. I wondered who Francine Eliot was going to eulogize next week, if she knew it already. Would she consider Thomas at all?

I asked Victoria what her favorite movies were, but she said she didn't really watch movies, only TV shows.

.   .   .

Lunchtime I spent mostly on my phone, refreshing my inbox every few seconds, *like the Facebook guy at the end of the Facebook movie,* I thought, but really like anyone anywhere at all times. The mundanity and the drama contained in such a small action. A flick of the thumb, not even, and you could give yourself a little heart attack waiting for a new message to appear in bold. Every time I refreshed, I thought that this would be it, that Francine Eliot had been hitting Send the moment I'd hit Refresh, and I could almost see her name appear in my inbox, faintly superimposed over the last email I'd received ("Caran d'Ache: New colors available!"), but it was always an illusion. I wondered if anyone had ever died while refreshing their inbox, and thought how interesting that would be for Francine Eliot to write about. I almost emailed her again to suggest she look for that person.

I wasn't supposed to wander too far from school, but I walked five blocks to buy cigarettes anyway. I'd smoked a few with Thomas before, in secret of course. He wasn't supposed to smoke with the cystic fibrosis, and he didn't really, just thought he had to live a little if he was going to die young. When he died, he'd had the same pack for five months. I'd finished it after the funeral, thinking they would be the last smokes I'd smoke, but that hadn't quite worked out.

The guy at the counter of the corner *tabac,* where they didn't ask you to show ID, told me I looked all melancholy, and I responded that melancholy was the happiness of being sad (Victor Hugo), and that I was at this moment feeling no form of happiness whatsoever.

"*Ouh la,*" he said. "I don't actually care! Maybe go write a song about it?"

He wasn't mean, though, kind of just admitting that he couldn't do anything for me, which I appreciated—the honesty.

So I gave it a shot. I didn't write a song, because I know nothing about music, but I tried a poem:

This is my first poem.
No matter what happens
Over the course of the next few lines
Never will I write
A first poem again.

I thought it wasn't too bad for a start, but it ended up putting a lot of pressure on whatever followed. The nobody from Francine Eliot's latest obituary didn't seem like such a loser anymore.

When my mother picked me up that afternoon, she made a comment about the cigarette smell. "You don't want to ruin your teeth," she said. "You have such a beautiful smile."

I had that big gap between my top middle incisors, *les dents du bonheur,* as they call it, "happiness teeth," like Vanessa Paradis. Because of my teeth, I'd known who Vanessa Paradis was before I'd learned the name of our president or anyone else famous. It was nice for a while, to hear "How cute! Just like Vanessa Paradis!" because I loved her (she was beautiful and no bullshit), but then, as years went by, I understood that it wasn't the teeth that made her beautiful but something from within, and that I didn't have that something, only the teeth.

"Vanessa Paradis is a smoker," I told my mother.

"Well, she has the means to whiten her teeth all the time, I guess."

"We do, too," I said.

We kept talking about it like that, like the main issues with smoking were cost and cosmetic side effects, and like happiness teeth were something to take special care of, even though I just wanted normal teeth, because I wasn't happy, and having happiness teeth when you weren't happy was a cosmic "fuck you." I'd asked my mom if we could fix them into being just regular teeth—the way Joy changes her name to Hulga in "Good Country People" because Hulga reflects her personality better—but she'd said no. I told her smoking kept me awake.

My father had mentioned a few weeks earlier that my issues could be related to my inner ear, and so we were on our way to an ENT now. I could tell that my mother thought it was a bit of a waste of time, but it was the first time my father had actually suggested something, so I think she wanted to reward him for participating.

The ENT seemed to have no idea why we would want his opinion, given my set of symptoms. We were in and out in fifteen minutes. While we were in there, Francine Eliot responded. She was sorry for my loss, and to hear that I was dying, blah blah blah, but she was under strict contractual obligation to eulogize only the newly dead (this week's or last), and so she couldn't write about Thomas, who'd been "gone" (I hated that she used the word) for a few months already.

I thought about Victoria, how I would've reacted to the email if I'd been her. I tried to have violent thoughts toward Francine Eliot. I imagined her in her office, responding to my email. "*Inventaire* is a time-sensitive publication." I imagined slamming her face into her keyboard, slamming and slamming until the squares imprinted on her skin, but I couldn't get into it. I fell asleep in the car on the way home.

At dinner, my mother pretended that my father's idea hadn't been too bad, that at least we'd ruled something out. I don't know why she insisted that he feel included in our quest. He was retreating more and more into himself, like fathers in the movies. He was just barely there. He was some sort of crisis solver for big-time companies, was good at it apparently, at observing in detail and spotting what the problems were, and he was supposed to, I think, know a thing or two about perseverance and resilience, but he never shared his knowledge with us about what made people happier or more effective. I guess we didn't ask, but still.

I asked my parents if they remembered the last time they'd tucked me in or read me a bedtime story. My mother said of course not, but my father had a clear recollection of the exact moment when he'd realized it had become ridiculous.

"I remember," he said. "You had a zit on your forehead, a real red-and-white one with pus, and I thought, Maybe she's getting too old for this."

"A zit?" I said. "How old was I?"

"I don't know . . . five? Six?"

"And I had a zit?"

"It was just one zit."

"Even babies can get acne," my mother said, before she took another one of her shortcuts and displayed a new way in which she'd misunderstood me. "Do you think if we went back to tucking you in at night, that would solve your issue?" she said.

I asked if they remembered the last time they'd read a bedtime story to Thomas, but neither of them did.

In bed, I read that week's obituary again, the blue-eyed failed poet's. I cried a bit, not for him, but because of his blue eyes, because they reminded me of the Michel Pastoureau lectures about color that Thomas and I had listened to on the radio during the first Covid lockdown, in March 2020. In the one about the color blue, Pastoureau had said that blue eyes had been seen as ridiculous in ancient Rome, the eye color of fools and idiots. Pastoureau didn't say this, but this was how Thomas had interpreted his words: being blue eyed in ancient Rome was kind of like having a mullet today, he'd said. I'd laughed at that for a long time. Thomas hadn't quite understood why. "What's so funny?" he'd said. "*You're* funny," I'd said. "*Blue eyes in ancient Rome were the mullets of today!* That's hilarious!" Sometimes I was too nice to him. I'd remember he would die before me and pretend he was funnier than he was, or smarter, but this wasn't one of those times.

I went to the kitchen for water and saw my parents dumb in the purple TV glow. They were on, like, Episode 98 of some show. I couldn't deal with TV shows anymore, they were becoming too long, and you never knew in advance how many seasons they would be renewed for. I like books better, movies, too, because you know when they'll end. Especially books, though. You hold the remaining pages in your right hand, you pinch them, flip through them. You get a sense of your progression.

"That was a good one," I heard my mother tell my dad. They couldn't see me, as I was in the darkness of our hallway.

"Watch another?" my dad said, and after launching a new episode he wrapped his arm around her.

I didn't think they were getting over Thomas. I didn't think they ever would. But it still turned my guts to stone when I saw them act normal.

. . .

The next day, after French, I asked Victoria if maybe she thought her anger issues could be solved by engaging in some actual violence.

"You mean, if I did beat the shit out of these people?" she said, fanning her list of enemies under my nose. She'd been working on it some more.

"Yeah. Like, maybe you wouldn't like it. Maybe beating them up would make the whole fantasy of beating them up disappear."

"Or I might like it a lot."

"Wouldn't you want to know?"

I told her she could beat the shit out of me if she wanted to. "As a test," I said.

She said I was crazy.

"I won't tell it was you," I said.

She repeated that I was crazy.

"Maybe we can help each other out. Maybe if you break my jaw, or my teeth or whatever, it will wake me up for good. And maybe it will make you realize you actually don't want to be violent, that actual blood is gross."

"Your teeth are cute."

"I didn't ask what you thought of my teeth."

"Makes you unique."

"I wouldn't mind new ones."

It took some more convincing, but Victoria ended up accepting my offer.

"Tomorrow after school," she said. "I'll bash your face in."

The following morning, I smiled at myself in the mirror, to see my teeth one last time before Victoria broke them, to make sure I wouldn't miss them. We didn't talk to each other the whole day. I didn't fall asleep at all, not even in German class. I was afraid of the pain that she would inflict later on. I kept on wondering how serious it would be.

When we met behind the school at five, like we'd planned, I told Victoria that maybe we ought to keep it that way: the threat of her beating me up had kept me from falling asleep, it seemed, and maybe it had provided her with comfort throughout the day? Maybe this was the solution to both our problems—to make a date every day for her to beat me up without actually having to go through with it? She said no, that she wanted to punch me right now.

It seems to me that I lost consciousness immediately, so I can't say whether Victoria enjoyed hitting me or not. Being knocked out was different from the sleeping fits. The images I saw there were more slideshow than movie, stills superimposed and morphing into one another without apparent logic. Rainbows became dollar bills at the center of which Vanessa Paradis's smiling face suddenly erupted, and then more rainbows turning to dollars. Which was weird, because I'd only ever seen American money in American movies, had never held a dollar bill myself. I half remembered my head hitting the ground only because it broke the cycle of rainbows, dollar bills, and Paradis. When my head hit, the image that appeared and stuck was that of an *Inventaire* obituary page with my name on it. I distinctly saw it. Not a photo of me, not a glimpse of what Francine Eliot would say about my short life, but my name. How did she find her nobodies? Did she just scan obituaries in local newspapers? And pick the dead person whose set of dates told a story? Would she recognize my name from my email to her? Were the names a factor when she decided which nobody to memorialize? Johanna Sahlins. Was it a good name?

I spent four weeks in the hospital, the first one mostly unconscious. While I was under for some other thing, they did a spinal tap and concluded that what I had wasn't narcolepsy. They rebuilt my teeth, gap and all, which I was pretty pissed about, but my mother said I'd specifically asked for them to be reset exactly the way they'd been. I was on a lot of meds, though, and I don't remember it.

When the police asked who'd done it, I pretended not to remember. I saw a new neurologist for the "amnesia" and had to draw another clock in an empty circle. I placed the hands at eleven-ten this time, which I'd read on the internet was what most people did.

For a week or so, in the middle of my hospital stay, I shared a room with an old woman with diverticulitis. She talked about the Holocaust a lot. I don't exactly remember what she said. I must have talked to her about Vanessa Paradis, because what I remember is her saying that Vanessa Paradis wasn't happy all the time, and that I should get over myself. The way she said it made it sound like she knew it for a fact, like maybe she'd been Vanessa Paradis's therapist or something. A friend.

My mother brought me the new issues of *Inventaire* as they came, but I didn't open them. I didn't want to know who'd died that week, where they'd fit in my binder.

Another thing the diverticulitis lady said was that I should stop comparing myself to others. That others should never be the measure by which I determined my own worth, because that pool was shit, other people were shit, and so it was setting a low bar for myself. When I asked her what I should measure myself against, she said fictional characters, that characters in books were less flaky than real people. Then she sort of spaced out and said that she missed her mother, that she couldn't quite remember her face. No one visited her the whole time she was there. At eight-twenty every night, she watched the stupidest show I've ever seen, some cheaply made soap whose scenes we were supposed to believe had taken place that very day, a show where the characters' concerns were supposed to mirror those of regular French people. The show had been airing every weekday for eighteen years, longer than Thomas had lived.

Victoria visited me once, but our mothers stayed in the room the whole time, so I couldn't ask if she thought beating me up had solved her problem. She gave me the latest on school life, like it concerned me, like I'd been part of it before. When she left, my mother said she was happy I'd made a friend.

At night, the old lady with diverticulitis pretended to be fed up with my stories (I regained energy around nine, long after visiting hours, and told her everything that crossed my mind about Thomas, how close we'd been, each other's only friends, really, what with the moving and changing schools all the time), but I think deep down she liked listening to me. I never stopped talking until I was sure she was asleep for the night. She was discharged ten days before me, and I kept watching her stupid show even after she left. I didn't change my mind about it, it was no *Léon* or *My Girl,* but maybe I had to accept that nothing was, really. Even *Léon* wasn't really the *Léon* I'd seen as a child. I didn't like the scenes they'd added in the new cut. And I had to forget they'd made *My Girl 2* if I wanted to enjoy *My Girl* again the way I had the first time I'd seen it. I didn't like it when they added stuff, or made a sequel just because. But I guess they had to.

Understanding the Science

"EVERYONE THINKS THEY'RE ON THIS BIG *JOURNEY* NOW," DEBBIE said, refilling her glass. "I've had it with the journey. I've had it with you people."

"I don't think I'm on a journey," Burt said.

"Self-discovery," Debbie added. "What a joke. Life's too short to find out who we really are."

It was the first time the six of them were getting together for dinner in over a year (since Maria's diagnosis), and after such a long time (and in celebration of Maria's news of remission) they'd expected to have more interesting things to tell one another, deeper things, but they were entering dessert territory now, a cake was on the table, and only superficial topics had been broached: Ervin's promotion, Jane and Burt's move to the suburbs, Katherine's recent purchase of a metabolism-tracking device—a pen-shaped item, the source of Debbie's rant.

"How much can you know about yourself exactly?" she said. "The therapy, the vision quests, the food-sensitivity tests . . . do we really need the data on metabolic flexibility, too?"

Jane, in Katherine's defense, said that the more you knew about yourself, the more useful you could be to society.

"Bullshit," Debbie said. "I call bullshit. Knowing whether Kat is in fat- or carb-burning mode doesn't help anyone. I'm not sure it even helps *Kat*."

As a result of Kat's declining cake five minutes earlier, no one had yet touched it. No one, Debbie included, really wanted to. They'd all overeaten already, drunk too much, made private plans to atone for it the next day. The cake presented a challenge, it stood there taunting them, and Debbie knew this, that you couldn't serve cake to a group of fortysomethings without causing ripples, but what else could she have done? *Not* offered dessert? She got it, no one wanted to put on weight, but this was a gorgeous princess cake, just gorgeous, she'd had to drive all the way to Andersonville to get it from that Swedish bakery everyone talked about. Staring at it now, though, she wondered if the cake didn't look a little bit like a tit, the smooth half sphere, the small pink marzipan flower nippling the top of it, and— Oh god, did *Maria* think it looked like a tit? Did Maria still have nipples? Debbie had been meaning to look it up, what exactly it was they took out in a mastectomy, but she hadn't had the nerve.

"I'm not on a journey," Katherine said. "I just want to lose a few pounds."

Back in the summer, she'd met a pretty famous actor at a friend's gallery in L.A., and they'd been dating long-distance since. The actor was a little younger than her. She didn't want people to think they looked wrong together. He was about to come spend time in Chicago, too, for a six-week shoot. It would be the first time they were in the same city for more than a few days.

Katherine changed the subject to the documentary she'd just seen, about flat-earthers, but this topic, too, made Debbie angry.

Debbie's anger at flat-earthers turned out to run deeper, in fact, than her anger at metabolic-tracking devices. It was one thing to *feel* the earth was flat, Debbie said, but that anyone could believe that a secret of this magnitude could've been kept from the public by scientists and governments for centuries, for *millennia,* even . . . No one could keep a secret for that long. Didn't people understand this?

"Why would Pythagoras have lied about the earth being round?" she said. "And Aristotle? And Eratosthenes? Why go through the trouble of pretending to measure the planet's diameter, going out planting sticks, measuring shadows?"

"Maybe they just wanted to impress their wives," Burt said.

"Were those guys even married?" Katherine said. "Weren't they all gay?"

Debbie rolled her eyes. She happened to know a lot about the Greek wives: Pythias had been a scientist (on her honeymoon with Aristotle, she'd helped him gather materials for an encyclopedia they were working on together); Theano (Pythagoras's wife) had been a mathematician in her own right.

Maria hadn't said anything in a while. She didn't think the cake looked like a tit. She didn't care how accomplished certain wives had been twenty-four centuries ago, either, nor had she seen the flat-earth documentary. She couldn't understand why such a documentary would exist in the first place, why someone would bother filming idiots displaying their idiocy. There was something aesthetically repulsive about it, wasn't there? About ridiculing people, amplifying their dumb beliefs, so that upper-middle-class Chicagoans like herself and her friends could feel alarmed and superior. Most things were aesthetically repulsive to her, though, if Maria was honest. Her aging friends certainly were. Not so much their appearance (they used the retinol creams and popped the antioxidants, they dyed their hair, they exercised), but their thoughts . . . had they always been so small? Maria was getting bored of them. She was getting bored of herself, too, but what could you do about that? You could do one thing, Maria knew, but she didn't have the guts. And for all that she'd thought of suicide as a teen, it had surprised her how determined she'd been to survive cancer when she'd found out it had come for her, to *see the world through* (those were the words that had appeared in her head then), as much of it as she could.

"And Eratosthenes was killed by the man whose wife he was sleeping with," Debbie said. "So, maybe *bisexual,* all these guys, but definitely not straight-up gay."

Who cared who'd been what and slept with whom? Maria wondered, but she knew everyone did—everyone but her cared about these two things. She was the outlier. She was so bored she started wondering what she would take in a fire. She knew what she would take in a fire at *Katherine's* place, but what would she save from Deb and Ervin's apartment if it went up in flames right this moment? There wasn't much to get excited about. Everything matched, nothing begged to be noticed. Katherine's apartment was much nicer, Maria thought. She wished they were having dinner there. Katherine had art on the walls, real art, from real painters. Not painters whose names anyone recognized yet, but soon. Kat was the best of the lot, really. After Maria's diagnosis, Kat had offered her everything she could— a shoulder to cry on, chemo drives, pharmacy runs, ice cream deliveries. Maria said no to all, but still. She appreciated the effort. She appreciated that Kat had kept trying, too, offering stranger and stranger services as the weeks went on—she could do Maria's nails if she wanted, she could read to her, she could teach her piano. The idea of piano lessons offended Maria at first—that she could be expected to learn a new skill while dealing with cancer. Wasn't cancer itself enough to learn from? she wondered after Kat said she could teach her. What else would be asked of her? Was she supposed to master Mandarin as well? Meet new people? Yet later that same day, mere hours after the piano suggestion, Maria had found herself in the shower, once again fighting the urge to feel the lump (had it grown? was it shrinking?), and when she'd extended her arms as far away from her body as possible, pleaded with the fingers at the end of them to stay still and not touch, to refrain from palpating, from inquiring, she'd realized (1) how thin her fingers had become and (2) that giving them something to do might not be such a bad idea. She'd started going to Kat's Mondays and Thursdays for piano lessons, skipping only one week when she went in for her mastectomy. Now that she was in remission, she wondered if Kat would want to keep teaching her. Already she was less available, but that had to do with the new boyfriend, Maria wanted to believe, not her newly recovered health. Kat was spending more and more time in L.A., or weekends on set with Adrian, and she always told Maria that she was free to come practice at her apartment when she was out of town—she'd given her a set of keys. Maria took advantage of Kat's empty apartment any chance she got. Sometimes she even spent the night there. She never told Kat when she did. She didn't necessarily practice much piano when she went, either, but mostly lay on Kat's tufted daybed, read from Kat's library, made tea in Kat's enameled steel kettle. Every little thing Kat owned was beautiful. In a fire, she would've taken the small painting of a woman in her bathtub that hung in the guest room.

Debbie choked on a sip of wine, and in the few seconds it took her to catch her breath, Ervin saw an opportunity to open up the conversation. His wife could be hard to stop when she'd had a few, and she always started early when they hosted (a first glass of wine while she gathered ingredients on the counter, a second while dinner simmered—by the time her guests arrived, she was usually four drinks ahead). Ervin asked everyone what their favorite conspiracy theory was.

Jane said it was global warming. Oceans rising.

"You don't believe in global warming?"

"I thought we were naming things *other* people didn't believe in," Jane said.

"Every time I hear about oceans rising, I think about the Steven Wright joke," Burt said. "*Sponges live in the ocean. I wonder how much deeper it would be if that weren't the case.*"

"Maybe the world would be saved if we grew more sponges."

"Or just one very big sponge," Katherine said.

She said her favorite conspiracy theory was Elvis alive. Ervin said Roswell, and Burt said God, which made Maria uneasy. Not that she believed in God, but her parents had, and she'd tried it herself, a handful of times.

It was going to be her turn to share. She didn't have a favorite conspiracy theory. What did that even mean? She thought her friends might not insist she come up with an answer, though. One good thing about her illness was that people had mostly stopped trying to change her mind once she'd said no. Whenever she said no now, everyone assumed the no came from a deep place of knowledge they couldn't access, that it was the no of someone who'd seen, not exactly the future, but something akin to the future, a shortcut to the end, and who knew what was worth her time and what wasn't.

"What about you, Maria?" Ervin asked. "What's your favorite conspiracy theory?"

She thought of her parents, who hadn't believed in evolution, who'd tried to tell her, when she'd expressed a desire to become a paleontologist after seeing *Jurassic Park,* that fossils had been placed on earth by God as a way to test people's faith.

Would they have called dinosaurs a conspiracy theory? Would saying "dinosaurs" now be an insult to her parents' memory?

The cake was still untouched at the center of the table.

"Why is it called a princess cake?" Maria asked, but Katherine's phone rang before Debbie could look for an answer on the internet, and because it was Adrian calling, everyone went quiet, trying to hear bits of the famous actor's voice emerge from the receiver.

"Adrian's in town!" Katherine said.

"I thought he wasn't coming till Sunday!" Burt said.

Adrian had taken an earlier flight to surprise Kat, but found no one at her place.

"Can he come over?" she asked Debbie. "Maybe he'll eat the whole cake. Adrian can eat anything."

The mood switched in an instant. They were going to meet a movie star! Jane and Debbie both pretended they had to pee, but really, they went to the bathroom to reapply their makeup.

When Adrian arrived, Debbie brought him a small plate and a spoon, even though he could've used any plate or spoon already on the table.

"This looks amazing," Adrian said. "Did you make it yourself?"

Debbie blushed and said, "Don't be silly." She cut him too big a slice, and thought as she did that the cake looked worse than a tit now, looked like a mangled tit. Adrian made appreciative sounds the moment the cake entered his mouth, and Maria assumed he was acting. Not enough time had passed for flavor to reach his taste buds and register in his brain.

Jane brought him into the fold and asked what his favorite conspiracy theory was, and Adrian didn't take a beat to think about it or pretend that the question surprised him: his favorite conspiracy theory was that he had a secret twin. With every new film he made, he explained, speculation erupted online as to which twin had done the work.

"That's creepy," Burt said. "I don't think I've heard that theory."

"The worst part is, I think my therapist believes it," Adrian said. "I feel like she's always trying to trick me, always quizzing to see if I remember this and that from a previous session."

"Why don't you fire her?"

"Because she's really good. She helps me to keep the right boundaries between my characters and my true self."

Maria's and Debbie's eyes met over the cake. Neither of them found the concept of therapy interesting—they knew this about each other. Debbie, on top of despising the idea of self-knowledge, believed that she was too complicated for therapy, and Maria felt the opposite, that one needed an interesting personality to take to a shrink, and that she didn't have one. Her dreams were not sophisticated layers of meaning, for example. Before a trip, she dreamed that she was packing a suitcase. Every time she quit smoking, she had pleasant dreams in which she smoked.

"I think it's more of a rumor than a conspiracy theory," Kat said, about Adrian's secret twin.

"What's the difference?"

"I've always wondered how rumors got started," Jane said.

They thought about it as a group. Did a rumor start the moment someone came up with it? The powerful men in an office, the bored children behind a tree? Or did it only start once a certain number of strangers had heard it? What was that number? It had to be tricky, launching a story into the world that you knew would get warped and amended, something whose nature it was in to be distorted. The main beats had to be foolproof. As the creator of a rumor, you had to pick the first people you told it to with utmost care. Burt wondered how many rumors got nipped in the bud—for each successful rumor, how many failed to take off?

"And why did the rumor that I have a twin make it?" Adrian asked. "What's so interesting about that?"

Maria figured he wasn't comfortable whenever a conversation strayed away from him for too long.

"Are you kidding?" Ervin said. "Two Adrian Kerrys! That's the definition of hope for the ladies."

"And the gentlemen," Kat added. "Adrian is quite popular among the LGBTQ community."

They agreed that rumors, like conspiracy theories, played on hope. Hope that there was always more to uncover, more to life than what one had been told, more meaning to it. More life. Everything had to be more than it was, have a secret layer that only truly enlightened people could see. Even the darkest of conspiracy theories held a promise.

"I guess I can see the hope in the twin theory," Debbie admitted. "Or even in Roswell. But where's the promise in a flat earth?"

"Oh lord. Not this again."

"I'm serious! Who would feel better if we suddenly were to find out that the earth is, indeed, flat?"

"The hope is to discover that everyone has been lying to you," Kat said. "Which then gives you an explanation as to why your life sucks. The hope is to put the blame on someone else."

"It gives you a chance to give up, too," Jane added. "If everything you were told is a lie, then you're free to give up on the sheep life you've been living and start anew. It's the ultimate fantasy."

"I don't have that fantasy," Burt said. "Why does everyone always want to quit what they're doing?"

"I don't know, Einstein, why did you quit med school? Because it's hard!"

"That's not why I quit," Burt said.

"It's fun for a minute, and then it gets hard," Jane insisted.

Maria wanted to ask why it was that Burt had quit med school, but Adrian jumped in before she could.

"I just played a heart surgeon in an indie film," he said. "I observed a couple surgeries back in May, to prepare for the role. That stuff is *wild*."

Maria's mastectomy had been in May, and though she knew it wasn't her surgery Adrian had attended, she became uncomfortable at the thought that it could have been.

"What type of surgery did you observe?" she asked.

Adrian was going for another slice of cake.

"Just a couple valve replacements," he said.

"Did you have to ask for the patients' consent?"

"They were *so* psyched to let me watch."

Maria struggled to find a response to that. She glanced in Kat's direction (was her boyfriend serious? did he really think his presence had made open-heart surgery better for the patients?), but Kat was focused on the new slice of cake on Adrian's plate.

"I'm going out for a cigarette," Maria ended up saying, and her friends looked at one another. Were they supposed to stop her? She'd never been a heavy smoker, but after her diagnosis, they'd all been relieved to hear that she'd quit.

"You sure you want to do that?" Jane asked. "I didn't know you'd taken it up again."

"I'll come out with you for one," Adrian said.

From the balcony, right off the dining room, they could've kept participating in the conversation, but Maria slid the glass door shut behind them, which muted all her friends at once. She'd needed to be away from everyone for a minute. That was in fact the main reason she'd started smoking again—a cigarette was always an excuse to get out: people, even nonsmokers, understood that a smoker needed to take a cigarette break once in a while. What they seldom knew was that the break was one the smoker was also taking from them. She resented Adrian for following her out.

"Can I ask you something?" he said, lighting Maria's cigarette. She didn't like it when people lit her cigarettes for her— lighting your own cigarette was half the fun.

"Ask away," she said, and instead of at him, she looked down at the street three floors below.

"What do you think Kat sees in me?"

What might it feel like, Maria wondered, to be so self-involved? She doubted it would be all that pleasant.

"I don't know," she said. "Kat is pretty private. We don't really talk about these things."

"What do you talk about?"

Maria thought about it for a moment. The past few weeks, they'd mostly talked about her apartment. Maria wanted Kat to help her redesign it, she couldn't stand the way it looked anymore, the sad eggshell walls, the smooth kitchen cabinets.

"Neither of us talks very much," she said to Adrian.

The wind in the trees made a sound that reminded her of the hospital, the pillow they'd given her there. The pillow had made this unnerving sound whenever she shifted her head on it, something between a ruffle and a squeak, like it was filled with Styrofoam bits.

"We did talk about you once," she remembered. "I asked Kat about actors, if she thought the idea of death was easier to accept for actors, because their youth had been recorded on film, the fact of their having been alive and in motion preserved forever."

"*Forever?*" Adrian said. "Who believes in *that?*"

He said he didn't think humans were going to last very much longer. His *youth,* as Maria said, would exist on film for a while, but soon no one would be left to watch it.

"All humans fantasize that their generation will be the last," Maria said.

"Believe me, I'm aware. I work in Hollywood: every other script I get is an end-of-the-world story. I'm shooting one of those right now." Maria showed no curiosity for the plot of the movie he was working on, so Adrian went on: "I didn't say *we* were going to be the last. Maybe humans will stick around for thousands and thousands more years, but it's a known fact that we'll disappear at some point, as a species. We don't know how yet, that's the whole thrill, but we know that we will. And then what difference will it make that I was young and did my own stunts in *Last Pursuit?* Or that I was in the film adaptation of *Cat's Cradle?*"

Maria had never seen any of Adrian's movies. She didn't suspect they were very good.

"I think after someone dies, there's solace to be found in moving images," she said. "For the family at least."

Adrian said she might be right. His mother had died when he was young, and he found it sad sometimes that there was no footage of her, only a few photos, that photos didn't help you to remember someone as well as home videos.

"What did your mother die of?" Maria asked.

"Cancer."

"Which kind?"

He hesitated to say it.

"The kind you had."

So, Kat had told him a bit about her. Maria looked away from the street and at Adrian, but she couldn't make out his expression. There were no outdoor lights on the balcony, and his face was turned left toward the moon now anyway, against which a flock of birds was flying high and toward warmer climates.

"I wonder if birds also have conspiracy theories," Adrian said. He'd read somewhere that people who studied birdsong noticed slight evolutions in a flock's repertoire after certain migrations, as if bird stories and vocabulary were amended according to what they'd learned from different trips. "I wonder if they have gossip."

"Do you like birds?"

"Not really," he said. "They creep me out a bit."

"Me too," Maria said.

Especially since dead birds had started showing up on the sidewalks again, she added, like they always did this time of year. She'd seen her first dead warbler of the season just yesterday, and the first dead warbler of the season always felt like a bad omen. She couldn't understand why migratory birds insisted on flying through Chicago on their way south. Studies had shown that Chicago was the most dangerous place for them. Every fall, they got confused by all the lights and reflections. Every fall, thousands of them hit windows and died. It seemed their birdsong should've included "Avoid Chicago" by now, she told Adrian. "Avoid Chicago at all costs."

"But maybe Chicago is part of their mythology," he objected. "Maybe their vocabulary does include something about the dangers of Chicago, and they know something bad might happen there, but it still has to be part of the journey. Like, they know it's dangerous the way we know that smoking and drinking are dangerous. We still do it."

The wind made that Styrofoam sound in the leaves again. Maria shivered. She'd thrown away all her pillows after coming home from the hospital; she hadn't ended up using the noisy one there, and realized that pillows weren't necessary for sleep, as she'd been led to believe since childhood. That human need for pillows was just another lie.

"The real question, though," Adrian said, "is do birds *know* that they're dinosaurs? That they've been around so much longer than us? Do they have any clue?"

Maria found it odd, this shift to dinosaurs. Adrian's commitment, since he'd stepped out on the balcony, to talk about the nothingness of humanity, the specks of dust they all were, made her wonder if he treated every change of locale as a new scene, an opportunity to inhabit a new type of character. He'd seemed so interested in himself back at the table.

"I used to wonder about that, too," she admitted. "I used to wonder if birds carried some kind of collective memory of the asteroid."

"Right? We always talk about the species that were wiped out, we mourn the T. rex and the brontosaurus, but when I was a kid, I was obsessed with the ones that made it, the birds and the turtles. The fungi. I always wondered what it must've been like for them, to survive all those years, alone in the dark. If they carried any sense of responsibility, or guilt, or regret. I think they did. I think they still might. Maybe that's why I find it hard to look at them for too long. They embody a form of regret: what the world could've been."

Maria thought that was a bit cheesy, but then maybe it was hard not to be cheesy when you talked about birds.

"My parents believed the world was six thousand years old," she said.

They might have also believed that birds merely sang throughout the day, she realized now, were constantly singing cutely, not alerting one another to potential dangers, not retelling old stories and cautionary tales.

"Six thousand years is still a good chunk of time," Adrian said. "It's still a frightening amount to consider."

Maria thought that was a nice thing to say. Or maybe condescending to her parents. She couldn't tell. Her cigarette was almost finished, and she didn't want to go back in thinking of them, or time, how much there had been and still was left. She asked Adrian what it was *he* saw in Kat.

Adrian turned toward the window, as if he'd needed to look at Kat to remember what he liked about her. She and Debbie were animated in conversation, Debbie making hand gestures like *Let me stop you right there,* Kat leaning forward to say what she was going to say.

"Kat . . . she doesn't think about this stuff," Adrian said. "She doesn't think about geological eras, what she's bigger or smaller than. She's content. It's an amazing thing to see."

Maria wondered if he knew about the metabolism-tracking device. It didn't seem to be on the table anymore. Perhaps Kat had hidden it before he'd arrived.

Kat broke up with Adrian before the end of his first week in Chicago. Coming back to her place after filming a stunt in which his character was thrown through a bay window, he'd talked for too long about his nostalgia for sugar glass, a type of prop that had years ago been replaced by something called breakaway glass. He just didn't like resin as much. Kat couldn't find it in her to pretend to care. The split was amicable. Adrian moved into Soho House that very night.

Over the following few days, he was supposed to film action

scenes on Lower Wacker Drive, but heavy rain flooded it, and production adjusted the schedule: a monologue Adrian dreaded was moved up three weeks. He was now expected to give it to the camera in about an hour.

"You're right," he said to the mirror in his dressing room. "I *am* a physicist."

Would the audience believe this? Well, they would've already been asked to buy the movie's plot, Adrian reasoned, that after Russia tested new secret weapons in Siberia, the earth had started spinning faster on its axis.

"I understand the science," he went on, "I know what is happening. What I *don't* know is how to explain it to my kid. I don't know how to tell my kid that if the earth keeps spinning faster and faster, that if the numbers keep rising at the pace we've been seeing, it won't just be satellites going off track, it won't just be shorter days and constant jet lag, tsunamis raging and plants dying and horses going mad. If my projections are correct, we'll reach terminal acceleration in a week. We'll become weightless, which will be fun, sure, but only for a split second, before we start flying around like bloody, literally bloody confetti. We'll hit the walls in our houses and die, we'll collide with buildings if we're outside, or trees, or other bodies, already dead bodies, just floating in the air. Is that what I should tell my kid? How do I get him ready for this? I'm a physicist, yes, but I'm a father first. Now tell me, what equations can I look at and solve to prepare my boy for this kind of death?"

Later in the script, Adrian's character did have a talk with his son, another twenty lines he wasn't looking forward to learning, especially given how much he disliked the child actor they'd cast to play alongside him. The kid had been chosen for his resemblance to Adrian, supposedly, but Adrian couldn't see it, was insulted that production hadn't found a better match.

His assistant knocked on his door. They were waiting for him on set.

Walking to the soundstage, Adrian heard a flapping sound and looked up at the thirty-five-foot ceilings. He spotted two pigeons in the mess of metal beams, looking down at the set. Their puffy chests brought to mind plump ladies at the opera, passing judgment from the comfort of their private box. He wasn't fond of pigeons, but seeing birds where they shouldn't be always cheered him for a moment. There was security to go through to get into Cinespace, but the pigeons hadn't bothered with it. Maybe they'd take the L and go to an indoor mall later, or to the airport, or to the movies. He'd never seen a bird in a movie theater, but it had to have happened.

The makeup artist did some touch-ups to his forehead, and Adrian tried to focus on his lines, to get in the zone. The only thing he'd liked about the script was a scene, much later on, where his character prepared for the erosion of gravitational power by strapping pillows against his and his kid's chests, their arms and legs. He looked forward to shooting that scene, and the ones that would follow, where he'd hang from cables in front of a green screen, padded in pillows. He hadn't known Maria when he'd first read the script (he hadn't even known Kat), and he would only ever think of her once more: when the time came to shoot that pillow scene. When they'd gone back to the table after their cigarette at Debbie's, Maria had told her friends about her newfound discovery that people didn't need pillows to sleep. She'd presented her act of throwing away all her pillows as a grand cathartic gesture, a step toward freedom, but everyone at the table had looked troubled by it. She couldn't go to bed without pillows, they'd said. They'd all seemed to believe it was unthinkable.

Adrian stood on his mark and waited for the director's go.

The pigeons were still up there, but they were restless now; they seemed to have sensed that something was about to start. Perhaps they were debating flying down toward the set for front-row seats.

Set today was a physics lab recreated on a soundstage, with many fine details, but also a gigantic periodic table of elements nailed to the wall. Adrian had expressed doubts about real physicists having a poster of the periodic table hanging in their labs, but his doubts had been brushed away by the director. "It communicates," the director had said.

Graceless

I KNOW SHE'S CATHOLIC BECAUSE THAT'S SOMETHING MY PAR-
ents make fun of, a little—the things she believes in, the things
she tried to have my father believe in when he was a boy. She's
never mentioned it herself, though. Her Catholicism. It feels
like I'm not supposed to know. When my sister and I go stay
with her in the summer, we're there a few weeks, three or four
Sundays. But Sundays come and go, and she doesn't go to Mass.
She could go to Mass—she could leave us with our grandfather—
but it's as if she doesn't want us to know that she is Catholic.

There are no crucifixes in her house, no signs of religious belief.
Only a small decorative plate on the mantel that says "Friendship is a pearl, our heart is its oyster," which I for years assume is
a Christian saying. On Friday nights, she watches *Thalassa,* a
show about the sea.

. . .

I do not understand what religion is, exactly. I am seven, eight years old. As far as I can tell, my grandmother is the only person I know who believes in God. Because of her singular status, I interpret all of her actions as symptoms, signs, or consequences of her faith. She's on her stationary bike every morning for an hour, so I assume pedaling is something that religious people do. No one else I know exercises. She doesn't drink, when every other adult I've met seems to do so proudly. She eats very little and denies herself sweets. My father (her own son) can't resist ice cream. She's the only person in my family who has blue eyes. Maybe having blue eyes helps one believe in a higher power. She is not funny, but she has a sense of humor. She laughs at my grandfather's jokes. Every time she does, though, it's like she thinks she shouldn't, so I tell myself that maybe Catholics are not supposed to laugh. She always tries to stop herself immediately. My grandfather attempts to wring it out of her for as long as possible.

One day, I'm picking tomatoes with him in the garden, and I ask if Grandma ever goes to Mass. "Oh, she goes," my grandfather says. He doesn't seem to think he's betraying her secret. "I take her every Sunday. Just not when you girls are here." My parents never said anything about *him* being Catholic. "You go to Mass, too?" I ask. My grandfather laughs. "No no no no no," he says. "I just drop her off, and pick her up when it's done." My grandma never learned to drive. Another thing Catholics can't do, I assume.

My sister makes fun of her at night, when we're alone in our room. "Who watches *Thalassa*?" she says. She also tells me, "When you die, it's done, it's like before you were born, there is nothing." My sister is only a year older than me.

We barely see our grandmother during the school year. During the school year, we take dance lessons, for no good reason. As far as we can tell, our parents don't care about dance as an art form. We certainly don't. We are not good at dancing. I don't think the idea that we could one day become better ever crosses our minds. Sharing a laugh about how much we suck at dancing doesn't occur to us, either. We are serious children. We suffer in silence. We're never next to each other in class, and I don't remember if this is at the teacher's request (an attempt on her part to spread out the badness evenly) or if my sister and I intuit on our own that we will stand out even more if we stick together, look even less gifted than we are. If our eyes accidentally meet in the mirror during dance class, we break contact immediately, allow each other her dignity. We understand on some level that we deserve better than this, than to be seen doing this. Every year, we start again at Beginner, with a new group of girls.

Sometimes, when we're at Grandma's for the summer, we visit her friend Jeannine. We bring homemade cookies, but Jeannine doesn't serve them back to us with the tea. She brings her own tin to the table instead, stale cookies that crumble in the mouth like teeth in a nightmare. In her living room, Jeannine has a pair of embroidered pillows that say "Grace" and "Mercy," and a portrait of Jesus Christ, but no one ever mentions them. I gather that being Catholic is bringing good cookies to people who only have bad cookies, and offering bad cookies to the people who already have access to good ones.

. . .

Before we go to Jeannine's, I always help make the cookies. I'm good at it. I burn myself once, though, taking the pan out of the oven. I run cold water on my hand for a minute, maybe two, but then my grandmother walks in and turns off the faucet. "I don't know about Paris," she says to me, "but down here, water isn't free."

She visits us once in Paris, but cuts her trip short and leaves two days early. The city's too loud, she can't stand it. She needs peace and quiet. I think what horrifies her the most is not the noise but that our parents let us watch *ER* on Sunday nights. "Are you sure this is allowed?" she asks us, but she still doesn't believe us when we say it is. She goes to our father for confirmation. "How can you let them watch this?" I hear her say through the wall. I don't hear my father's response, but when our grandmother crosses the living room again, she looks angry and hurt. I pretend not to notice and keep watching. I try to understand what upsets her so much about *ER*. It's full of death and helplessness, yes, but there's a beauty to it, too, it's like ballet, everyone in position, everyone moving to where they should be. Except with actual stakes. Sometimes, though, the doctors do everything right and the person still dies.

I don't get better at dancing with time, but I learn that grace is not a fictional quality, reserved for princesses in fairy tales. It's all around me in the changing room, emanating from girls who live a few blocks away, go to schools I've heard of. The graceful girls seem comfortable in their own skin, happy to

have a body. They seem to know what to do with it. My sister
and I have grown up under the impression that the body is just
a thing to feed and wash and drag to class. A thing to ignore
except for when it gets sick. We never sit up straight. We splash
on couches, we sneeze loudly. When we clean up after dinner,
there are crumbs all over the tablecloth, purple wine rings by
our parents' plates. I imagine the graceful girls from dance class
don't even produce crumbs eating a croissant. If a croissant
crumb falls as they eat it, they surely pluck it out of the air,
incorporate it seamlessly into the long choreography of their
lives.

My grandmother boasts to Jeannine that we are doing splendidly
in school. Perfect report cards. I am ten, maybe eleven. I want
to tell Jeannine that her cookies are gross. I look at the portrait
of Christ instead, try to feel something about it. I look at my
grandmother after that, and it strikes me how beautiful she
must've been. She is still beautiful. The blue of her irises is soft
at the edges; it seems to lightly spill over the white of the sclera,
like a halo, like cooked blueberries in a cobbler. I wonder if she
thinks I'm ugly, with my brown eyes, my enormous teeth. I tell
her she has beautiful eyes, and ask whom she got them from.
She says she doesn't know, that she never knew her parents. This
is news to me, but I don't think she understands that. She seems
to think I'm taunting her. Jeannine starts crying. Between sobs,
she tells us that she knows her parents are in a better place, but
she still misses them every day. My grandmother is embarrassed
for her, or perhaps just annoyed. "Come on, Jeannine," she says.
"Not in front of the girls."

. . .

In the changing room, so close to the graceful girls, I feel double ugly. I try not to stare, but I study them, the way they move. I don't realize yet that a person can't fake grace. I still think I can learn it. Hands seem like a good gateway to grace, so I start there. I focus on my hands while I change from street clothes to dance clothes. One thing I've noticed is that grace looks effortless, and my first challenge is to relax my hands, to think of them as lighter than air, dandelion tufts in the wind, but it's hard to put on a leotard without tensing the fingers. At home, I try to stand straighter, to walk light as a cat. "You look constipated," my sister says. She understands what I'm trying to do. "You'll never be like them, you know?" She doesn't mean to be cruel. She just wants to save me some time.

A graceful girl talks to us in the changing room, and it feels like being at once blessed and condescended to.

"So, you guys are *sisters*?"

"We are," I say.

I'm always the one talking. My sister, for all the opinions she holds, is even shier than me.

"Do you do everything together?"

"Just this," I say.

I am ashamed that anyone might think we're taking dance seriously, so I add: "We're better at other things. Like, she's really good at foreign languages."

"That's cool. What about you?"

"I'm good at history," I say. "And math. Things like that."

"Oh, so, you guys are more the intellectual type."

I don't like the word "intellectual," but I take comfort in hearing it from the graceful girl. She can tell we don't fit in, but she's created a space for us to make sense in, an explanation for our difference.

When my father gets sick, he doesn't tell my grandmother how serious it is. When he dies a few months later in the loud city she swore never to visit again, I wonder who will deliver her the news. My mother says my aunt will. My aunt only lives an hour away from my grandparents, and is already on her way. I try to imagine her driving through the quiet landscape, crossing the river, parking in the gravel driveway, my grandmother already on the threshold, having heard the car from a distance. I can't imagine it.

At my father's funeral, there's nothing religious. My grandmother must have thoughts about this—her own son, no prayer. But maybe she doesn't. Maybe she's not thinking at all. Yet I worry that we're doing it wrong. What if we're doing it wrong? I expect her to say something afterward, but she maintains her cover. She will never speak of heaven and angels. I figure that part of having faith is keeping it to yourself. Maybe she prayed alone, and that is enough.

The following year, at my grandfather's funeral, there is a priest, there are prayers. I wonder if he started believing at the end of his life, or if this is all for her benefit. I don't pay attention to the priest. I think about my grandfather's garden the whole time. Parsnips, cardoons, nashis, all those fruits and vegetables I would've never known about if he hadn't shown me how to grow them.

. . .

Years pass, and there is no time left on the schedule for dance lessons. We quit. For school, I move to a city I only know from watching *ER,* on the other side of the Atlantic. On the plane, looking down at the water, I think about how much more than me my grandmother knows about this particular ocean and every other, from watching all those episodes of *Thalassa.* Yet I'm the one crossing it.

In the new city, in the new country, people on the street offer to pray for me. I say I'm good, I'm all set, and I wonder if she's ever done it, my grandmother, prayed for me, and if so, on what occasion.

I meet a man who asks am I not curious? Have I really never read the Bible or gone to Mass, just to see what it was like? Even *he* has gone to Mass, he says, and he is Jewish. I am ashamed to be called uncurious (to me, a capital sin), but I tell him he doesn't understand. Her Catholicism is something my grandmother has always kept to herself. If she chose not to take us to Mass with her, it's that she thought we didn't belong there. It is out of respect for her that I don't try to uncover what she wants to keep hidden. "But what if it speaks to you?" the man asks. "What if you start believing?" I say I won't. "How can you be so sure?" I tell him faith is like grace, you either have it or you don't. I could go to church and ape the others, I could sing along with them, if there are songs, but I will forever be the one doing clumsy pas de bourrée in the background while the graceful kids do something pretty front and center. I understand I believe this as I say it.

The documentary series *Thalassa* goes on, but it only airs once a month now. I don't know whether that means TV is entering a new era, or if the mysteries of the ocean are running scarce. I wonder what my grandmother does on those Fridays *Thalassa* isn't on.

I write letters and talk to her once a month. She is lonely. I want to ask if her faith is helping, if it ever has, but it sounds like too dumb a question. I'm afraid she'll think I'm making fun of her.

I don't go to her funeral. I am stuck abroad—visa issues. I don't ask my sister about the ceremony. We just talk about our grandmother on the phone, how hard her life had been, no parents, a dead son, a dead husband. I think we both hope it wasn't as hard as we imagine. I think even though it sounds simplistic, we both want to believe that her faith made it bearable. My sister asks about life in America, if I really plan on staying there forever, with all the guns and the Jesus freaks. I tell her I have heard shots a few times but not seen a gun yet. She laughs and says, "So what? You won't believe it till you see it?" I have to laugh at that, too. She is pregnant, but hasn't told anyone but me and her boyfriend yet. We make plans for the baby, who we assume will be a girl. My sister expects her to be a prodigy. Piano and music-theory lessons the minute she turns three.

"What if she hates it, though?" I say. "What if she hates it like we hated dancing?"

To my surprise, my sister tells me she didn't hate dancing. She just hated being so bad at it.

"Even still," she says, "I think it's important to suck at something early on. Forges character. Helps you recognize what you're actually good at, later, if such a thing presents itself. You still learn a lot by sucking at something."

"Yeah? And what exactly did we learn from being so bad at dancing?"

"A sense of space," my sister says. "That perseverance doesn't always pay off. That we were utterly graceless."

"What a useless quality," I say, trying to convince myself of it. "When has grace ever helped anyone? Who's ever had to dance anyway?"

I don't expect her to give an answer to this, but she considers the question seriously.

"Everyone in *They Shoot Horses* has to dance," she says. "As long as they keep dancing, they'll be warm and fed."

"Right," I say. I try to summon images from the movie, but instead of Jane Fonda's face, it is my grandmother's I see.

I ask my sister if she thinks any of the graceful girls from dance class ever became professional dancers.

"Bless their souls, poor little dimwits," she says, though I remember her being pretty deferential to them at the time. "I hope they all did."

Colorín Colorado

Should They Hear This?

THE DAY THEY CAME FOR THE INTERVIEW, I WOKE UP TOO EARLY, thinking about Bernard Loiseau. This happens when I'm nervous—not thinking about Loiseau, specifically, but thinking in my sleep, waking up mid-thought.

The thought was in fact a memory. I write fiction now, mostly, but back in the nineties I worked for a magazine in New York, one that sent me to France to profile Bernard Loiseau, after he earned his third Michelin star. I was picked because I was half French and spoke the language, not because I was good. But I wanted to be good, and writing a profile was a major step for me, so I did a lot of research on Loiseau. I concluded that interviewing him would be easy: the guy was funny, passionate, generous in his answers. The piece would write itself. A piece that wrote itself was dubious to me, though, even as a mostly inexperienced young writer. I needed to introduce conflict, I thought, something abrasive, get Chef Loiseau off balance. I asked him about food, of course, but then I quickly jumped to questions of ambition, of jealousy and envy. Those were the kinds of things that were on my mind at the time. I was seeing too many people around me sign book deals and make connections while I was stuck cataloging everyone else's successes in hundred-words-or-less reviews for our culture pages. That was my story back then: twenty-four years old and already bitter. I don't remember exactly how I phrased it to Bernard (he'd asked me to call him that), but I remember the sentiment, I remember wanting to get this honest man, this man who'd done nothing but work hard and make it to the top, to talk shit. I wanted to know if he was angry at another chef's success, if there were dishes that others got famous for which he thought were crap.

"Do your readers need to know this?" Loiseau had answered, the way he'd answered all my questions—not taking a split second to think about them.

"Pardon me?"

"Your readers—should they hear this? Do they *want* to know this?"

He didn't mean to shame me, I don't think. His dimples were still showing. I changed the subject. We talked for another hour. I observed dinner service. I watched Loiseau shake hands with every single one of his employees after it ended. I felt inadequate the whole time. Not because I was a journalist in a three-star kitchen but because I was a journalist who hadn't once asked herself what her readers wanted to know. I'd operated under the assumption that my readers would want to know what *I* wanted to know. In Loiseau's case, I was probably right—probably my readers would want to know which chefs he hated, who he thought was a hack. But did I want to write for people who wanted to know this? For people like me? I quit and moved back in with my father, back to Chicago. I never wrote the profile. In my father's guest room I wrote a novel about bitter journalists in Manhattan. It was surprisingly well received.

Now, thirty-some years later, woken up by a memory of Loiseau asking again, "Should they hear this?," I was at my kitchen table, watching videos of him on YouTube. I kept the volume low so as not to wake my husband. It was still pitch black out, the birds weren't even up yet. I watched Loiseau talk about success ("I'm on top because being on top is the only thing on my mind"), I watched Loiseau peel carrots, cook sole and mashed potatoes. I watched him being asked what came first, the chicken or the egg, and heard his confident answer: the chicken, of course. *La poule, bien sûr.*

At some point, the trash collectors came. I heard my husband get up, our bedroom door creak, the sounds he made in the morning. No one brushes his teeth for longer than my husband. You think it's over, but then it starts again, more vigorous than before. There's some spitting and heavy throat clearing, too, which I try not to think about. He smokes a lot. I launched another Loiseau video.

"What's that guy so happy about?" my husband asked, when he joined me in the kitchen.

"He's poaching eggs," I said.

This got him interested. Eggs interest him. We watched in silence as Loiseau spoke of egg curvature. When it ended, my husband saw as well as I did which videos YouTube suggested I watch next. They were all talk-show clips of my former student Addie. Addie interviewed about her films, Addie interviewed about success. I'd been watching cooking videos for an hour. YouTube should've suggested Paul Bocuse, Alain Ducasse—there was no reason for it to come up with Addie. I felt betrayed by my computer, that it would so casually let my husband know how much research I'd been doing on her the past few days. Computers know too much about us, of course. I understand that certain people find comfort in that, but it's hard for me not to think of the machines as intently trying to shame us, the way they give other people glimpses of our search histories, or allow that family-vacation photo to slip into our PowerPoint presentations.

"He looks like Gandolfini a little," my husband said, of Loiseau. He was letting me save face, walking away from my screen to make us coffee. "Who is it?"

"It's that chef I interviewed a hundred years ago. Bernard Loiseau."

"Oh yeah," he said. "Bernie the Bird."

My husband and I met not long after my journalist years, but I almost never spoke of them. I'd mentioned Loiseau only once, in 2003, when I heard of his suicide. My husband had instantly translated his name back then, too. "Bernie the Bird." *Oiseau* being one of perhaps a hundred French words he could recognize.

"He killed himself, right?" he asked now.

I confirmed and closed the YouTube tab. I understood as I did so that in a few months, when the documentary about Addie came out, the documentary for which I was about to be interviewed, I would be offered recommendations to watch it, or clips from it, perhaps the very clips in which I would be talking about her.

"He looked like a nice guy," my husband added. "Bernie the Bird."

"He must not have thought so," I said.

Colorín Colorado

I met Addie the year my fourth book came out, a collection of stories. I was teaching by then (I still am), and she was an undergraduate student, taking Fiction Writing for the first time. The roster said Adriana, but she insisted we all call her Addie. It had long stopped surprising me how intent Americans were on having everyone they met use their diminutives, how intent on projecting friendliness right away. *Scratch that,* they seemed to say if you used their whole name. *It's just my name, it's just something my parents gave me.* I'd come around to the Sams, the Dans, and the Steves, but it felt a shame to shorten Adriana, and so for a while I didn't. Addie corrected me every time.

After the first day of class, she stuck around to make sure she'd understood how little would be expected of her. Really? she asked. All she had to do was write two short stories? For the whole semester? I told her that two stories were a lot, that some stories had taken me years to write, and, for a second, Addie made a face like something smelled bad, like I'd opened a Pyrex of egg salad.

"I don't mean I spent years working nonstop on one story," I explained, already defending myself, already modifying the wisdom I'd just tried to impart (writing took time, writing was serious). "I'm always working on several things at once."

"What about novels?" Addie asked. "How long does it take you to write a novel, on average?"

I said there was no average. I'd written my first novel in eight months, my second in six years, my third in three.

"There's always an average," Addie said. "The average of the numbers you just gave me is about thirty-eight and a half months. That's the average time it takes you to write a novel."

I was silent for a moment. I guess I was trying to do the math she'd just done, adding all the months I'd suffered through, then dividing them neatly.

"It's a long time," she noted.

She herself had written nine novels in high school.

By the following week, Addie had read everything I'd ever published. She stayed to talk to me about it after class. She tried not to be insulting, but she was twenty years old. She was still looking for meaning everywhere and hadn't found any in my writing. It was all about normal people to whom life happened, she said. I said I was sorry my books hadn't touched her, and I meant it. I was always sorry when people felt they'd wasted time reading me.

"You said in class that fiction was a stream of causes and consequences," Addie said, "but your stories, they're always just about people talking and thinking."

I had indeed just told my class about causes and consequences—repeated the dyad cause/consequence, cause/consequence too many times, clapping my hands every time I said "cause" and every time I said "consequence," while one student took furious notes, worried he might let one slip, as if he thought I'd been listing the exact number of causes and consequences a good piece of fiction should contain.

"Thoughts and language have consequences, too," I told Addie.

"Maybe," she conceded. "But in your stories the consequences of language and thoughts are always just more language and more thoughts."

Addie, I would later learn, wrote crime novels. She wrote about rape, dismembered women, violence leading to revenge leading to epiphany leading to closure.

"I guess I didn't understand why they were *stories,*" she added, about mine.

What she was saying, albeit politely, was: Why did you bother?

Should they hear this?

"They're well written," she went on. "But it's like there's no beginning or end, really, only middle. At some point, it just ends, like . . . colorín colorado."

"Like what?"

"Colorín colorado. It's something we say in Mexico at the end of children's stories. *Colorín colorado, este cuento se ha acabado.* It's kind of our version of *And they lived happily ever after.* Except it doesn't mean anything at all, so it's confusing."

Because the word combination "colorín colorado" carried no meaning and had been chosen only because it rhymed with "acabado," Addie had grown up thinking that she was missing the point of every story.

"I'm sure you understood the stories fine," I said.

I didn't know if I was talking about my stories or those from her childhood. I was always dumb and exhausted after teaching. I wanted to go home. Watch a movie with my husband.

"What makes you decide when a story is done?" Addie asked. She wasn't tired. "When do you decide the message has been conveyed?"

"I object to the word 'message,'" I said. Messages were for ads and propaganda, I didn't say. Messages were for politicians. For Hollywood. For babies. For selling something to someone you considered a little or a lot less intelligent than you. "Art is not here to give lessons."

"What is it here for?" Addie asked.

I remember avoiding eye contact. Looking down at my satchel, wishing I had more things to pack back into it. That peculiar mix of feelings—shame and superiority in equal measure.

I knew what art was for. I just didn't think it was the kind of thing you said out loud.

"Art is—" I stopped right away. I could feel my face redden, the shame overcoming the superiority. I was fine with people not understanding art or what it was for. I had friends like that. It was the people who didn't and wanted to that worried me. I felt they were trying to trick me, to expose the charade of my life. Because maybe I *didn't* know what art was for, after all. Maybe *Addie* knew, and she was about to humiliate me with the answer. Maybe my conviction existed only when left alone in the dark and disappeared the second someone asked for it to come out.

"It's okay to write plot," I ended up saying. "This class is about asserting your own taste. Recognizing what you like and why you like it."

"But what about *your* taste?" Addie said. "Is that what happened to you? You didn't like plot, and so you just decided to do without it?"

"I love plot," I said. "I'm just incapable of conceiving of one."

"When's the last time you tried?" Addie asked, but she didn't wait for my answer. "You should try again."

She wanted to make a deal: she would write a story in which people just talked if I wrote one in which something happened.

"That's not how this class works," I said.

"I know. This would be between us."

She thought it was too sad that I had given up on plot. She thought that there was a chance I'd be good at it now, for some reason.

"We change all the time," she said.

She needed to believe this a little longer.

I surprised us both, I think, when I said I'd give it a shot. I would write a plot-heavy story and share it with her. I heard myself thank her, too, the way I sometimes thanked people who bumped into me on the train.

"Thank you, Adriana," I said.

She said it was Addie.

The Aliens in Skokie

The camera crew arrived at ten A.M. sharp. The men were immediately at ease in my apartment, took control of the living room with the confidence of movers on moving day. They had a job to do. A frame to set up. I was the one with no business here. I made coffee, I made tea, but no one went near either.

Around ten-thirty, the director sat me on the couch and asked for my story.

"My story with Addie?" I said.

"No, just your story for now. Just a warm-up."

Two cameras were pointed at me, but I don't think they were rolling yet.

"I don't know where to start," I said. "My father was from here, from Chicago. My mother was French."

"That's amazing," the director said.

It was a stretch, but I told him I actually used to do what he did. Interview people. I said, "I used to write profiles for a magazine."

"Who's the most famous person you ever interviewed?" he asked. "We just did Jennifer Lopez last week. Very nice woman, very down to earth."

"Well, no one near that," I said. I couldn't say Bernard Loiseau, now that the name Jennifer Lopez had been produced.

"You could tell she was genuinely sad about Addie," the director went on. "Even off camera."

I should have said earlier that Addie died last summer. I'm bad at this. I should have led with that. Addie died on set while filming the last part of the trilogy that had made her famous. Although that's not correct: it wasn't the movies that made her famous but the videos she'd posted in the years before—short, extremely low-budget adaptations of the crime stories she wrote, in which she played all the roles (victims, witnesses, cops, lawyers, and perpetrators). Addie had gained a cult following while still in college, and worldwide attention not long after she graduated, when one of her "films" was shared by a then influential (now disgraced) comedian. He'd meant to make fun of Addie (for the bad lighting, the terrible sound effects), but the internet had shamed him for shaming a young woman, an unknown artist, and declared Addie's work fearless and radical. Studio interest had followed naturally after the buzz, a streaming-platform contract after that. Cinephiles and critics, unsure what to do with Addie's work, had deemed the person herself a fad, but now her premature death at the age of thirty-four was turning her into an icon of sorts, her art (it was now art) into something that would last and define our time, in retrospect. I suspected Addie would get a reel, not a still, in the Oscars' "In Memoriam" segment next month.

"Let's put you in the armchair, actually," the director said to me. "I love the almond green. It will be nice with your gray hair."

He made a phone call while the crew rearranged the shot. They were done before him, and one of the cameramen said he was going downstairs for a cigarette. I told him it was cold out, and he could just go into my husband's office. I regretted it immediately. My husband wouldn't want anyone left alone in his office. I would have to keep the cameraman company while he smoked, which he would take for what it was: a sign that I didn't trust him. Unless I smoked with him, I thought, as we walked together to my husband's office. Then he would think we were bonding. I hadn't smoked in years.

"This is nice," he said, lighting his cigarette by the window. "I haven't smoked indoors since college."

I took a cigarette from an open pack on my husband's desk. Perhaps I could just hold it for a minute, I thought, pretend that I wanted to smoke and then pretend to change my mind, keep the charade up long enough that Jay (his name was Jay, or maybe J., come to think of it) wouldn't question my motives for keeping him company.

"It must be pretty depressing to come film me after Jennifer Lopez," I said.

I'm not sure J. heard me. He was staring at my husband's shelves, at all the books. He asked if I was a teacher.

"I'm mostly a writer," I said, though I'm not sure what I meant by "mostly." I spent more time teaching than writing. I made more money teaching than writing.

"What kinds of books do you write?"

"Just old-school novels," I said. "About made-up, normal people."

"I love it," J. said. "Nobodies are the best kind of people."

He pulled a book from my husband's shelves but put it back immediately, as if he'd mistaken it for another. His affect was exactly that: you start waving at someone you think you recognize on the street, but it's not him at all. He asked me how novelists went about making up people. "Do you take a lot of meetings with nobodies, to soak in their randomness?"

I don't know why he insisted on saying "nobodies." I'd said "normal people."

He told me he'd met an interesting nobody the night before.

"Older lady at the bar," he said. "I wasn't flirting."

The older lady had played a song J. liked on the jukebox, and they'd started talking, finding that they had a lot in common. They'd both just been to Mexico, they both loved musicals.

"Then, out of nowhere," J. said, "she tells me she was abducted by aliens a few years back."

It was the first time he had really talked to someone like this, J. said, someone whom most other people would have deemed insane, but because they'd just been bonding over normal things, he'd engaged with the alien-abduction story, and surprised himself, not *believing* it, exactly, but being interested in meeting the woman within the memory she was sharing. He didn't want to make fun of her, even in his head—he truly wanted to know where the abduction had happened (Skokie), what the woman had seen (shadows, five-knuckled alien fingers), how long it had lasted (only a minute or two before the aliens had thrown her off the ship—she'd broken a hand in the fall). The abduction had happened shortly after Michael Jackson's funeral, in Los Angeles, the woman had explained, an event she'd considered attending but had ultimately decided would be too much for her, emotionally. She'd watched the service at home on TV, alone. She'd cried all day.

"And then the aliens came for her," J. said. "You can't make that shit up."

"Obviously someone can," I said.

"I mean, yes, someone can, but you can't make *her* up, is what I'm saying. The emotional older lady who cries for Michael Jackson and gets abducted by aliens. There's no connection there. It would be too much in a book, no one would believe it was the same person."

He ashed in the metal ashtray my husband and I had brought back from France the last time we went. I'd just quit smoking back then; the smell had started bothering me. We'd thought that the hinged cover on the ashtray would keep the problem contained.

"Novels always want to simplify," J. went on. "Here's another example: because of novels, we pretend to agree people think in whole sentences. *She thought, I thought* . . . and then a perfectly shaped observation. But, like, if I'm on a date and I say something stupid, I just want to disappear, right? I don't actually think the words *I want to disappear.*"

"You remind me of Addie," I said.

"How so?"

"It's something she could've said."

"Everything is something anyone could've said," J. said. "That's my point."

I missed my husband in that moment. And J. was right, I didn't think the words *I miss my husband,* but a series of external stimuli (what J. was saying, the flat winter light turning the white bookshelves gray, the hum of the fan that expelled the cigarette smoke out onto the street) transited through my brain and bounced around in my body as emotions, shortcuts to old memories. Landing back on earth, J. had said, the lady had broken her hand. The only bone I'd ever broken was in my left hand, years ago, in arguably opposite circumstances. My husband and I had gone to bed holding hands (we were still a young couple), and he'd squeezed mine too hard in his sleep. Even through the pain, I'd thought it was a great story—*He held my hand so hard it broke*—but my husband had made me promise never to tell anyone. People would think he was secretly violent, he'd said, and I a brainwashed wife making excuses for him. Recently, though, over dinner, he'd told the story to an old friend of ours, and I'd realized it had been more than twenty years. Bernard Loiseau was still poaching eggs then, and I hadn't yet met Addie. Now they were both dead, and I couldn't remember the last time I'd gone to sleep holding my husband's hand. He was likely taking his break now, smoking outside with his grad students. Picturing him made me want the cigarette I was holding. I hadn't truly considered lighting it before. Could lighting it turn me back into the heavy smoker I'd once been? Did it really have to be all or nothing?

"You know," J. said, "I'm a teacher, too."

I assumed he gave classes on technical film stuff—lenses,

focal lengths—but, when I asked where he taught, he looked far into the distance and said, "Everywhere," and I understood he was high as a kite.

Touching the Ceiling

The week after we made our pact, Addie came to me after class having written not one but three stories in which nothing happened. She asked for my action-packed one.

"I thought I had the whole semester," I said.

She gave me a two-week extension.

Her stories were all about her grandmother. In one, her grandmother showed Addie how to make flan. In another, they went to McDonald's after a doctor's appointment. In the third, they made twenty piñatas in their garage, fulfilling a last-minute order from richer neighbors. The stories weren't great, but I thought that, if Addie got rid of 90 percent of the metaphors— the grandmother's "papery skin," the "bleeding sunset," if she took a hard look at "the flan was shivering on the plate"—and cut the dialogue in half, she could be left with something worth starting from. The piñata story was the most promising. It was actually so focused on one thing (the making of the piñatas) that I became jealous. For all that I praised concision, I sometimes had trouble keeping my stories contained. There were no metaphors or useless descriptions in the piñata story. The balloons Addie and her grandmother inflated to form piñata base shapes were just that: balloons. Once full of helium, they rose up to touch the ceiling—not to brush it, not to kiss it—and, when time came to work on a new piñata, Addie and her grandmother simply pulled on a string to bring a balloon to their level and pasted layers of newspaper on its surface with a mixture of flour and water, repeating the process balloon after balloon while the previously lathered ones dried. The story went nowhere, but it did so at a fascinating pace. When the shells had hardened and holes for pouring candy were cut out, the balloons inside the piñatas popped with the intensity of gunshots (an image that jumped to the reader's mind, not one that Addie used). The story also gave you instructions on how to make something, and so, no matter what you thought of it, you hadn't wasted your time reading it. You'd learned the steps to making a piñata, and that was more than what most writing gave you.

When I next saw Addie, I told her to keep doing that, to see where it led, to perhaps apply the same focus to the flan story, if she wanted to make this a larger project, a series of shorts in which she made different things with her grandmother, but she stopped me.

"I'll never write about myself again," she said. "It's too hard to hear what people think of your life. I don't know how you do it."

I told her I didn't. My stories weren't autobiographical.

"You know what I mean," she said. "People *think* they are. Because they could be."

I said that writing was supposed to be hard, and that she should keep digging at the piñata story—there was something there. She could add fictional elements if she wanted, murders, even, if it felt comfortable.

"You keep them," she said, when I handed her back her pages with my notes. "I never want to think about these stories again."

She might have said, "Do whatever you want with them," I'm not sure. Not that it would change much. Not that I'm looking for excuses. A year or so later (Addie had graduated by then), I used about seven hundred words of the piñata story in my novel *Six Corners*. I put them, pretty much verbatim, in the mouth of one of my characters, as a childhood memory. It was supposed to be a placeholder, something to help me move forward before going back to tweak later—you know the plagiarist story. I was convinced that the stolen part would jump out at me when time came to revise, but it flowed, it fit with the rest of the novel, and it stayed. I almost cut it at the last minute, not because I had stolen it but because I worried I'd get in trouble for using a cliché of Mexican life for a Mexican character. I told myself that was my crime—not the plagiarism but bringing piñatas into it. Why not have the character wear a sombrero while I was at it? Sing "*Ay, ay, ay, ay, canta y no llores*"? I asked my husband if he thought it was a problem, to have a Mexican American character making piñatas in Pilsen with his grandmother as a child, and he said it depended on the writing. He didn't see anything in the writing that was wrong, he said, or condescending, or essentializing, or exoticizing. It was just a strong scene. Simple and moving. I didn't mention that I hadn't written it.

I didn't get in trouble. The novel sold well, but not well enough for any kind of controversy to arise. As for the plagiarism, no one but Addie could have noticed, and I doubt she had time for contemporary fiction. She did send a message of congratulations when the book came out, though, teasing that in the time it had taken me to produce 250 pages, she'd made and posted thirteen short films on YouTube, become an internet celebrity, and signed a Hollywood deal. She concluded her email the way she'd concluded all emails since graduation: "You still owe me a story!"

The Real World

I tried to hold up my end of the bargain back then, to give Addie a story in which things happened. I tried writing about a missing child, about blackmail . . . I even tried a World War II story. Every week after class she asked me what I had, and every week I gave her a list of aborted ideas. When the semester ended, I said, "You win," but Addie said it hadn't been a contest. She made me promise that I would keep trying for plot. She gave me her personal email address. I don't think I meant to use it, or to send her a story, but maybe I did. In any case, I didn't try again until *Six Corners* came out. I must have thought at that point that finally sending Addie a story would absolve me, or at the very least (if Addie ended up suing me for the words I'd stolen) offer plausible deniability. If she accused me of anything, I could pretend that I thought we had an understanding, that the stories she'd given me in class were mine to use, and the one I'd sent her, hers. In order for this line of defense to work, however, there needed to be a story by me in Addie's inbox. I got to work.

A week or so later, I received a call from another former student, John. He wanted to apologize for the way he'd behaved in class years earlier.

"Are you doing the twelve-step thing?" I said.

I was joking, but John confirmed.

"I was an idiot in college," he said. "I wasn't living in the real world."

The way I remembered it, John had once said in class that I shouldn't be teaching writing, because I'd never had a bestselling book.

"I humiliated you," he was now saying to me on the phone.

He hadn't.

"You have nothing to apologize for," I said, but John had a script to go through.

He explained that he'd been sober for a year. He went through the list of all the substances he'd ingested since high school, matching different drugs to different behaviors. Alcohol had made him mean to women, cocaine violent toward friends.

"I don't want to sugarcoat how much of a dick I was," he

said. "I never hit a woman, but I punched through walls next to them. I enjoyed scaring them."

In an attempt to care about what he was saying, I tried to remember what John looked like. He had sharp incisors, I believed. A weird bump on his neck, big as a quail egg. Tattoos spilling out from his T-shirt—a howling wolf, a bird.

"I found God," he went on, and I heard him unzip something, his hoodie, perhaps, as if God had been under there all along. "I tried to kill myself, and He saved me."

Instead of reaching out to make amends to those he'd hurt, John could simply have appreciated his luck at that point, but the option didn't sit well with him. "That's not how the real world works," he said.

It was the second time he'd used that phrase, "the real world." He meant "the movies," of course. That's not how it worked *in the movies.* But the real world? As far as I could tell, John had experienced a pretty basic version of it. He'd expected consequences for his actions, like in books, like in movies, and nothing had happened. People had gotten over what he'd done, or plain forgotten about it. That was how the real world worked. Not everything you did mattered, not every conversation was remembered by the rest of the cast. Most bad deeds went unpunished. You got away with a lot. But John had wanted to be wronged back, to be asked to explain himself in a long monologue. Hunting down those he'd wronged (or those he thought he'd wronged) was his last-ditch attempt to not be alone with his shame and regrets, to make it all mean something. No one was asking him for an apology? The steps now gave him an excuse to force one on us, to force us to listen to him again. He was still a bully.

I forgave him for his in-class comment, and he asked if I had

Addie's number. He wanted to apologize to her for something, too. I told him I didn't have it and hung up.

It was one thing to feel used in someone else's redemption montage, but had John called me only to get Addie's contact information?

A conversation like this would usually have ruined my focus for the day, but I was too angry not to try to use the anger. I went back to work on the story I planned to send Addie as retroactive payment.

The story was an exaggeration of the reasons I'd left France at age twelve: my mother's death (she'd been in a car crash with a man she shouldn't have been in a car with), the shame it brought to her parents, the family feud over who got what. In the story, I made my mother's family even richer than it had been—and my and my father's banishment a steeper demotion. Not that it hadn't been steep.

I planned to end the story right there (my exile to America with poor Dad), but I wanted to see what happened if I deviated from real events, if I wrote a version of me who took action, who sought revenge against her mother's family. I had my protagonist grow up to be tough, excel at boxing, study law at Harvard, defend high-profile criminals. After many years, instead of going back to France to interview Bernard Loiseau, she went at a wealthy client's request, to help him mount his defense in a murder case. I had my character hesitate at first (she'd decided long ago to never set foot in France again!), then do the professional thing ("I have a job to do"). I had her thinking she'd be in and out, but got the plot to catch up to her, her family's past emerging in the client's files, her mother perhaps still alive, having been forced to fake her own death after getting in with the wrong crowd . . . I didn't shy away from cliché. The story became a novel—to this day, my bestselling work. I never sent it to Addie.

Rock Bottom

Last time I saw her (the last time I would see her) was when I attended a literary festival in New York. Addie lived there, and showed up for my talk on Stanley Elkin. The organizers had given me carte blanche—an hour on the author of my choice—but I could tell that Elkin had disappointed them. It wasn't a name that would draw crowds. On the same stage, panelists before me had talked about motherhood, about "writing from the body," about identity. It had gone well. When I talked to the same audience about the supreme quality of Elkin's verb choices and sentence-shape variations, the emotion that arose from his ac- and decelerations . . . many people left the room.

Afterward, Addie came up to tell me how much she'd liked my talk. She'd always enjoyed hearing me break apart paragraphs, she said, to see how much I cared about words. She said it like it was a quirk, like I belonged in a museum for knowing grammar and sticking with it. And perhaps she was right. Perhaps grammar was passé. It seemed more and more writers (including writers whose style critics praised) were treating its rules as ballpark suggestions. Browsing through one of the books by the author who had been onstage before me, I'd read the following sentence: "From the outside, our love is an impregnable fortress, only we know the truth—peace on the surface, the illusion of calm waters: below it, we fight about a misplaced dish." The sentiment was easy to grasp, of course, but would correct syntax have weakened it?

Addie and I went for a walk and talked about precision in language. Addie tried to humor me, to make fun of what I kept calling lazy writing by offering a silly defense of it: "Wanting verb to agree with subject is so *reactionary!*" she said. "There is no subject anymore. Everything is fluid." She was laughing, but I wondered whether she had a point. Maybe it wasn't lazy writing, after all. Maybe there was intention behind it.

"Isn't grammar just like a corset?" Addie went on. "Didn't we all agree to get rid of those? Who wants to see tits pushed up to shoulder level anymore?" She pushed up her own breasts as she said this. "Who wants to read tight sentences?"

It had rained and the streets smelled clean. Addie had just finished shooting her second film, and she seemed happy— happier than I'd ever seen her.

"Who wants form over content?" she said. "Don't we all want freedom? Isn't this the twenty-first century? Who wants thoughts expressed clearly? Who wants clarity? Who wants *thoughts?*"

We lived in the century of feelings. Blurry emotions. Blobs of interiority spilling out. Everyone was unique and infinite, everyone wanted to be understood, and no one had time to shape and carefully carve out explanations. It was a fast-moving train, being alive, knowing people, Addie said. You hopped on and grabbed onto what you could.

I couldn't tell whether she was still disparaging the aesthetic she described or agreeing with it now. I hadn't seen her first movie. I didn't know how her writing had evolved, what she stood for these days.

"Remember John?" she asked me.

Addie had seen him recently, and she told me that his sobriety hadn't lasted. Since our phone call a few years earlier, he'd relapsed and recovered, relapsed and recovered.

"John keeps hitting pause on his life, hoping that it'll give people time to really look at and understand him," Addie said. "Meanwhile, the train is moving without him. Isn't that sad? He wants to be understood."

Did he think the rest of us were?

"Maybe if John's syntax were perfect, people would understand him better," I said.

"That is such an elitist thing to say," Addie said.

We stopped at a mini-mart for gum. Addie liked to chew gum while she smoked. She said all the face movement was conducive to new ideas. The place sold piñatas shaped like cartoon characters, and for a moment I thought that Addie was onto me, that she'd planned this, the stop at this specific piñata-selling store, and was going to confront me about stealing lines from her old story.

"The problem, of course, is that you can never understand anyone else," she said, looking up at the piñatas. "And you can't tell people how to see you, either. That's not how it works. Our brains can only hold about a hundred different people, did you know that? After a hundred, it starts typifying. You're the fifth Canadian I meet? You'll be packed with Canadians. The third guy I know to go through a twelve-step program? Let me show you to your quarters. There's no room that I can build to John's exact specifications up there." Addie tapped at her forehead. "The human brain refuses to know anyone deeply. It's like it knows it's a bad idea."

She'd been staring at a SpongeBob-shaped piñata since we'd come in.

"How do you get them down?" she said. "I can't see any strings."

I told her they were piñatas, not balloons. They weren't floating.

"They're hooked to the ceiling," I said.

"Right," Addie said.

I couldn't tell what she was on. I'd never been interested in knowing that kind of thing—not even with my mother. My mother—I couldn't put my eyes in my pocket when she came home trembling and delirious, but nothing said I had to stare at her, either.

"How do you say 'hit rock bottom' in French?" Addie asked me. "Like, literally."

"*Toucher le fond,*" I said.

She said it was the same in Spanish, that French and Spanish speakers merely *touched* bottom, didn't *hit* it. She was still talking about John, how many times he'd used the phrase with her, a cliché he'd at least spared me.

"It's so American," Addie said. "This idea of momentum. Even when Americans are collapsing, they do it at great speed."

For "hit" did imply speed, didn't it? And "rock" a hard impact. A hard impact that had to jolt you awake if you'd been sleeping, a speed to take advantage of—all you had to do when you reached rock bottom was give it a good kick. Whereas in our language, Addie said (and I noted the use of the singular), the surface you landed on remained unspecified (was it sand? was it quicksand?), and the gentleness of the word "touch" left it unclear whether you were even conscious when you got there. It left wide open the possibility that you might never go back up to the surface.

"And he tried to kill himself!" Addie added, about John, from under SpongeBob's cardboard feet. "What a moron! Who does he think he is? Suicide should only be for geniuses and the terminally ill, don't you think?"

Who was being elitist now?

"I think it should be for everybody," I said. "The option, I mean."

The cashier asked us if we wanted a piñata today. I guess Addie and I had been looking at the ceiling an unusual amount.

"Not today," I said, and the man seemed to understand reasons behind my refusal that I hadn't hinted at.

"I'll take one," Addie said.

We walked out with the SpongeBob piñata. We walked for miles, all the way to Brooklyn. Every time Addie lit a new cigarette, I offered to carry the piñata, but she kept refusing. We talked about some famous actors she'd met, how tall or short they really were. We talked about art, and where to live. There were so many options, Addie said. She was in New York because she'd grown up hearing that was where artists went, but artists lived everywhere now. In New York, you found only the ones who complained that the city wasn't what it used to be.

"They were already complaining about that in my day," I said. "It's a trick, to discourage newcomers."

At a crosswalk in Dumbo, Addie noted three things: (1) night had fallen; (2) artists who moved to New York used the demands of the city as an excuse to stop making art; and (3) she didn't know what to make of her piñata.

"I don't know why I bought this," she said.

She thought perhaps we could fill it and find a kid whose birthday it was. We encountered a party store a few blocks later and followed through. We bought miniature versions of all the candy bars in existence, we bought M&M's, confetti, and small plush toys. At the checkout, the cashier wanted to charge us for the piñata itself, but Addie said we'd bought it in Chelsea.

"Why would you buy a piñata in Chelsea and the filling in Brooklyn Heights?"

It was hard not to hear judgment in his voice, yet the question seemed valid: we hadn't found anything special in Chelsea—his store carried the same piñata.

"It takes time for a plot to come into focus," Addie said.

The cashier didn't ask any more questions.

We filled the piñata on the sidewalk, giving some of the treats away to amused passersby. Two teenage girls recognized Addie and asked for an autograph. It was all good fun until something about the candy hole started bothering Addie. She brought the piñata under the streetlight's weak orange beam and stared into it.

"It's just a fucking cardboard box!" she said. "Someone just pasted crêpe paper on a cardboard box!"

"As opposed to what?" I said.

"They didn't even use a balloon!"

She sat SpongeBob on a stoop and explained to me how piñatas were made, the importance of the balloon, the balloon as scaffolding for the papier-mâché shell. Once the shell was dry, she said, you burst the balloon underneath. It had fulfilled its role.

I didn't know whether to pretend I was hearing this for the first time, remind her of her story, or say that I had myself written about the piñata-making process two novels ago.

Addie said that, when she was a kid, her grandmother had always let her burst the balloon, but that they'd consistently disagreed on what to do with it afterward. The grandmother wanted to take the limp thing out; Addie wanted it to stay in, for children to find on the ground later among the candy, when the piñata broke. She thought it was the real prize, that leftover knotted piece of rubber, the piñata's origin story, trapped within it until the whole thing was destroyed. It all started and ended with that primordial knot.

"Everyone is cutting corners now," she said. "What kind of origin story is a cardboard box?"

She sat on the stoop next to the SpongeBob piñata. She

hadn't included any of this about the knot in her story back then. It wouldn't have been as interesting if she had, the symbolism too on the nose.

"Do you remember the story you gave me once?" I said. "About piñatas?"

"I never wrote about piñatas," Addie said. "Must've been another one of your Mexican students."

"It was part of our pact," I said. "It was a really good story."

She couldn't have been less interested. She took her face in her hands, and I worried that she was going to cry. After a minute, though, I worried that she'd fallen asleep. Her breathing had slowed. The air coming in and out of her kept getting caught on the same patch of mucus in her throat, and I thought of amber, of trapped insects. We still had bags of candy in our hands.

"You're bleeding," I said, and that got Addie out of her state. A red line trickled from her nose, between her ring and pinkie fingers. She wiped the blood on her shirt. I wanted to call her a cab, but she said we were only a few blocks from her house, and asked me to walk with her the rest of the way.

Addie's place was devoid of books and full of lamps. Arc lamps, tree lamps, piano lamps, Tiffanys, low-hanging fixtures. Many were on already. Shadows moved in confusing ways, but visibility was high. She switched on a couple of new lights when we walked in, according to principles that remained unclear to me. She poured us bourbon and disappeared upstairs, to change shirts. After twenty minutes, I went to check on her. She'd fallen asleep in the bathroom. I washed her face with a towel and warm water, which half woke her. She nodded when I asked if she wanted me to put her to bed. I didn't know it would be the last time I saw her. She didn't ask me to stay by her bedside (in fact, after I found her in the bathroom, she didn't say another word), but I sat there anyway, until she started snoring evenly.

On my way out, I turned off only the lamps I remembered her turning on. She'd left the piñata in the foyer, next to our shoes, and I considered getting rid of it, letting her wonder in the morning if she'd dreamed the whole thing. I'd encouraged her to leave it on the stoop earlier, or to give it to the next family that walked by, but she'd insisted on taking it home. We couldn't give a cardboard box to a kid, she'd said. This wasn't a real piñata. It wasn't real.

Eggs in a Basket, Eggs in a Hole

None of this did I tell the cameras, in my living room, from the almond-green chair. I talked about Addie's work, how playing every role herself in her first movies had been the opposite of egomania. I made up something about the human struggle for coherence, how we'd all once had the experience of not quite recognizing ourselves. How Addie's early work had taken that idea to an extreme. I said things anyone else could have said about her.

When the crew left, I felt empty, the way I did after teaching. Whatever I'd been afraid of hadn't happened—no one had confronted me, no one had asked me point-blank if I'd ever stolen Addie's writing. I tried to convince myself that the emptiness I felt was relief, and the relief lightheartedness. I whistled as I did the dishes. I checked the time and the weather—two hours until my husband came home, thirty-two degrees. If I walked to campus, I could catch him after office hours, ride the L home with him.

I took Grand all the way downtown. For a few blocks, the wind carried a smell of cocoa from the Blommer Chocolate Company. I was glad not to have lit that cigarette with the cameraman earlier. If I ever smoked again, it would have to be with my husband, I thought, when he made me a cocktail, or when a book of his or mine came out. He was working on a book right now, about synoptic compositions in Greek art. Synoptic compositions had always interested him—in fact, he'd told me about them on our first date. They combined different timelines in a single image, telling a story or a myth in such a way that the eye could catch all of its main beats simultaneously: a battle being planned, fought, and won all at once; a man dying and his funeral. I often felt like my husband's fascination with the synoptic said something about the way he perceived time. It did often feel like he knew something I didn't about the future. For example, he'd started saying only weeks into our marriage that marrying me was the best decision he'd ever made. He'd repeated it many times since. I always pretended to be flattered, but the truth was, it made me uneasy that he could be so sure I wouldn't one day hurt him beyond repair, or be the source of his biggest disappointment. He liked his life and was confident that the future stood still, waiting to give him more of the same, whereas I either moved headfirst and in terror toward what came next or showed it my back, eyes on the past, like the Angel of History being pushed into the future by the storm of accumulated catastrophe. How different could my husband's view of time be that he knew how to judge his decision to marry me before I died, or he died, or something ended? How could I ask him such a question without alarming him?

I made it to school and ran into Eric, my husband's favorite PhD student, in the lobby.

"I hear they came to film you this morning!" he said. "How does it feel to be a movie star?"

I wondered why anyone said things like that. Maybe I made him nervous. Even though he studied art history, Eric had once asked my opinion of a novel he was writing, and I hadn't been as encouraging as he'd hoped. His novel had been about the characters in famous works at the Art Institute coming alive at night—Hopper's nighthawks waxing lyrical at the gift shop, Grant Wood's stern farmer wandering the hallways with his pitchfork while his daughter experienced profound transformation studying Van Gogh's bedroom in Arles. The book was full of useless details about famous painters. I'd told Eric that the adage "Write what you know" didn't mean that he had to write *everything* he knew about what he knew. We hadn't really spoken since.

In the lobby now, I told Eric how exhausting it all was. How no one should ever have to be on camera.

"Did it feel intrusive?" he asked. "Did they ask you weird questions?"

"I can't tell why they wanted to interview me at all."

I knew Addie had thanked me in a speech years ago, when she won her first award, but, apart from that, there wasn't much out in public to connect us. I told Eric they'd interviewed Jennifer Lopez . . . why would they come for me?

"Why interview the college professor?" I said. "In these situations, you go for the first-grade teacher, the drama teacher from high school . . . those are the important ones. No college professor ever made an impact on anyone's life."

I was standing precisely where I'd been when I learned of Addie's death—facing the glass doors to the street, bulletin board and elevators to my right. I'd been on my way out for fresh air during a class break when I found out.

"That is nonsense!" Eric said. "Your husband, for one, has had a tremendous impact on my life."

"Grad school is different," I said. I wasn't sure where I was going with this. I usually tried to think before I spoke, but that guardrail was gone now. "College professors, though . . . we come in either too early or too late."

The bulletin board was advertising the film club's feature of the month, and the poster of *E. T.* got me wondering why it was that we could only imagine aliens with long fingers, like that poor woman had—the one who'd been abducted in Skokie. Perhaps Eric would know. Or my husband, who I realized could be on his way down right now, since Eric had left his office minutes ago and hadn't mentioned another student going in after him. I became certain that my husband would be in the next elevator to open on my right. I could almost see him there, the way I could almost see that moment in the past when I learned that Addie was dead. I'd wanted to cancel the rest of class that day, but to do what? I'd gone back in, thinking I wouldn't be able to talk to my students about pacing and tension and imagery, but I had. I had been able to. I'd been able for an hour to forget that Addie had just died, the same way I'd been able, for countless days and months before that, to forget she was alive. Running errands, saying things, looking at herself in mirrors. It's a cliché to have characters forget that their mother has died, to have them try to give her a call years after the fact, but in my experience it's much more common to forget that someone we know, or used to know, is alive and breathing somewhere.

One of the elevators was coming down from the fourth floor. In a few seconds, its doors would open on my husband, I knew that now. He'd be surprised to see me, but not alarmed. He'd know nothing had gone wrong with the interview, wouldn't even have thought to worry that anything could. I would never tell him about stealing from Addie. In that way, it was already possible to say that stealing from Addie was the worst decision I'd ever made.

The elevator dinged, a sound similar to that of our old cooking timer, the one my father had used every morning of his life when soft-boiling eggs. Six minutes. It was one of two egg dishes (if you could call a soft-boiled egg a dish) my father had taught me to make—along with eggs in a basket, which my husband called eggs in a hole. With a cookie cutter or a small drinking glass, you made a hole in the middle of a slice of bread. You heated a tablespoon of butter in a pan. Once it melted, you added a few drops of olive oil (my father's secret). You fried the slice of bread in the butter-oil mixture for a minute before breaking an egg over the hole. You added a pinch of salt and let the egg set, a minute or so. You flipped the whole thing, cooked for twenty more seconds. You served immediately.

Acknowledgments

Thank you to the following people for their good cheer, patience, and vision:

Willing Davidson
Jackie Ko
Adam Levin
Caitlin McKenna
Emily Nemens
Amy Schroeder